HAT TRICK

MARIA LUIS

HAT TRICK

BLADES HOCKEY

MARIA LUIS

ALKMINI BOOKS, LLC

The NHL's most charming player is ready to score a hat trick on and off the ice...

As the star forward for the Boston Blades, I've earned a reputation for no-strings attached hookups and a mean slapshot that has all the ladies purring -- but it's never been the one woman I want to see all fired up and ready to score.

Boston's own Ice Queen Gwen James has had my emotions all tangled up for years. I've played the games. I've sat on the sidelines.

No matter her reasons, I'm done being benched.

When she approaches me for a second chance, I accept on one condition: she's got to prove she's all in.

No kissing. No sex.

It just might kill me to keep my hands to myself, but it's time Gwen knows what it's like to beg.

At the end of the day, I play to win, and I want what no other man has ever had...her heart.

Copyright © 2018 by Maria Luis of Alkmini Books, LLC

All rights reserved.

No part of this book may be reproduced in any form or by any electronic or mechanical means, including information storage and retrieval systems, without written permission from the author, except for the use of brief quotations in a book review.

Cover Photographer: Sara Eirew Photography

Cover Designer: Najla Qamber Designs

Editor: Indie Editing Chick

Proofreaders: Tandy Proofreads; Dawn Black

❦ Created with Vellum

To all the Regina George's out there in the world, this one is for you.

Good job, honey.

1

GWEN

BOSTON, MASSACHUSETTS

*L*ike mother, like daughter.

Is it wrong that I'm desperately hoping that the old adage doesn't have a lick of truth to it?

My mother, Adaline James-Fuller-Benn-Corwin, thrusts one hand out from beneath her scarlet red sheets. "He's *gone*." Her palm claps down on the fluffy pillow, and I still haven't had a peek of her face.

Might be for the best. From the streaks of black mascara painted across the pillow, I can't imagine this morning has been the easiest.

Unfortunately, we've been through this before. Four times and counting. And, considering my mother's track record for picking husbands who exit stage right in favor of one of her friends . . . well, we'll probably be here again soon enough.

I settle a hand on her shoulder. At least, I *think* it's her shoulder. She's got so many duvets and pillows and sheets on the bed, it's tough to tell. I give an experimental squeeze. "Mom, Ty Corwin was an asshole and he never deserved you."

"But I love him."

Is love even real?

To many, I'm a coldhearted bitch.

I prefer to think of myself as a realist who sometimes likes to paint myself in happy delusions when the going gets tough. But to my mom . . . . I sigh and pull back, glancing over at the clock seated on the gold-leaf fireplace mantle.

After a lifetime of playing Adaline's mini-me, I've slowly come to realize that women aren't the enemy. Sure, my mother has a shitty friend-making track record. You'd think that after visiting the same country club where you meet both your friends *and* your husbands, it'd be time to fish in some other pond. Not for Adaline. I tend to think it's the comfort zone factor. Ritzy, upper-class Bostonian gentry mingling with other ritzy, upper-class Bostonian gentry.

Is it any wonder that her relationships implode on the regular?

At this point, Adaline's monthly sojourns with her friends is like Morse code for orgies. Okay, not quite orgies. But, still, we're looking at *Jerry Springer*-level stuff—the events aren't even classy enough for *Maury*.

According to my mother's peers, there's nothing wrong with trading out husbands like a bad hand in poker.

Personally, I think it's safe to say that my mother's opinions can't be trusted.

At the knock on the door, my chin lifts and I meet the gaze of Manny, my mother's longtime butler. "Your car is waiting downstairs, Miss James."

Miss James—formalities aside, Manuel O'Carlo is the only father figure I've ever known. If it'd been up to Adaline, no doubt I would be dead from pure neglect. "I've got—"

Another hoarse cry rips through the room. "I can't

believe the snake bastard! Goddamn snake bastard, sleeping around on me. Can you fucking *believe* it?"

Oh God, here it comes.

Manny and I trade side-eye glances, neither of us particularly wanting to inch closer and ward off the impending storm. He makes a little sippy-cup motion with his fingers, squinting his eyes.

I shake my head—I don't want tea right now—and step forward.

He retreats, miming taking bigger and bigger gulps, just before he whirls around and escapes down the hall for afternoon tea he'll never deliver. No doubt he'll park himself right by the front door and wait there until I'm ready to leave.

Damn you, Manuel.

As much as I want to escape right along with him, I know that I can't leave Adaline like this. Even though I'm Zoe's maid of honor, and *even* though the engagement party has started ... my gaze flits to the clock again.

Now.

The engagement party has started now.

Crap, crap, crap.

Time for my special poison of tough love.

My fingers slip over the blanket and I give one powerful yank, revealing my mother's tiny body huddled in a ball of despair. "Mom." Her sniffles increase in volume as she buries her face in the pillow. "Mom, talk to me."

"He's a rat-snake bastard, Gwenny. Fuck him."

If only she'd sung that tune when Rat-Snake Bastard Ty Corwin proposed—despite the fact that he'd been dating Adaline while still wearing a wedding ring from his then-wife.

"You're right," I say, swallowing the fight, "he's a dick,

Mom, and you shouldn't be spending even a second thinking about him."

"A rat-snake, tree-loving bastard, Gwenny." She heaves a sob, and the sound squeezes my heart. "He's a vegan. How can a vegan cheat on me?"

"Because he's a rat-snake tree-loving bastard, Mom, and that's their specialty." And because infidelity is all encompassing—vegans included. I don't say that. No point in riling her up even more. "Okay, time to get up. You need to shower."

"I don't want to shower."

God help me.

My eyes squeeze shut and I count to ten. *One . . . two . . . three . . .*

"Gwenny, why are you wearing a dress?"

Because I'm supposed to be at my best friend's engagement party, celebrating happy love that I don't know exists, but instead I'm here being shown, once again, that it doesn't.

"My friend is having an engagement party."

"Did you tell her that all men are rat bastards?"

"I haven't had the chance."

Her blond hair rustles against the pillows. "Never lasts, Gwenny. It never fucking lasts. Her man will walk out on her as soon as that ring is on her finger, just like my Ty did. But it's not the men—they're weak. What about the women, your friends?"

Once upon a time, in a far, far away land—all right, let's cut the shit. Honestly? My mother has been spewing her gospel for years now. Probably since my dad left her because he couldn't deal with her antics. And, sure, I spent a good number of years believing everything she told me.

How could I not?

From the age of eight onward, when my mother was on

her second marriage, I watched each subsequent husband leave her for women Adaline considered close friends. I watched it all happen, and then I digested my mother's warnings—women could not be trusted—and I reacted accordingly.

What I never saw then, and what has taken me years to truly accept, is that Adaline Corwin is no better than any of her so-called besties. Tangled webs don't have shit on the group my mother runs in. Adaline has stolen her friends' husbands, and they, in return, have taken hers.

It's bat-shit crazy.

Totally nuts.

And I want no part in it.

"Gwen." My mother finally lifts herself from the bed, her blond hair hanging in front of her face like that creepy girl from the movie, *The Ring*. "Gwen, what do we always say about other women?"

On a day that I'm supposed to be celebrating my best friend's engagement, I'm not playing into my mother's games—not even when she's reeling from another inevitable divorce. Ty Corwin is the fourth in line, but I doubt he'll be the last. Christmas is only weeks away, and I bet with every fiber of my being that she'll have someone new chasing after her by New Year's Day.

Nothing ever changes with Adaline Corwin.

But I've changed.

"I've got to go, Mom. I'm sorry and I love you, and I'll be back in the morning but I can't miss this."

I bend to kiss her forehead, sweeping her knotted blond hair back from her face as I do. She turns her face away, unwilling to even give me a slice of affection. Feeling a little chillier than I did when I showed up two hours ago, I head for the stairs.

Manuel is waiting for me by the front door, as predicted, and from the uncomfortable expression on his face, he's heard the whole thing go down. Still, the man has a heart of gold, and he only offers me a small smile. "Ready to go, Teacup?"

My childhood nickname.

I fight back the sting of tears and accept the arm of the only man in my life who has ever appreciated me for *me*, and not for what's between my legs. "Let's do this, Manny."

But as he helps me into the car, and I rearrange my dress around my legs, I can only think one thing: I might have changed, I might not view other women as the devil incarnate any longer, but one thing will never change.

Love is still, unequivocally, horseshit.

2

HUNT

I'm fucking late.

I'm never late. Call me Mr. Punctual, if you want, but I've made it this far in my life by playing it easy, chill—the guy everyone wants to be around because I don't make a fuss. Ever.

Then days like today happen, and shit hits the fan.

Between my brother calling me for another "business" loan and my washing machine eating the dress shirt I'd planned to wear . . . not to mention the fact that I ran a red light and got pulled over, and oh *yeah*, apparently, there was the matter of two unpaid (forgotten) tickets on my record.

It's safe to say that Mr. Chill has been replaced with Mr. Get The Fuck Out Of My Way.

My dress shoes eat up the concrete pavement, frozen over with ice, as I maneuver my big body through the throngs of people waiting their turn to take a spin around the makeshift ice rink in the Boston Commons. The fact that I'm not stopped a single time for an autograph or a selfie goes to show that I'm not acting myself today.

My reputation as the NHL's most charming forward is about to be blown to smithereens in favor of returning to my roots: just plain, old Marshall Hunt, Pissed-Off Bostonian.

"Excuse me," I mutter, planting a hand on some dude's back and giving him a little push to the side, "coming through."

The sight of the front door of Cheers Restaurant might as well be the Stanley Cup right now, I'm so thankful to finally have it within reach. My teammate, Andre Beaumont, is having his engagement party on the second floor of the property, which, from what I understand, isn't associated with Cheers.

Even so, I'm Beaumont's best man and I'm currently . . . I dig my cell phone out of my slacks to check the time, letting out a low groan when I realize that the festivities began an hour ago.

Fucking fantastic.

A body bumps into mine just as I'm about to cross the street. Instinct has me reaching out, wrapping an arm around a set of slim shoulders to keep the person from tumbling down to the icy pavement.

And then I catch it—the scent of lemon, delicious and tart. There's only one person I know who ever wears that perfume.

Gwen James.

I glance down at her vibrant red hair and think back to a time when she was blonde. Honey blonde, none of that platinum hue for her. But it's been years since then—six, to be precise—and the honey blond curls I used to imagine fisting as I settled myself between her legs are long gone.

"Excuse me," she says, her husky voice both familiar and totally foreign all at once. "Sorry about that."

She tries to untangle herself from my grasp, but I clamp down, keeping her lithe figure pressed against my side. "So nice to run into you this chilly evening, Gwen. Heading to the festivities?"

Her head jerks up at the sound of my voice, and those beautiful blue eyes of hers go momentarily wide before narrowing. "Marshall."

I grin at her clipped tone. I opted to go by my surname the minute the Blades drafted me from Northeastern University. Besides my brother, Gwen might be the only person I'm still in contact with who calls me "Marshall."

Coming off her lush lips, I love it.

Though I'd prefer to hear her moaning it while we're fucking on my bed, but hey, I've been hoping for that outcome since I sat behind her in Accounting 201, my sophomore year at Northeastern. When it comes to me, Gwen James has done a pretty solid job of ignoring all my attempts to take her out on a date.

Which means that having her up against my side right now? Yeah, I totally plan to live in the moment.

I give her hip a little squeeze, enjoying the way her brows pull low like she's not sure if she likes it or if she wants to knee me in the balls. "You didn't answer my question, Gwen."

"I'm not playing your games today."

God, it's so much fun to tease her. After the shit day I've had so far, it feels like I've suddenly won the lottery I never even entered. Ducking my chin against her ear, I murmur, "I'm sorry, did I issue you an invitation to play my games?"

I hear her teeth clack together. "We're late."

"What's another five minutes? I'm sure Zoe and Beaumont will be ecstatic when they see us walk in together."

"We're *not* walking in together."

"What? Embarrassed to be seen with me?" There's always time for a first. I've gained a bit of a reputation over the last few years for only dating supermodels. I'm not going to deny it—the rumors are true. But what can I say? Supermodels work a chaotic schedule just like I do. There aren't hurt feelings when I'm on the road for a week, and I definitely don't get my briefs in a twist when a photoshoot or runway show has them taking the red-eye to Paris.

They live their lives, I live mine.

When, and if, we're in the same place at the same time, we hook up.

It's a win-win situation.

There's only been one woman I'd ever consider changing my ways for, and it's the one currently trying to escape me.

So much for a romantic stroll through the gentle snowfall.

With a sigh, I lift my arm and she doesn't waste her opportunity. Her fuck-me heels sink into the ice, puncturing the frozen water the same way she takes on her adversaries. Quickly, without a single regret.

Screw it—I'm not wasting my first opportunity to be alone with her in years. I catch up to her in two strides and we cross the street together. "I know why I'm late," I murmur, "but what's your deal?"

Her lashes sweep down, and I'm not sure if she's trying to watch her step or avoid making eye contact. "I . . ." She blows out a deep breath. "I don't want to talk about it, Marshall."

She never has.

In her eyes, I've always been the too-charming, too-young jock. And, yeah, she'd be right about that. But unlike what most people think, I do have a brain rattling around in my skull—a surprise, I know. Concussions from playing hockey or not, I'm not a meathead.

Just like how I know she's always been more than what she shows off to the world: standoffish and ice-cold.

I shove my hands into the pockets of my slacks. "Anything that I can do to help?"

That stops her.

Her stride pauses, just as she's reaching for the wrought-iron railing to Cheers's front stoop. "Why would you want to do that?"

Cocking my head to the side, I say, "Definitely doesn't have anything to do with your prickly attitude, that's for sure."

She snorts, and then takes the stairs. "I prefer feisty."

Unable to help myself, my hand goes to her back. Just to make sure she doesn't fall. Safety and all that. "Feisty? Is that so? In some circles, they might even go so far as to throw out the word 'bitchy.' Not that *I'm* calling you that, of course."

Her shoulders twitch under her trench coat. "Of course."

I grip the door handle and pull it open for her to step through first. Heat blasts my face, reminding me that even as a professional hockey player, five-degrees Fahrenheit feels like my own slice of hell. As warmth returns to my bare fingers, I tell her, "I'd be willing to lend an ear, if you wanted —for a price."

Blue eyes flick up to my face, and for a moment, I'm convinced that the impenetrable Gwen James is going to break into a smile. But then she just shakes her head, purses her lips against happiness, and quips, "I know your price, Marshall, and I'm not interested in being shackled and chained to your basement walls."

Fuck, but she's witty when she wants to be. I chuckle

softly, enjoying her subtle teasing, and step to the side as an attendant offers to take Gwen's jacket. "You've heard the stories, huh?"

"Every single one."

"And?" I prompt as she slips the coat off her shoulders. "Feelin' a little turned on?"

The coat is whisked away and, Jesus, Mary, and Joseph, I die. Right then and there, I'm fucking dead. Because Gwen James has always been unbelievably gorgeous to me, even in the jeans and university sweatshirts she once wore to class because she couldn't be bothered to doll herself up for two hours of hell on earth.

But right now . . . I take her in, *all* of her, not bothering at all to hide my once-over. It's a game we've played for years, and even if it hadn't been, I doubt I could hide my appreciation. In theory, her red dress should clash with her red hair. It doesn't.

The material is silk, like rippling water over her bare skin, and though it's wintertime in Boston, Gwen's dress can't be described as anything other than "slinky." Thin, hardly-there straps arch over her shoulders, and the front V-neck is deep and enticing. A slit creases the skirt, and I spot a toned thigh slipping through.

Like Gwen, the dress is classy with a sexual edge—and a very clear reminder that I've never stopped looking and have never been given the opportunity to touch.

Unfortunately, my cock has never gotten the memo, and even now, in the middle of fucking Cheers, I'm hard as a rock.

Gwen's fingers to my chin snaps me out of it, and I meet her gaze unapologetically. Her plum-painted lips move, and I register the words just as she steps away toward the stairwell leading up to the second floor.

Feeling turned on, Marshall?

She knows I am. And for the first time since I've met Gwen, I decide I'm not willing to play our games anymore.

The woman owes me a date, and I plan to finally collect.

3

GWEN

Ba-dum-ba-dum-ba-dum.

The sound of my heart thudding in my ears blocks out the low murmurs and clinking glasses as I enter the wood-paneled room above Cheers Restaurant. Hockey players swarm the Victorian-era space, most of them balancing white porcelain plates on one palm as they shovel finger sandwiches into their mouths.

A few years ago, when I first started working for Golden Lights Media, Boston's top PR firm, I'd been in awe of the environment.

In other words, big biceps, crooked grins, and the ever-present threat of hot men dropping towels and showing off the goods.

The Blades are a newer franchise within the NHL, less than a decade old, but you'd never know it based on the talent of the team.

Including Marshall Hunt.

Just the thought of him sends my pulse into overdrive, and I throw a quick glance over my shoulder at the empty doorway.

His big body fills it a moment later, shoulders so broad I'm surprised he doesn't have to turn to the side to fit through. His brown hair is trimmed short on the sides, a little longer on top. *Perfect to grab when*—no, no grabbing ever. Against my will, my gaze continues to track him in a way I didn't allow myself when we collided outside.

Navy-blue fitted suit and shiny dress shoes. I watch as he strips off his jacket, revealing a crisp, white button-down. Blunt fingers that have never once touched me sexually undo the buttons at his wrists before slowly rolling up the sleeves to expose corded forearms.

Just then, his pewter eyes lift and hone in on me.

I feel that look like I've been doused in boiling water, and I suck in a deep, uneven breath.

There's no missing the way the corner of his mouth hitches in a half-smile.

Marshall Hunt knows he's undeniably sexy, and he doesn't bother pretending otherwise.

For years he's pursued me, on-and-off, depending on whether we're in contact. Besides the fact that I'm three years older than him, he also witnessed the most humiliating experience of my life.

He witnessed me at my lowest, when my heart was scraped raw, and I learned very quickly that everything my mother had ever whispered in my ear was true.

Sexy or not, I'm not the type of person who enjoys ruminating in my mistakes—unfortunately for Marshall, my brain has lumped him in with that experience, right or wrong. And even if there are times when I can't help but think *what if?* I'm quick to push those crazy daydreams away.

Based on his track record for being the NHL's version of

Leonardo DiCaprio, dating Marshall would no doubt be the equivalent of dating Ty Corwin.

It would only be a matter of time before someone else caught his fancy and he moved on to a new model, both literally and figuratively.

I dip my chin in acknowledgment and turn away. I need to find Zoe. Or my other close friend Charlie.

Anyone, really, who *isn't* Marshall.

I don't search long. Charlie Denton can always be found near food, and after scoping out the buffet table, I see her curly blond head bent over a display of red velvet cupcakes.

My feet diminish the distance between us, the sound of my six-inch heels clipping across the nineteenth-century hardwood floors drowned out by deep masculine laughter.

I step up beside her. "How many have you had?"

"Truth?" Charlie asks, not even turning her head.

"Always."

"Two. I'm trying to decide if I want a third or if I want to switch gears and go for the chocolate-covered strawberries instead."

I laugh and bump her hip with mine. "The strawberries, obviously."

"Cupcake it is, then," she murmurs with a wink at me, and then plucks one out of the display.

There was a time, not even that long ago, when Charlie and I were more likely to tear at each other's hair than crack jokes. I'm at fault for that one, like always. Adaline screwed me up in ways that I can't even begin to fathom some—

No. No passing the blame to someone else. First thing I'd learned at therapy when I began going last year. Some days, days like today when I've listened to my mother spew her bullshit, it's hard to remember to take an active role in my decisions.

Think of me as a reformed Regina George, except that the reformation period is never quite done. Something always pops up to remind me that my progress hasn't been as steep as I'd like to think it is.

"I saw you walk in with Hunt."

Cupcakes. I need sugar. After the day I've had, I'm in desperate need of a pick-me-up, not to mention a distraction. *Stop thinking about how good Marshall looks.* A nearly impossible task, really.

I shrug off Charlie's comment and dive for the closest dessert. "We didn't walk *in* together."

"You were, like, four steps ahead of him." Charlie's gaze doesn't waver from my face. "Did you two come together?"

We've never come together, at all. Oh, God. Now is *not* the time to start thinking about sexual innuendos with Marshall Hunt at the forefront. "You and Zoe need to stop trying to throw us together, Charls. I'm not interested."

That wasn't quite true. If Marshall and I were on Facebook, our relationship would definitely be marked as "it's complicated." From the first moment that he sat behind me in an accounting class at Northeastern, my focus has always been elsewhere. Back then, it was on . . . Well, it doesn't really matter. Not anymore. Point is, objectively I can see that Marshall Hunt is a damn good catch. The dimples don't hurt his sex appeal, either.

But finding a guy attractive doesn't mean you want to date him. I don't want to date Marshall. Sometimes, yes, I think about the possibilities—usually when my walls are down and I've thrown back a few glasses of wine—but, rationally, I know it's not a good idea. I've spent the better part of a year avoiding the dating scene altogether. I wanted to focus on the new me, the me I *want* to be, the me who isn't anything at all like Adaline Corwin.

I can't do those things if I'm falling into bed with a six-foot-two hockey player with a slow, easy grin, and a heat in his eyes that would tempt me into never leaving his bedroom—especially not if the Blades' very own Casanova then dumped me to go back to one of his leggy women.

I'm not in the market for a broken heart, now or ever.

Not to mention that the love thing? I'm still not convinced it's real.

Charlie chuckles at my denial. "How long have you been telling yourself that you aren't interested?"

My shoulders stiffen at her wry tone. "I'm not."

"Wait, hold on, is that your . . . yup, that's your nose growing, Pinocchio."

"I'm not—it's not—" Flustered, I stare down at my untouched cupcake. Life would be so much easier if my two best friends didn't want to see me shackled and hooked up just like the two of them. I know they *mean* well. They want me to be happy. And I am happy—mostly. I'd probably be happier if I didn't have them throwing Marshall at me whenever we're in a group setting.

Not that Marshall is any better. The man is utterly relentless—charming, yes, but relentless nevertheless. If I were a weaker woman, I'd give in. Sleep with him once and then send him on his way. If I were still up to my old ways, I'd probably do just that.

The worry comes in when I think about becoming needy just like Adaline—that one taste of Marshall will never be enough. And that, when he leaves, I'll crash and burn just like my mother. Or worse, that I'll be back to my old tricks again and crush him without even realizing it.

"Gwen."

I meet Charlie's gaze, someone I've known even longer than I've known Marshall. While Marshall has seen me at rock bottom, Charlie has personally borne the brunt of Old Gwen. When we first started hanging out, along with Zoe, I was convinced Charls was just yanking me along, biding her time to strike perfect revenge for all the shit I pulled on her. But, no, Charlie Denton is just . . . good, all the way to her core. The sort of good that I desperately want to be.

I put up a hand, cutting her off. "Don't say it."

Her lips turn up in a grin. "You don't even know what I'm going to say."

Shaking my head, I mutter, "You're an open book, Denton. Trust me, your thoughts are all over your face."

She laughs loudly, a boisterous, full-belly sound that is so typically her. "No wonder Duke always knows when I want to jump his bones. My lust is all over my face."

Feeling the mood lighten, I add, "I'm pretty sure he looks your way and you immediately start panting. Thankfully, your boyfriend is a little more circumspect as a client. If I signed you, the world would know when you're begging for sex."

"Who's begging for sex?"

The Mountain, otherwise known as Duke Harrison, appears behind his petite girlfriend. Once upon a time, Duke and I dated—if you can even call it that. A few dinners here and there and one awkward make-out session does not a relationship make. Not my best moment. *Are they ever?* Swallowing, I force a bright smile. "Your girlfriend is—tell me, Harrison, what do you see when you look at Charlie's face?"

Catching onto my game, Charlie winks at me and then presses her chin to the top of her hands. She flutters her eyelashes ridiculously, then goes all out by biting her bottom lip and . . . is she squinting?

Duke, typical guy that he is, frowns. "Did you get something in your eye, babe?"

Charlie huffs. "I'm smizing."

"Smizing? Is that a new mascara or something?"

Stifling a laugh, I open my mouth and then am soundly cut off by the one man who never fails to make me question everything about myself.

Marshall slings a muscular arm around Duke's shoulders, leaning in as if to impart a big secret. "Nah," he says, his gray eyes bright with mirth, "it's model lingo. She's smiling with her eyes. Get it? Smile. Eyes. Smize."

Duke's brows lower. "That's the stupidest shit I've ever heard. Who made that up?"

"Tyra Banks," I put in, growing warm under the weight of Marshall's stare. "*America's Next Top Model*," I add. "Ringing any bells?"

The Mountain looks at me blankly.

I turn to my friend. "Your boyfriend's knowledge of reality TV is sorely lacking."

"I think we should be asking, instead, why *Hunt* knows what smizing is." Charlie taps her nose and then points at the Blades' star forward. "Wanna tell us your secrets?"

For a moment, so quick I'm almost convinced it didn't happen, Marshall's gray eyes grow somber, the laughter banking. My heart stutters. Marshall is an open book—he's not one to hide what he's thinking, and the man is full of so much good humor that it's hard to imagine him hiding anything at all.

Then he grins, his dimples creasing his clean-shaven cheeks. "Charlie, a man never tells."

"You do," Duke snorts. "You can't keep a secret to save your life."

Except that he has for years now. He's kept *my* secret,

and I've never even asked him to. As if knowing the direction of my thoughts, his gaze fixes on me. "Some things are sacred." He blinks, and the darkened cast in his expression lifts like an unraveled veil. "And some things, like my dating reputation, keep me informed on the smizing habits of models everywhere in the world."

Everyone laughs at that—just as Marshall intended, I'm sure—and then he's turning to me, dropping his arm from Duke's broad shoulder, and stepping close. My breath hitches as I reflect his approach by inching back.

His dimples wink with a quick, easy grin. "Running, Gwen?"

I shake my head. "Never."

"Prove it."

Duke and Charlie's laughter fades, and my best friend clears her throat. "Hmm, is that Zoe I hear calling my name? Gotta go!" She wraps a hand around Duke's arm, despite the fact that the man would follow her to the ends of the earth, and sashays her way into the crowd.

Traitor.

I fix my gaze on the artfully displayed desserts. In a tone that acutely reminds me of the Old Gwen—in other words, painfully hoity-toity—I say, "Didn't we go through this once already today? This game thing is not happening."

But Marshall surprises me.

"Dance with me." His voice is rough around the edges, its undercurrent a true Bostonian slant that speaks to his childhood in Southie. I haven't heard all the stories, mostly in an attempt to keep our lives untangled, but I've heard enough to know that his life hasn't always been one of supermodels, million-dollar contracts, and international hockey stardom.

Once upon a time, he'd been dealt a hand of foster care,

petty juvenile crimes, and a surprising talent for staying upright on skates when he and his buddies stopped up the gutters in their old neighborhood and waited for the shallow water to freeze over.

A free ice rink.

"Commandeered" skates.

My gaze catches on the gold Rolex encircling one thick wrist, a Rolex that the Blades' GM gave him when he came up from the farm team.

Marshall Hunt has come a long way from his roots.

So have you.

I withhold a wince. I don't suspect that my transformation is nearly as noticeable to the outside eye as his.

"Gwen?"

Glancing up past his wide chest, to the buttons he's undone at the column of his throat, I meet his pewter eyes with a little shiver. *Remember, you are* not *interested.* Staring at masculine perfection makes it hard to remember that fact. "There's no music playing," I finally say.

There is, but the soft jazz isn't exactly inspiring any of the partygoers to break it down on the dance floor. Instead, everyone is still shoveling food into their mouths as they toss back the endless supply of booze.

"Once upon a time, you didn't care if you were the only woman belting out 'It's Raining Men' with just the jukebox as your partner-in-crime." He holds out a hand, palm up. Even with a foot separating us, I can make out the hard callouses that scar his flesh. "Dance with me, Gwen."

I can't.

It has nothing to do with my interest in Marshall and everything to do with me. His words are a stark reminder that I'm no longer that carefree girl who was willing to climb on top of tables in dirty barrooms, singing outrageously at the top of her lungs.

That girl has been gone for a long time now, replaced by bitterness and tension and a fake superiority complex. And even if I'm no longer quite the latter anymore, either, I'm still not the girl he remembers from college.

She's disappeared, and I'm not quite willing to jump into the fire to pull her back out.

My heart lurches at the sight of Marshall's hand slowly falling back to his side, and I feel that increased distance between us acutely. *Take his hand, take his hand, take his hand.* The words flip on repeat in my head as the handsome smile on his face fades. With a cool expression, his mouth flattens into a firm line.

"Right. Have a good night, Gwen."

It sounds so final, but this . . . this is what I wanted, right? To cut the cord?

"Marshall," I start awkwardly, "listen, I'm sorry. It's not—"

His gaze hardens. "Spare me the *it's not you, it's me* speech."

But what if that's actually the case? I want to say. *What if, for once, I'm trying not to follow so directly in my mother's footsteps? What if I can't get my mother's pestering about traitorous best friends and good-for-nothing husbands and skin-deep loyalty out of my head?*

I don't get the chance.

Marshall's hands go to his lean hips, and he lowers his head, lashes sweeping down as he stares at the floor between us. His chest expands with a deep breath and the words that follow claw at my heart.

"I'm done, Gwen. We've been doing this for years now. Me chasing you; you pullin' away. I'll admit I haven't been a saint, but I'm done watching you flit from douchebag to douchebag without ever once looking at me. *Really* looking at me. I'm younger, so what? You've dated guys twice your age. I witnessed a painful time in your life? So *what*, Gwen. It happened six fucking years ago." His gaze cuts to me, and I feel that look like a punch to the stomach. "Get over it. Don't get over it. Doesn't matter to me. If you need me, you know where to find me. Until then, I'm done playing games."

My brain scrambles for words, any words that I can possibly say to stop the impending train wreck but I've got nothing. Zip. Zilch. Nada. My heart pounds erratically in my chest, my skin grows clammy, and then I watch as Marshall shakes his head, as though disappointed to realize that I don't have the balls to take a leap of courage, before giving me a two-finger salute and stalking off.

I don't expect tears to spring to my eyes.

I don't expect to feel the sudden loss in my chest from his sudden departure.

And I *certainly* don't expect the new mantra which has kicked off in my head: *what have you done, what have you done, whathaveyoudone?*

It's quite easy to see what I've done.

I've singlehandedly pushed away the only man in my life—aside from Manuel—who has seen beneath my icy (read: bitchy) exterior to the woman who's been lost for years.

A hand presses to my back, and I immediately catch the scent of Zoe's perfume. It's the one I convinced Andre to buy for her birthday a few months back when he dragged me to the mall in search of the perfect "presents." Plural, not singular.

I can't stop myself. I lean back into that hand, into our

friendship, and Zoe catches me with an arm around my waist. I may not have known her for years, but this girl, she's become as close to a sister as I'll ever have.

"What did you do?" she murmurs in my ear, echoing my own thoughts as she fits a champagne flute into my hand.

What *didn't* I do?

In advocating the "love is horseshit" slogan, I may have inadvertently ruined my only chance at discovering that the exact opposite is true.

I search the crowd for familiar broad shoulders. No luck.

I tip the flute up to my lips for a healthy swallow of the bubbly.

"Everything," I say to Zoe, "I screwed up everything."

4

HUNT

"So, you and Gwen put on quite a show at my engagement party last night."

I'm flat on a bench press at the Blades' training facility when I hear Beaumont's wry remark. I don't answer immediately. Hell, I don't even know what to say because he's right. Not only did Gwen and I put on a show, I lost my temper for the first time in what feels like forever. I never lose my cool, not anymore.

I learned impulse control around the time Northeastern recruited me and took me out of the shithole where I'd been surviving.

Still, staring down at Gwen's pained expression as I lit into her . . . I hate that. I hate that I made her feel *less than* when I've been trying—for years, at that—to show her that she's *more* than all that icy attitude she hands out like candy. I've seen glimpses to the woman underneath that hard shell of hers when she thinks no one is watching. I've seen her give without comment about how it might inconvenience her. Gwen tries damn hard to keep up the Ice Queen façade

—is it wrong that I'm tired of trying to crack what I know is just a front?

Six years of doing the chasing with sporadic-as-hell glimmers of hope has worn me down.

I take a deep breath, preparing myself for my final push of the morning. Weight-lifting is my thing. Some people like cardio. Some people like sitting on their asses and working out their thumbs flipping TV channels. Me? It's all about arm curls and dumbbells and bench presses. If I didn't spend my days training for the Blades, I'd probably be one of those crazed CrossFit nuts.

Seems like my own slice of paradise.

Metal clangs against metal as I set the crossbar back on the rack. Then I swing myself into an upright position and meet my best friend's gaze. If you believe the media, I'm the white light to Andre Beaumont's dark shadows, the angel next to his Belial, the ball of sunshine next to his stench of sulfur.

The media knows shit.

Beaumont plays hard on the ice because it's required of him. And, yeah, the guy hasn't always been the most chipper fellow on the block, but the last eight months or so have done a lot to ease the bleakness from his black eyes. His girl Zoe has done that.

And last night, instead of playing up my special platter of sunshine and laughter, I let frustration get the best of me.

Me and Beaumont? We're not as different as everyone would like to think. I'm just a lot better at hiding my demons behind a charming smile and a playboy lifestyle.

"I'm sorry about that, man," I say, the only peace offering I've got. I could promise him my firstborn, but the way things are looking, I'll be single for life. The models are great, but all those relationships are casual.

I've been hanging onto the thread of hope that one day Gwen James will look at me, reach for the zipper of my jeans, and say, "It's always been you."

Hey, a guy can dream, right?

Beaumont casts a quick glance at our teammates. We've been conditioning for an hour now. Every day playing for the Blades is somewhat the same. Early morning skate, followed by cardio, followed by weights. Most of the guys have got music blasting into their skulls via their headphones; a few lazy-ass stragglers are preening in front of the mirrors as they arm-curl an equally lazy-ass ten-pound dumbbell. Keep that up and they'll be back on the farm team before the season even gets fully underway.

"Hunt," Beaumont says, turning back to me after he's apparently satisfied no one's eavesdropping, "you made her cry."

My stomach sinks, even as I force myself to maintain a neutral expression. "You're delusional," I mutter darkly. "Trust me when I say that Gwen James doesn't cry."

Wrong. She has, albeit two times.

I don't blame her for either of them. That first situation six years ago tore her to shreds. It'd hurt to see her feel so strongly about another guy; it'd hurt even more to know that I'd had a hand in her humiliation. Just because it'd been an *indirect* hand didn't change the outcome.

Tears were tears and hearts were shattered.

Gwen can play the indifferent card with everyone else, but for the length of Accounting 201, we'd become friends of a sort. Friends who met up for lunch and studied together. Unfortunately, "friends" is as far as we've ever progressed. Any attempts on my end to call her out on friend-zoning me, when it's clear there's an attraction on her end, have been shut down.

I bat Beaumont back with a wave of my hand so I can snag my Gatorade bottle off the floor by his foot. Popping the lid, I guzzle the blue liquid and try not to think of Gwen crying.

Damn. Can't do it. Dropping the bottle to my knee, I scrub the heel of my hand across my mouth. "Did she actually cry?"

Beaumont shifts. Since he's more mountain than man, the movement obscures my line of sight to our captain, Jackson Carter, who's watching us both. Carter is a true vet: thirty-four years old. He came to us at the start of last season from the Dallas Stars. Appropriate, since the guy is "cowboy" all the way.

"Well," Beaumont hedges, "she did *look* like she might cry."

I lift my gaze to his. "But she didn't?"

"Eh . . ." He points to his face. "There may have been a tear. Maybe two."

I almost laugh. It's just like Beaumont to try and make me feel better, even if it's by way of making me feel like a dick first. More than anyone else on the team, he knows how much I want that woman. "Like I said, Gwen doesn't cry. But thanks for making me feel like an asshole anyway."

We wrap up the rest of training, completing our circuits, listening to Jackson Carter as he tells us to be prepared for our game against the New York Islanders in two days. It's at home, which I definitely don't mind—although not for the same reasons as everyone else. While my teammates have their family in the Friends-and-Family section of TD Garden, I've got . . . well, to put it bluntly, I've got no one.

Except for my older brother, who's more likely to hit me up after the game in the hope for some cash. Since I've earned myself a solid spot on the first line during the last year, Dave has come to only one game.

He spent all three periods hitting on my teammates' wives and girlfriends.

It was his first and only time sitting with the families. If he comes to watch me anymore, it's not on my dime and I'm not aware of it.

After a quick shower, I pull on a pair of jeans, a worn Blades T-shirt, and my favorite leather jacket. Once everything is stowed away in my locker, I'm heading out the door. Usually I'll catch up with some of the guys, maybe grab some lunch at this badass Italian place just around the corner from the training facility. I'm not feeling it today—between Dave hounding me for more money and the whole Gwen showdown from last night, the need to kick back with my teammates is nonexistent.

Nope.

Not today.

The air is frigid as I exit the arena, and my skin tightens like someone's slid ice cubes down the ridges of my spine. Heading for my truck, I don't notice the figure standing next to it until I'm feet away, jangling my keys against my leg and looking up from my cell phone.

I'd recognize that red hair anywhere.

What the hell is Gwen doing here?

My stride slows, and she must hear the tread of my heavy boots because she glances up from her phone with a strained expression. The loose curls of her hair are frizzier than normal. Even her clothes, which are usually perfectly tailored, look disheveled today.

Her slim, knee-length skirt is off-center, the row of buttons not aligning with her belly-button. Her flouncy shirt is half-tucked into the skirt. And, hell, the woman is wearing flats.

Gwen James is a stiletto kind of girl.

I haven't seen her in anything else since Accounting 201.

Be casual, man.

Right. Be casual. How's that even possible when all I want to do is muss Gwen up even more? With my fingers. My tongue. My cock.

I purposely slide my gaze down her trim frame, taking in my fill, before slipping my phone into the back of my jeans and cocking my head to the side. "Fancy seeing you here, Miss James."

Her blue eyes flick away from my face, but I suspect the aversion has less to do with checking me out and more to do with hiding her flushed cheeks—a flush that has nothing to do with the chilly weather.

"Marshall," she says somewhat stiffly, sliding her hands down the length of her skirt. "I was hoping to run into you."

Had she? I squelch down a burst of pleasure, stomping the bastard hard into the ground. I'm done with the hope. I meant what I said last night. Shoving my hands into my jeans' pockets, I tilt my head toward my truck. "Looks like you found me."

The flush burns even brighter, and this time I know damn well the freezing temperature isn't responsible.

"Yeah, I . . ." She visibly swallows, and I realize that I've never, not once, seen her so at odds. Gwen is the epitome of ice and class, a concoction that keeps her nose in the air and her true feelings wrapped up in steel walls.

But this Gwen . . . the messy, uncertain Gwen standing before me? Well, color me intrigued.

Wanting to push her a little more, I lift my brows in a show of deliberate patience. "You are . . .?"

Her red hair is shoved indelicately behind one ear. "I'm here."

She's pretty much told me nothing. I nod slowly. "Congratulations. You lookin' for a trophy or something?"

White teeth sink into her bottom lip. I suck down a groan and force myself to stop thinking about those lips wrapped around my cock. Never gonna happen, that's for sure.

"I, um." Gwen shifts her weight, tucking one foot behind her opposite calf like she's nervous to have me see her this way. "Listen, I . . . So, this is officially a lot harder than I thought it would be."

I watch her expectantly, giving her nothing. Oh, how the tables have turned. Plus, I doubt she's here for anything *us* related. If anything, she's probably here on her boss's bidding. Walter Collins has been trying to lock me down into hiring Golden Lights Media for a year now.

I'm not interested.

I've already signed on the dotted line for another firm— a firm, I might add, that took me on even when I was still on the farm team, when the Blades had yet to pull me up onto their official roster.

"Okay, okay." Gwen shoots me a glare, like I'm the one at fault for her halted speech. I hear her mutter something that sounds *suspiciously* like, "I can do this," and then she's straightening her shoulders, thrusting her full breasts up and out, and announcing, "I'd like to take you up on that offer for our date. The date that I won from the charity auction last spring."

Shock clamps my jaw shut.

But now that Gwen has opened the gates, proverbially speaking, she doesn't stop. She steps to the side, head down, tucking her hair behind her ears. "I know that I sort of . . . you know, turned you down rather harshly. I'd told Zoe I didn't plan to bet on you, and I *know* the money was going to first responders, but I just couldn't . . . I mean, it's never been about your looks." She offers an awkward *ha-ha*, her blue eyes skirting up to my face before swiftly darting away again. "You're handsome. And young. Oh, God, what I *mean* is—I already said that. The *I mean* thing, I mean. I just did it again." Her eyes go wide as though begging me to end her misery.

I don't.

Let the misery continue.

I fold my arms over my chest and keep up the mute act. I like this Gwen. Hell, I *really* like this Gwen.

She huffs out a heavy breath, repeating the tuck-the-hair motion again. There's no more hair to tuck. It's already been plastered behind her ears. But she's nervous. For the first time in years, I think I may be witnessing Gwen James come undone.

Over me.

Does sweet justice actually exist? I think it does.

"So, yes, I turned you down repeatedly. That's on me. I was going through . . . life? Yeah, we'll go with life. But I listened to what you said last night, Marshall, and I realized that I'd like to go on a date with you. It'd be nice. I mean, I *think* it would be nice. We won't know if we're compatible until we go out or whatever. To be honest, I'm not even sure a relationship is the best thing. Does love even really . . . it doesn't matter." Her shoulders hike up, her flouncy shirt fluttering around her breasts.

Blue eyes meet mine, hopeful and nervous.

"Will you go on a date with me, Marshall?"

I stare down at her—the woman I've crushed on like an idiot teenager for half my adult life—and say the one word I never anticipated telling her.

"No."

5

GWEN

"I can't believe he said no."

Both Charlie and Zoe roll their eyes, two nights after Marshall's rejection. We're seated at a high-top table at our favorite bar, and not even my favorite Pinot Grigio can soothe the sting of his firm "no."

"I can't believe he said no," I repeat, motioning to a passing cocktail waitress for another round. "How could he even do that? How do you go from asking someone to dance one night to shutting them down the very next day?"

"Easy," Charls says, surprising me. She snags my wine glass and downs what's left. "Sorry, not sorry," she tells me, pointing the glass at me when my mouth falls open. "We've been listening to you repeat the *same phrase* for thirty minutes now. I can't take it anymore."

I turn to Zoe, the bride-to-be. Instead of glowing radiantly like every bride should, she's feigning sleep, one hand holding up her head. Clapping my hands together, Zoe puts on a good, performative jolt like I've startled her awake.

"What?" she says, glancing around. "What did I miss?"

Charlie snickers, and I resist the urge to kick her in the

shin. "Oh, nothing. Our beloved Gwen is still talking about Hunt."

"About how he turned her down?" Zoe replies, reaching for Charlie's glass of wine. In other words, *my* glass of wine.

"Yup."

"Oh, huh, guess I didn't miss much then."

"Is this pick-on-Gwen night or something?" Smiling politely at the cocktail server as she drops off our second round of much-needed booze, I turn back to my friends. "Why don't you two have my side on this?"

Charlie and Zoe exchange a look, and it's one that I can't read. After a sip of her fresh Manhattan, Charlie props her elbows on the table and stares me down. "Do you want this easy or hard?"

I give an awkward laugh, knowing both of my friends aren't the sort to beat around the bush. "Is this where I make a bad sex joke? That's what she said, and all that?"

Zoe scrubs a hand over her mouth like she's fighting off a smile but doesn't want to encourage me. "No," she says, lips still twitching, "this is where we tell you that we love you. You know we do. But this is all your fault."

Charlie nods her curly blond head in agreement. "Totally your fault. What did you expect when you've strung the poor guy along for ten years now?"

"It hasn't been . . ." Knowing that neither one of them is going to care about the fact that I haven't even *known* Marshall for ten years, I add, "Correction. I've never strung him along. Not once."

"Lies." Charlie points at my wine. "Take a sip."

"Is this a new drinking game we're playing?"

"It is tonight." Charlie pushes the wine glass toward me with one finger to the base. "Now, how about that time three months ago when you made sure to order his favorite kind of wings when we were having dinner at Zoe's?"

They've got to be kidding me. Since when does an order from the local chicken-wing joint equate to relationship-*anything*? Clearly, the two of them are absolutely, irrefutably bonkers. Which, to be honest, isn't shocking.

Charlie thrives off being the life of the party, as much as she pretends to be the quiet wallflower decorating the furniture. She's hilarious, friendly, and snarky enough that most people are caught off-guard when she opens her mouth and trash-talks with the same caliber as a professional hockey player.

Zoe's not much better. Sure, she can be quiet in group settings—unless she's got a drink or two in her—but she's just as much of a snark-master as our girl Charls.

So, it's with a bit of trepidation that I murmur, "It was *wings*, you guys. Fried chicken, of all things. I didn't offer him my left kidney."

"Would you?" asks Zoe, lifting her brows. "Because Hunt would do that for you."

"Give me his kidney?" I shake my head. "Wouldn't happen."

"You sure?"

"Well . . . yeah." Am I sure? I certainly *think* that I am. Yes, Marshall hasn't made an effort to conceal his attraction to me over the years. But attraction isn't nearly the same thing as *caring* about someone.

"Drink time!" Charlie shouts, giving me The Look. The one where she's both triumphant and tipsy, and I'm pretty sure she's swaying in her seat. "You need a plan," she adds, most definitely swaying now. She tries to pass it off like she's dancing to the beat, but while hip-hop blasts from the bar's speakers, Charls looks like she's wrapped up in a slow-jam number from prom night.

She's even got her arms wrapped around her belly.

We should probably get ready to call it a night. I'm not feeling all that sober myself. I blame Marshall for this—because in the span of five minutes, he managed to undo everything. I have my role in our relationship; he has his. When I hook up with guys—which hasn't happened in months—they're always older, separated from their wives, and way too busy with their careers to think about me for longer than it takes for us to do the deed. I don't do younger guys *or* men with a penchant for long-term crushes. That's not my style; it's *never* been my style.

But then Marshall walked away, closing a door I'd ignored for so long, and . . . maybe I'm feeling a sense of regret for missing out on what could have been. Maybe I secretly liked the chase, and now that he has no plans to keep up the game, I'm desperate for any sort of connection with him.

Maybe you just don't want him to walk away.

I bring my wine glass to my lips for a swallow of the cold, irrefutable truth—that I didn't mind ignoring Marshall's advances when I always assumed he'd be there.

And now he's not.

Like my friends so eloquently told me, I have no one to blame but myself.

"I need to woo him."

The song switches over the loudspeaker as I speak, and my slurred words come out an octave louder than is socially acceptable. Heads swivel in our direction, curious glances painting everyone's expressions as they sip their cool brews and watch the spectacle unfold.

Cringing, I draw my shoulders down and bury my face into my hands. "Oh, my God. I can't believe I just said that."

Zoe pats me on the shoulder like I'm a good dog. "Glad you're finally admitting what we've known all along. You've screwed up, bad."

"Wooing is a great plan," Charlie jumps in, tapping the top of my head so that I'll meet her gaze, "as long as you do it correctly. And if you're serious."

"Why wouldn't I be serious?"

Her head cocks to the side. "Um, maybe because you've had *countless* of opportunities to take him up on any of his offers to go out with him, and you've turned him down just as many times. I don't think it's out of the realm of possibility to consider that you're just interested because he's no longer pining after you?"

"I don't think he ever *pined* after me," I mutter, nevertheless feeling the sting of her words. I can't help but wonder if they're true. Anything's possible and I'm definitely wasted right now. But . . . there's *also* the fact that the last two days have been alcohol-free, and I still haven't been able to rid myself of the hollow feeling which gripped my soul the minute Marshall dismissed me.

"He pined after you," Zoe confirms with a nod and a toss of her long, dark hair. "Pining was definitely involved. Fact is, Gwen, here's a little tough love. You're perfectly comfortable living the single life. I mean, I'm actually rather convinced that you enjoy it. When you do date, it's always casual and rarely lasts longer than a week or two."

While the words ring true, they also ring loud, as though I'm witnessing more of my sins being paraded out in front of me.

Bitchy Gwen James. Icy Gwen James. Horrible Gwen James.

I know my faults, every last one of them.

Clearing my throat, I say, "That's what I do, Zo, you know this. No-attached sex means there aren't any hurt feelings when we go our separate ways. I don't think I'm cut out for the ever-after sort of thing."

"Then what are you doing sulking about a lost opportunity with Hunt? If you don't want to date or get into anything more permanent, what's the point?"

I don't know.

I don't know.

I think of my mother, who I plan to visit tomorrow. She's been divorced multiple times, and yet she still jumps into new relationships with complete abandon. In a way, I almost envy her for that. Because in that respect, the apple might as well have landed in another continent.

I trust men to—excuse my language—fuck my body. Hell, I even trust them to make sure I orgasm. But I don't trust men to choose me over someone else. And, if I'm being honest with myself, perhaps that's always been my issue with Marshall.

I choose men who don't want me for the long haul. They walk away faster than I can blink and I do the same.

Marshall . . . Marshall wouldn't end things so heartlessly, not with me. But when he does leave—they always do—I don't think I could recover from that. Not really. Not in the same way that my mother can rant and rage for a few weeks before finding a new man to marry.

There's a seedling of doubt cracking my armor, a quiet question of *what if?* What if Marshall didn't abandon me? It helps that my best friends are happily in relationships, too, although I know Charls and Zoe would never, ever consider hooking up with a guy I wanted to date.

They're not like that.

Marshall isn't like that.

"I think I'm an idiot," I announce.

"Agreed." This from Zoe. "Question is, what are you going to do about it?"

"Go after what I want."

It's time to woo Marshall Hunt.

6

HUNT

There's something to be said about living in the same city where you were conceived, born, and raised.

I use the word "raised" lightly.

Because as I sit in my older brother's shitty-ass apartment only two blocks from my old foster-care house, I can't help but wonder how I managed to pull myself out of this hellhole. A determination to succeed, maybe. A fear that I'd end up just like my brother, Dave. An innate knowledge that if I allowed myself to linger too long in the memories, they'd fist my shirt and never let go.

One minute I'm staring down at a chipped mug full of rum, and in the next I'm drowning in the past.

Coming here to Dave's apartment always does this to me, and our routine never changes. He calls, needing something and, inevitably, I come running. When it comes to my brother, I operate almost exclusively on guilt. We both know it's the only reason I show up—that, and a naïve but still lingering hope that he wants to see me because we're family.

I push away the mug with a sigh. "I'm not writing you

another check," I tell Dave, forcing myself to meet his bleary blue eyes. "I told you that last time."

"Nah," my brother says, dragging his fingers along the side of his pockmarked face, "you said you'd *think* about it. Big difference, bro."

Bro.

Like he really gave two shits about me growing up or like he even gives two shits about me now. It wasn't until Northeastern recruited me that Dave started popping into my life again for something more substantial than a "hello." By that point, I'd seen enough of Boston's seedy side to know that Dave was bad news all the way around.

The way he scratched at his nose, a telltale sign that he was addicted to coke and God knows what else, was just the tip of the iceberg.

Dave sits forward in his chair, elbows on the table as he snags my rejected mug. He downs the rum in one go, Adam's apple dodging downward, without even a wince. Porcelain meets wood with a *clank!* and then my brother is looking at me earnestly. "Let's do it together, bro. Can you imagine if we created a genius app? You've got the funds. I've got the brains."

His accent is just as thick as mine, so that "together" sounds a lot more like "togethah." I've done what I can over the years to soften the Boston in my voice, mostly so I don't have to answer to idiots asking me to "pahk the cah in Hahvahd yahd." But Dave is completely unaware of all that, and he speaks as brashly as he fights on Friday nights down in Brockton.

Yeah, he doesn't think I know about that. But I do.

The missing teeth here or there were good indicators to start—those that weren't already gone from the drug use, anyway.

Swallowing my growing temper, I pull on my charming façade. Pissing off Dave usually ends in him threatening to bash me over the head with the closest object. "How're your other businesses going? You gotta be a little too busy to add on more right now... don't you think?"

I can see him pondering this, taking the time to plot out his next move. I'm not at all surprised when he opens his mouth and lies like a motherfucker. "Not too busy for my baby bro. Who do you think I am?"

A drunk. Cheat. Liar. Thief.

I may have missed one.

He must read my thoughts in my expression because his lips twist in displeasure and he gives up all pretense. "C'mon, dude. I fuckin' need the money, alright? While you're out on the ice scoring hat tricks like you're shittin' out baby unicorns, some of us have to make a real living."

Because, apparently, having grown-ass men pummel me on the ice isn't a *real* job. I roll my eyes, my hands going to the table in preparation to get the hell out of here. "You already owe me close to fifty-k, Dave. I'm not looking to sink anymore cash into plans that aren't going anywhere but to your addictions."

It's a low blow, I'll admit.

And it's absolutely the wrong thing to say.

Dave climbs to his feet, swaying from the booze. Drunk or not, he's still a big dude. Almost as big as I am—his fighting keeps him muscular even if the alcohol has his waistline bloating like a pufferfish.

"You don't know what you're talking about," he growls, coming around the table with jerky steps. "You got the fuck outta here, bro. You skipped out of Southie faster than I take a piss most days." He shoves his face close to mine, and the scent of rum is overwhelmingly sweet. "You think you're some bigshot now, huh? Who knows that little Marshall Hunt, fucker of all supermodels and the NHL's golden boy, is nothing but a—"

My vision clouds.

Keep calm.

I don't keep calm.

The old me, the angry youth, shoves to the surface as my hands go to Dave's chest and push. Hard.

Thanks to the drink, his balance is shot and he stumbles backward. Crashing into a chair. Tripping over a stray sneaker. Falling onto his ass.

Mouth curving in a snarl, Dave lifts a shaky finger to point at me. "You know what makes me feel better each night?" he demands, voice quivering with undiluted rage. "The fact that every game, I'm hoping you'll lose. That you'll keep on losing, night after night, until you're booted off the Blades... and you're right back here with me. Surviving."

I don't want to admit it but his words freeze my heart with the fear that drives me every day. I play hockey because I love the sport, but I'm not delusional—I bust my ass in the rink, in the gym, because the alternative is *this*.

Dark-paneled walls. The stench of cigarettes and booze. The tiny apartment seated over a convenient store more known for the number of armed robberies occurring within its walls than any of its inventory.

My stomach heaves, both out of guilt for escaping and also for that damn fear that never fails to tighten my skin.

"How much?" I rasp, hating myself for giving in yet another time.

The slant of Dave's smile is like a right hook to my face. Once again, I've been played right into his trap.

Marshall—zero.

Dave—fifty-thousand dollars and counting.

He rests one wrist across his bent knee, casual and cool the way he wasn't five minutes ago when he was whispering prayers that my livelihood would be stripped from me. "Just ten, this time."

I'm not stupid enough to think he's talking about a crisp Alexander Hamilton. I need to get the hell out of here before I agree to re-mortgage my house for him. "I'll transfer it to your account," I mutter, grabbing my cell phone off the table.

I barely make it to the door before my brother is laughing like a maniac and shouting, "Love you, bro!"

Yeah, joke's on me.

I'm out of the rancid apartment in seconds, yanking the door shut behind me as I head for the stairwell.

Once upon a time, I used to fully believe that I could outrun my past. My mistakes. Dave is a constant reminder of how *not* true that's turned out to be. The more success I have on the ice, the more my brother is there, waiting, to collect on what he thinks is owed to him.

And maybe . . . maybe there's some truth to that. But after seventeen years, I'm pretty sure my debt has been paid —if debts are even supposed to exist among family. They do in mine, which I guess is all that matters.

Not for the first time do I wonder what it'd be like to belong to a family like Duke Harrison's. Not only does he have both his parents, but they support him. Even his mother, who has a phobia of flying, has started conquering that fear by forcing her husband to book flights from Minnesota, where they live, to our games along the west coast.

Hell, if we're looking at my teammates, Jackson Carter probably has the sweetest deal. Parents who think he hangs the world. An equally doting wife. My captain might be an asshole on the ice, but off it, he's the quintessential Texas gentleman.

I brace myself for the brisk cold air when I step outside Dave's building. Trash bags line the street, broken glass bottles are scattered within the snow, and even the colors of the buildings are bleak. Gray, mostly, with a few brick ones mingled in.

Without even realizing it, I find my feet taking me in the opposite direction of my truck. I don't stop until I'm staring at the house where I spent most of my teenage years.

It looks just as awful as it did a decade ago.

My foster parents don't live here anymore. We don't keep in contact, so it's just as possible that they've moved out of state as it is that they're dead. I feel a stab of guilt at the thought. Sue and Marty Gottim weren't horrible people; they just hadn't cared about the kids in their care.

Maybe they had, when they'd first started out working with the system. But, by the time I came around when they'd been in their sixties, time had worn them down. Hell, *I'd* been worn down.

I'm so lost in my thoughts that I almost don't hear my phone ringing. I dig it out of my pocket, still noting all the ways the Gottim's old triple-decker hasn't changed as I answer the call.

"Hunt," I say, as I catch a flutter of a window curtain on the first floor.

Time to go.

"Marshall?"

I have no control over my body, and my cock stiffens at just the sound of Gwen's breathy voice over the phone. As I step away from my childhood home, I walk briskly back to my truck, head down against the bitter wind.

"You've never called me," I say. "To what do I owe this pleasure?"

"Of course I've called you before."

Guess she's still stuck on the first bit.

I shake my head, even though she can't see me. "Negative, Ghost Rider. Not a single time and we've known each for, what? Five years?"

It's been six, but I'm a bastard and I want to know if she'll say something.

"Six," she corrects, and warmth spreads in my chest. "Never mind that, I'm pretty sure I've called you at least once."

"Give me an example."

"Uhh . . . maybe when we used to study together?"

Her hesitation is like victory thrumming in my veins, and I let out a low chuckle. "I'll let you off the hook, Miss James. What can I do for you? I'll be blunt, though, I'm all out of fucks to give today. Fair warning."

She laughs, and I can almost see her tucking her red hair behind her ears. I miss it blonde, but the red is hot, too. More appropriate, maybe, given the fact that she's a spitfire in designer clothing.

"You should tell me about it."

Throwing a quick glance to my left and right, I jaywalk across the street. "Tell you about what?"

"Why you've got no fucks to give."

Is it wrong that I feel a little suspicious over that? My stride slows as I approach my truck. I don't even know how to best respond. Gwen doesn't call me. Ever. She doesn't ask me about my day or wonder why I might not be in a good mood.

Simple fact is, I don't trust her sudden change of heart.

I climb into my truck, tugging the door shut. The

moment the engine kicks into gear, I'm cranking up the heat. Hockey player or not, I'm not a fan of my balls freezing into nonexistence from the cold. "Gwen."

"Marshall."

I resist a smile at her perfunctory tone and cut straight to the chase. "Why are you calling me?"

There's the sound of squeaking on the other end of the line, like she's shifting in a chair. "Can't I call a friend?" she finally says.

"Are we friends? Last I checked, you were avoiding me like the plague."

"I wasn't . . . I'm not . . ." She blows out a heavy breath. "There's this *thing* tonight, and I was wondering if you might want to go with me."

My pulse kicks into gear. Is Gwen asking me on a date—again? I run one hand through my hair. There's a good chance I've entered the Twilight Zone. No other explanation for it. "What's this *thing*?"

"Ice sculptures," she clips out quickly. "I saw it online today while I was at work, and I've never been. I thought, maybe, it might be fun to go with someone."

I want to ask if I was her first choice or if she's asking simply because no one else will go with her. I don't, mostly because I'm not about to show her my ace. Namely, that I'm way more intrigued by her proposition than I should be after she turned me down the other night.

After everything with Dave, I want this. Hell, I *need* this. Skimming my palm over the steering wheel, I seal my fate with five words. "Where should I meet you?"

7

GWEN

Twinkling lights wind through the trees above me as I wait for Marshall in Boston's historic Faneuil Hall. Clasped between my hands is a Styrofoam cup filled with hot chocolate; clamped between my legs is a second one for Marshall.

I don't even know if he likes hot chocolate.

Bringing the cup to my lips, I blow away billowing steam and brace myself for a hot sip. I need the scalding heat, anything to keep myself from obsessing over one thought: what in the world am I doing?

Asking Marshall out on a date—for a second time in a week?

I'm not even the sort of woman who asks a man out at all.

But here I am, camped out on a bench along one of Boston's busiest tourist spots, waiting for the NHL's most charming playboy to come and find me. Laughing awkwardly, even though I'm alone, I tap my cell phone to life and peer down at the text he sent me ten minutes earlier.

Parking now. What are you wearing?

He could have easily asked where I'm sitting—answer to that would be next to the Starbucks because I am nothing if not a traitor to every Bostonian around.

"That's not his way," I mutter to myself, sipping more of the hot chocolate.

I've known Marshall for years, and my first memory of him isn't hockey-related. No, not at all. Accounting 201. While I'd known even then that PR was my future, I'd still been required to take certain business courses.

Accounting it was, then.

On the first day of class, Marshall sat directly behind me. Big, muscular. Without even knowing who he was, it'd still been obvious to me that he was an athlete. Mere mortal men don't look like they can bench-press women over the age of twenty.

Marshall did.

His desk had creaked with his shifting weight, and the next thing I knew, his face was in my periphery, grinning devilishly as his full lips formed the words, "Gotta pen I can borrow?"

My eyes had caught on the pen hooked behind his right ear. "Think you've got that one covered," I'd told him dryly, "but nice try."

Marshall Hunt wasn't a quitter.

For the next week, he purposely stalled by the doorway next to the trashcan. Only when my gaze clashed with his did he theatrically dig out a pen from his backpack and drop it into the garbage.

Every day I gave him a new pen.

The next day, he trashed it, making sure I witnessed the travesty to poor pens everywhere, and then asked me for another.

As a way to start up conversation with you.

Seeking out my hot chocolate like it's spiked with booze, I try not to think of the disappointment in Marshall's pewter eyes when I'd clued him in that I wasn't single a few weeks into the semester, and that I was dating his teammate.

Ironic how we've come full circle.

"Gwen?"

I jolt at the sound of his voice, though I've been expecting it now for nearly fifteen minutes. My gaze lifts from my cup and collides with the bulge in his jeans.

He's *right* in front of me, literally inches away.

And so is his jean-covered package.

Feeling heat rise to my cheeks, I hike my gaze up past his belt buckle, the Blades hoodie spanning his wide chest, and then up to his face. Chiseled features greet me, along with an arched brow and a twinkle in his gray eyes.

Oh, yeah.

He totally caught me ogling him.

Embarrassment mingles with pride as I purposely take a long pull from my drink, daring him to call me out for my shameless once-over.

Thankfully, he lets me off the hook with a flashy grin and a nod to the cup between my legs. "That for me? You shouldn't have, Gwenny."

Without waiting for an answer, he drops to his haunches, without a care to anyone who might be watching. The air vacates my lungs in a swift exhale when his big hands settle on my knees and then inches them wide.

The hot chocolate drops from its tight hold, right into his grasp, and in the smoothest move I've ever seen, he slides his free hand up my thigh, blunt-tipped fingers skimming my skirt. He watches me over the rim of the cup as he takes a long pull of his drink.

Hat Trick 53

The moment is over within seconds.

Marshall takes the empty spot beside me on the bench, his hands wrapped around the Starbucks blend, his thighs spread wide, his right pressed to my left. Totally casual, as though he hasn't made my legs quiver or my heart race with *something*.

Need. Lust.

Two things I've always been very careful not to allow myself to feel around Marshall Hunt.

I'm so consumed with sudden images of him between my legs in a very different NSFW-way that I catch only the tail end of his sentence: "How long have you been a wannabe Aaron Burr?"

I blink, turning to him. He's got a beanie hat pulled down over his ears. I *want* to say that it makes him look younger than he already is—like he's back in college—but that'd be a boldfaced lie.

The hat only accentuates his handsome, pretty-boy features. The straight slope of his nose, somehow unbroken from countless battles on the ice. The square jaw. The high cheekbones.

He belongs on a billboard.

Realizing that he's watching me, waiting, I scramble to think of something to say besides *you've made me horny and I don't know what to do about it*. I don't say that, thank God. Instead, I opt for the safer, "What do you mean, Aaron Burr?"

He holds up his cup, giving it a little side-to-side wiggle. "Starbucks, Gwen. As a local, you know better than to betray our beloved Dunkins."

Funny how I'd thought the same thing as I purchased our drinks.

"Not that I'm complaining," he continues with a wink in

my direction. "It's cold as a witch's breast out here and this definitely helps."

"Tit."

He lowers the cup to his thigh. "What?"

"Tit," I repeat, hating the fact that he's managed to throw me off-kilter. I glance at the crowd wandering past, heading for the sculptures along the harbor, and wonder how no one has noticed that the Blades' new favorite player is within their midst. "The phrase is, 'cold as a witch's tit.' Not breast."

Marshall only crosses his leg, his left ankle on his right knee. His smile is slow, flirtatious, and just before he tips the cup back up to his lips, he murmurs, "I know."

Of course he does.

And, *of course*, he would find a way to mess with me. Some things never change, just like with the countless pens I handed over, only for him to deliver them straight to their pen graveyard. I lick my lips, tasting the light gloss I swiped on earlier. Gray eyes latch onto my mouth, as I say, "You *would* find a way for me to repeat the word 'tit' multiple times."

He gives a low, masculine laugh. "Worth it."

I swallow a smile. "Anyone ever tell you before that you're a jerk?"

"Once or twice."

"Only once or twice?"

His fingers tap out a rhythm against his raised calf. "Pretty sure you're not supposed to insult your date, Gwenny. It goes against every date code there is."

Just like that, he manages to deflate my ease.

I'm on a date with Marshall Hunt.

And I'm not even stressing over his celebrity-status as a pro-athlete. Nope. The only thing bouncing around my skull is, *I'm on a date with Marshall Hunt, the guy who drove me nuts all senior year and hasn't stopped since.*

Okay, maybe "drove me nuts" isn't entirely correct.

It's just that . . . over the last six years, Marshall has always popped up at times when he's least expected.

A random date I'd gone on with a man nearly twice my age. One minute I'd been contemplating whether or not I actually wanted to sleep with the successful real estate broker, and, in the next, Marshall was pulling up a chair and sitting beside me, introducing himself to my date and ultimately ruining everything.

There was a year or two in our timeline of sort-of-friends where we'd had no contact. But then the auction had occurred last year. The Blades had "sold" themselves off to the highest bidder, all in the name of charity for Boston's first responders, and Zoe had bartered me off to Marshall.

Once again renewing our years' long push-and-pull.

Needing another moment to work over my thoughts, I finish off my hot chocolate, which isn't so hot anymore, and then tuck the cup between my legs, just as I'd done to his.

"I'm surprised you even agreed to meet me tonight," I say, going for honesty. Another rule of life I've thrived on after countless therapy sessions. "You were pretty clear the other day that you were no longer interested."

I sneak a glance at him, hoping to see something in his handsome expression that'll tell me I'm wrong, that he still wants me.

And if he does? What do you plan to do with that knowledge?

My cup crumples as my knees dart inward.

I don't know. I don't know what I'll do at all, but for the first time in my life, I'm flying by the seat of my pants—or skirt, as the case may be. All I know is that the panic I felt when he walked away at the engagement party is not something I want to experience again.

Marshall plucks the cup from between my knees, holding it up with a raised brow before basketball-tossing it into the trash bin opposite us. Naturally, he's got dead-center aim, and it disappears into the depth of waste.

"I had a pretty shit day," he says, repeating the NBA-worthy throw with his own cup. "Figured if there was anyone out there who could make it better, it'd be you."

Unexpected warmth squeezes my heart. "That's so sweet—"

"As friends."

What? My mouth falls open, and there's no way that I look anything but ridiculous right now. "What do you mean as *friends*?" My voice emerges loud enough that a few people walking past slow down and crane their heads to look back at us.

"Lover's spat," Marshall tells them with a little finger wave in our direction. He goes as far as to wrap his arm around my shoulders and yank me up against his hard body. "You know how it goes."

You know how it goes?!

What is he—is he . . . I can't even get my thoughts to straighten out, I'm so flustered. But I do manage to untangle myself as I shoot over to the far side of the bench. *Breathe, breathe, breathe. Do* not *revert back to the Old Gwen.*

It would be so easy to do just that. To lay into him with a sharp tongue and a one-liner about not needing him as a friend, that I have plenty of friends (I don't), and that I especially don't need his *friendship* when he led me to believe that this was, in fact, a date.

But I refuse to be that person.

This is a test, that's all.

A test of my self-control and respect for my self-worth, and there is no way I'm going to give him even the smallest glimpse into my shock . . . and, yes, my disappointment. I press a hand to my chest, feeling the erratic pounding of my heart through my coat. Yup, disappointment exists.

I'm not happy about it.

Determined to show how unaffected I am by his announcement, I flick my red hair over my shoulders and make a point to meet his gaze. "Friends is good. I mean, we haven't even gone to the sculptures but I can already tell that . . ."

I purposely dangle that unfinished sentence in his face, letting him make of it what he will.

Marshall doesn't let me down.

Square jaw clenches. Pewter gray eyes narrow.

No doubt about it, if I played hockey and he was coming my way, I'd be down in the fetal position in three seconds flat.

Model-handsome or not, he's got the whole *I-will-make-you-piss-yourself* glare down to a T.

Not that I've pissed myself.

Nor do I intend to.

"What's that supposed to mean?" he says, voice hard.

I pretend to admire my cuticles, turning them this way and that. He will *not* see how much I was looking forward to tonight. Obviously, I was mistaken—Marshall isn't a forever kind of guy.

He's not even a *now* kind of guy.

Not when push comes to shove and I finally throw myself at him.

Guess he wanted the chase like every other guy in existence.

To my surprise, he captures my wrist, halting my inspection of my manicured nails, and tugs me forward, toward *him*.

I don't have the chance to preserve my balance.

My palms land flat on his thighs, my thumbs dangerously close to that bulge I came face to face with earlier. A ridiculous *oh!* escapes my lips, and my tits, as he so expertly convinced me to say earlier, graze his hard chest.

Between the icy temperature and the fact that Marshall's warm breath whispers against my forehead, is it any wonder that my nipples turn into hard peaks? Thank God for heavy winter layers because otherwise ... well, you know.

Diamonds, my friends.

My nipples are as hard as diamonds right now.

Forcing nonchalance into my voice, I quip, "Can I help you, Marshall?"

His hands slip up from my wrists to my shoulders, and I fight off a shiver. A shiver from the cold, *obviously*. It has nothing to do with the hotshot hockey player a breath away.

"You wanted tonight to be a date."

I don't fall for his cool-as-a-cucumber tone. "You obviously didn't," I retort, trying my best not to give in and sniff his cologne like a crazy lady. "*Friend*."

"You do realize that I've been trying to make this happen for years now, right? And then the *minute* that I decide I'm no longer playing our games, you decide that you suddenly want me?" The heat of his palm coasts down, down, down, over my back. I don't have a chance to miss the loss of him before he's cupping my butt, and this time ... this time the *oh* that trips off my tongue is more lustful sigh than anything else. "Exactly," he continues huskily, "you want what you can't have, Gwen."

No. The word reverberates in my chest. *No, no, no.* He's

lumping me in with who I've been, the self-centered woman with an icy shield of armor. "Marshall—"

"So prove it."

My nails bite into his thighs as I rear back to meet his gaze. "What?"

"That you want me." His gray eyes glitter with an inscrutable emotion. "If you want to date me, if you *really* want to see where this might go, it's on you this time."

Hadn't I said this exact thing the other night? That I need to woo him?

Although, to be fair, that was the plan tonight.

Marshall Hunt has always been one step ahead of me.

"Okay." I swallow, hard. "Okay, I can do that."

"And we're not hooking up until I know you're in this for real."

Is it possible for your head to burst from too much blood pounding furiously through it? Humiliation, pure and raw, clouds my vision and unsettles my stomach. Good thing I waited to eat, in the hope that Marshall and I might grab something, because I feel utterly sick. Nerves, I think. Also a good deal of self-disgust that I've done so much harm to others in my life that *this* is how Marshall figures he can trust me.

Ahem. I think that was the sound of my heart splintering.

I avert my gaze, nodding to myself like *yeah, yeah, makes all the sense.* When, in reality, my heart is screaming *what do I have to do to* not *be treated like my mother?*

"No hooking up," I mutter, stealing back my hands to push my hair behind my ears. "Got it."

My shoulders twitch when I feel strong fingers cup my jaw, softly encouraging me to meet even softer gray eyes.

Marshall's thumb brushes my bottom lip, and I fight the urge to touch my tongue to the calloused flesh.

"I want you, Gwen. You have no fucking idea how much I want to taste you." His accented voice thickens into a low growl. "I want your nails carving down my back as I take you, and I sure as hell want to know what it's like to have you come all over my cock." He leans in, his mouth nearly brushing mine, tantalizing me with the endless possibilities, before he retreats. "But I want what no one else has ever had."

A shiver ripples down my spine. I tell myself that it's the cold. I tell myself that it has nothing to do with the heated passion in his eyes and the way my core pulses with need. I've never, not once, felt the way that I do in this moment—like I'm on the cusp of something huge and I'll never be the same once I take what he's offering me. "And what's that?"

"You." That one word steals the breath from my body and I blink back the sudden sting of tears. He continues, both with his thumb caressing my mouth as well as with his words. "You've never hidden the fact that you give your body to others. I'd be a hypocrite to judge you for that, but I want more than just your body. I want your heart, and that's not something I'm willing to share."

"And if I give it to you? My heart?"

His lips turn up in a naughty grin. "I'll score a hat trick, Gwen. I'll let you make of that what you will."

A hat trick . . . the hockey term plays on repeat in my head. *When a player scores three times in one game.*

As if waiting for all the puzzle pieces to slide into place, he laughs when my eyes go wide at the sexual undertone of his voice and then he plants his hands on his knees to stand. Looking down at me, he holds out one hand, palm up in a silent offer of truce. "Show me the ice sculptures?"

I eye his proffered hand, then slip my palm snuggly against his.

Game on.

8

HUNT

"That sculpture is *supposed* to have hard nipples, Marshall."

I make a show of glancing up at the frozen mermaid in front of us, jerking my head to the nipples in question as I nudge Gwen in the side. "She's turned on, Gwen. Leave the poor girl alone to her horniness. This is a judgment-free zone."

The throaty groan Gwen releases is all kinds of sexy. "It's made out of *ice*." She waves a gloved hand at the boardwalk of ice sculptures against the backdrop of the twinkling harbor. "They're *all* made out of ice. Get your mind out of the gutter."

Around Gwen, my mind is permanently in the gutter.

I lean down, allowing my breath to whisper across the shell of her ear. "You think she's dreaming about Eric right now?"

Goosebumps erupt over her flesh, and I swallow a chuckle.

"Eric?" she echoes.

"Yeah. Prince Eric—Little Mermaid's boyfriend. Ringin' any bells?"

Chin tipping back, she glances up at me with a roll of her eyes. "I can't believe you just turned a Disney movie into an R-rated porno."

"A *porno*?" My hand flies to my chest, and I go all out trying to uphold the mock-affronted glare. "Gwen, we haven't even hit PG-13. Don't challenge me."

"I'm not—" Her pursed lips break into a wicked grin, and she dances away from me, her boots tromping in the snow. "All right, let's do it."

My teeth rattle as my jaw clamps shut. "Let's do what?"

Her blue eyes flit side to side, taking in the children screaming bloody murder as parents stalk down their offspring. Couples stroll through the night, faces tipped back as though expecting snowflakes from the otherwise dry night.

Everyone is way too consumed with their own lives to overhear us, but Gwen nevertheless starts back my way again, swinging her hips and stripping off her right glove.

The glove is clutched in her left hand, and, when she's within reach, she surprises me by hooking a bare finger into the neck of my sweatshirt and tugging me down to her level. Gwen isn't short but I'm taller. Broader. It goes against every instinct in my body not to drag her into my arms and finally learn what it's like to kiss Gwen James.

But then I'd be going against my own rules, and there's no way I'm doing that.

If she wants me, then Miss James is going to have to show me the old-fashioned way. I expect to be properly courted.

Courted, really? Did the cold officially cut off your dingleberries?

With her breath warming my face, Gwen declares, "I challenge you to find something raunchy about every sculpture."

What I *want* to do is demonstrate how every thought I have of her is raunchy. Obviously, that's not a go—yet.

Wrapping a hand around her wrist, I rub her chilled skin between my two palms. "I'm in. *All in*. But you have to do the challenge with me. Each time you can't think of something, that's another date I collect from you."

Her blue eyes warm even as she ducks her head. "Going for a hat trick, Marshall?"

"Always," I vow. Releasing her hand, and therefore severing our connection, I stuff my hands into my sweatshirt pocket as I stroll down the pebbled path. Over my shoulder, I toss back, "Don't worry, Gwenny. Each time you best me, you'll earn a kiss."

"Breaking your cardinal rule already?" she teases, sashaying to catch up with me. Her scarf comes undone around her neck. To my surprise, she leaves it as is, as though content to just *be* instead of constantly pulling herself together.

I like it.

More than I should.

"I'm not breaking anything." With a palm to her lower back, I direct her to the next sculpture. "I'm not kissing you yet. But you can start your tally now, if you want."

"Oh, I want. Now stop talking so I can find the sexiest damn thing about this block of ice. One butt-whooping is about to be underway."

Laughter reverberates in my chest. "Yes, ma'am."

I don't miss her grimace. "Please don't call me that. It reminds me that I'm—"

"Old?" I offer, finally letting my hand drop from her back. "Ready for your social security to kick in?"

She flashes me a surly glance but I see straight through the icy veneer.

I face the sculpture, a God-knows-what slab of frozen liquid that I *think* might be a Christmas tree but looks a lot like Jabba the Hutt from *Star Wars*. It's woefully lopsided, and I'm careful to keep my attention on the ice when I respond. "I think you like that I'm younger than you."

With sharp motions, she jerks her glove back on. "I think you're delusional."

I rock back on my heels, and I can feel a grin threatening to break free. "You gotta be how old by now, Gwen? Thirty-five, at least? Which would make you, what? A decade older than me?"

Her side-eye would be withering to a lesser man but I stand strong. One redhead won't do me in, no matter how gorgeous she is. "So, if you had a kid, would that make you a MILF?"

It's that comment that does it.

She turns to me with gloved hands raised, miming strangling me. A moment later, she's bent over, hands on her thighs, feminine laughter slipping from her lush mouth. In between gusts of joy, she grinds out, "You're ridiculous, Marshall. Utterly ridiculous. And you know I'm twenty-eight, you jerk."

I match her stance, planting my palms on my thighs as I slide up next to her so that we're shoulder-to-shoulder. "I should probably take the time to point out that our Christmas tree sculpture looks like it's into some BDSM."

Thumbing a tear from her eye, Gwen stands tall, hip popping out, arms crossing over her chest. "Those are supposed to be holiday lights, Marshall."

"You sure?" I point out the frozen etchings crisscrossing over the shaved ice tree. "Looks like chains to me."

"Garland, maybe?"

"Chains, Gwen. Like the kind the media likes to think I have in my basement."

With another quick glance at the BDSM tree, she skirts around another couple and heads for the next sculpture. In two strides, I'm at her side, just as she asks, "How did that rumor even start?"

The old-fashioned way—with a lick of truth to it. Not the *complete* truth, mind you, just a sliver.

I rub the back of my neck, debating the best way to tell the story. "It all started when I first got on with the Blades, back when I was on the farm team. We had this . . . I don't even know what you'd call it."

Her brows arch with curiosity. "A sex shop?"

I chuckle. "No, not a sex shop—cutouts. We had cardboard cutouts of every player who'd been recruited by the Blades but hadn't been called up yet. They usually stayed at the rink, but one night a couple of the guys got wasted and they stole a few."

"Yours included?"

I nod, slowly. "Yeah, mine included. Well, bastards that they are, the idiots brought them down into my buddy's basement. He dimmed the lights, got some candles, chained all that cardboard up to the wall like something out of *Fifty Shades of Grey*. Pretty sure rose petals were an addition. I don't even know how many photos they snapped, but before the end of the night, those pictures were hitting every tabloid site on the internet."

Her smile is slow and tempting. "And, *voila*," she murmurs, "a sex fiend was born."

"Exactly." I meet her gaze without a hint of shame. "You

disappointed I have no plans to lock you up in my lair, Gwen?"

"Considering that you have no plans to lock me up at all, I think it's safe to say that I'm not any more disappointed now than I was an hour ago."

Fuck, I love her dry wit. It hooked me years ago and has the same powerful effect on me now. I desperately want to take her hand and pull her in close to see if she's got just as much attitude between the sheets as she does out of it.

But the point of the challenge I issued her isn't just to cut us off from sex. I meant what I said about wanting her heart. It'd be all too easy to take her home tonight and strip off her clothes. She'd let me, I know that. And we'd both thoroughly enjoy what would happen next.

The thing is, it's easy for her to accept our mutual attraction. Lust, however inconvenient at times, isn't rocket science. It's human nature to look at someone and find attributes about their body that turns you on.

It's a lot harder to do that with emotions—and, emotionally, that's where Gwen's walls have always existed. The second time I witnessed her cry was at her father's funeral. As I'd pulled her into my arms, I'd recognized that a woman who could feel so strongly about a man she barely knew had the capability for unshakable love.

If she let herself fall.

You mean, if she let herself fall for you.

I meet her gaze, wanting to say so much but not even knowing where to start.

She saves me the trouble by burrowing her hands into her coat pockets and smiling up at the black sky. Softly, so softly I almost miss the words, she whispers, "I needed this. Thank you."

Vulnerable Gwen is not a side of her that I see often.

Like a string pulled tight, I waver a moment before stepping close. Not *too* close, but close enough that I can see her breath curling into the cold air.

Don't give in, man. Don't touch her.

I mimic her pose, shoving my hands into my sweatshirt again. "What did you need?"

Her lips quirk up at my husky tone, and when she dips her chin again, her red hair slips forward over her shoulders like strands of silk. "A chance to be me." She shrugs, offering me a hesitant smile. "It doesn't happen . . . well, ever, really. My fault, of course. I have a bad habit of not letting anyone close, including you."

My heart squeezes. I know how much it cost her to admit that, to show the softer side she rarely allows anyone to see. "Come to my game tomorrow night."

I don't know if she's more surprised by the invitation or if I am.

"I—" Clearing her throat delicately, Gwen says, "I thought I'm the one pursuing you?"

Yes. No. Fuck it, I don't even care. "Then say you'd like to come to my game tomorrow. I might be nice and know someone with tickets."

She laughs at that, her teeth flashing white in the darkness. "You do know that I could easily snag tickets if I wanted them, right? I wouldn't have to pull any strings."

I cock my brow, challenging her. "But would it be as romantic as me leaving you tickets for the Family-and-Friends section?"

Gloved hands go to her hips, and she tilts her head to the side, as though considering my offer. Then, "Will I have the chance to take you out after the game? To continue my wooing?"

Wrong as it may be, given the fact that we're surrounded

by kids under the age of ten, my cock hardens at her words. "You can woo me whenever you want, Gwen."

"Great!" She squeezes my arm, once, and then steps back. "I have plans to up my kiss tally. Be prepared to do something crazy tomorrow evening."

"Does it involve chains?"

She rolls her pretty blue eyes. "Only in your dreams, Marshall."

But she's smiling as she says it, and for once, I think Gwen James and I are on the same page. Finally.

9

GWEN

The following night, TD Garden is utterly wild as the Blades hit the ice against the Pittsburgh Penguins. And when I say wild, I really do mean bat-shit crazy to the nth degree.

Even seated in the Family-and-Friends section, along with Charlie and Zoe, the arena is boisterous and unruly. Towels stamped with the Blades' blue and silver colors are thrown down onto the ice. I've seen at least two people wearing faux penguin heads. And, not to be overly dramatic, but I've been called a "goddamn Blades sucker" at least three times now.

Full confessional: I love it.

I haven't always been a hockey enthusiast. In fact, it's safe to say that while growing up with Adaline, I fully believed hockey players scored touchdowns. It was all tomato-tomahto to me. A goal is a goal, right?

Working for Golden Lights Media for the last few years changed all that. My PR firm single-handedly represents most of the players for both the Blades and the Boston Bruins, the city's other pro-hockey team. Learning the sport's terminology ensured I didn't look like an idiot in front of high-paying clients. Somewhere along the way, I also learned to fully appreciate the game itself.

Which is why I feel no shame at all in screaming like a lunatic when Andre Beaumont illegally cross-checks an opposing player into the boards. "What are you *doing*?" I shout, cupping my hands around my mouth. "Get your head out of your ass, Andre! Seriously!"

He might go by the nickname, King Sin Bin, but that doesn't mean the Blades can withstand Beaumont taking another turn in the penalty box. We're already trailing behind by two, and from the way things are shaping up, it doesn't look like we'll be pulling ahead tonight.

Not that Marshall hasn't tried. The man has already scored twice: once by jockeying the puck around the net before sailing it into the corner pocket; the other time when Lady Luck shined down upon him as the puck hit the pipes and then rebounded into the net behind the goalie's right shoulder.

Maybe I shouldn't admit to it but seeing Marshall in his element is damn sexy. Whenever the camera zooms in on him, I alternate between staring at his sweaty face, loving the determined look in his eyes, and also scoping out the way he handles his stick.

Foreshadowing, if you will. I have a feeling he's packing below the belt in the best way possible.

Someone taps me on my shoulder, and I turn to find Zoe staring at me with a shit-eating grin on her face.

Ahem.

I jerk my thumb over my shoulder. "Sorry about that . . . Just, you know, got carried away."

She maintains her silence.

I hold open my arms. "I love you?"

Charlie leans around Zoe, a cheese-covered nacho halfway to her mouth. "If Zoe doesn't love you back for dissing her man, I'll love you for her."

Have you ever heard of a heart sighing? My mom used to tell me that when I was a kid, generally in reference to her husbands. But for me, it's the support from my two friends —even if I did totally just "diss" Zoe's fiancé. In my defense, it was a crappy move that gave the Penguins an upper hand with a power play.

"Oh, I'll love her," Zoe shouts over the din of the crowd, "but not until she comes forward and confesses. I want to know what's going on with her and Hunt."

My cheeks warm, and I immediately reach forward to snatch a nacho from Charlie's seemingly endless supply. "It's good," I mutter, popping the chip into my mouth and rearranging my Blades ball cap on my head. "You know."

"We don't know." Zoe bumps her hip with mine. "Spill, girl. This is more fun than binge-watching *Vanderpump Rules* for an entire night."

"Now that's a lie," Charlie says. Her gaze tracks the players, and I know she's dying to be down near the ice, as close to the game as possible. For the sake of friendship, however, she promised to leave both her audio recorder and notebook at home.

One glance at Charlie's antsy sway back and forth, especially with every slapshot that flies at the Blades' net (and therefore at her boyfriend), and it's clear she's itching to write tonight's game into an epic article for *The Boston Globe*.

"Did you kiss?" Zoe asks, going in for the kill without preamble.

"No." I bite my lip, trying to decide if it's best to come out with the truth—that Marshall has no plans to fulfill the promise in his heated gaze until he knows that he can trust me. Letting out a sigh, I slip my fingers into the butt pockets of my jeans and avert my gaze to the ice, where Marshall has just won the puck in the face-off. "He wants to know that I'm not going to, I don't know, screw him over."

"Before he kisses you?"

Though I keep my eyes locked on Marshall, I nod at Zoe's question. "As we all know, my track record isn't full of unicorns and rainbows. I don't blame him for wanting to be sure I'm all in."

"And you do? Want to be all in, that is?"

How can I explain that last night, despite the fact that we'd done nothing but stroll together along the harbor, was one of the best nights that I've had in a good, long while? Forget that. How can I explain that I've been so shortsighted all these years?

"He's a good guy," I finally say, though the words are woefully inadequate to explain how I'm feeling. Which is probably sixty-percent excited and forty-percent *what-the-hell-am-I-doing?*

The latter exists only because I've never been in this position before.

I've never allowed myself to consider the prospect of *more* with anyone, least of all not with a hotshot athlete like Marshall.

"C'mon," Charlie says, holding out another chip coated with cheese, "open up and I'll give you a nacho. Yes, it's bribery. I'm fully aware."

Bribery among friends. I almost want to laugh. Instead, I watch as Marshall avoids being slammed into the boards down on the ice. His number, 22, flashes on his jersey as he turns away, shoulders pulled low. The Penguins' enforcer comes barreling toward him, but Marshall is quick—the quickest player on the ice—and the next thing that I know, he's skating down the length of the rink. His stick swings back and then sails down as he sends the puck skidding toward Jackson Carter, the Blades' captain and the team's right wing.

One push off Carter's skates, and then another and another. Helmet ducked, black gloves clenched around his stick, the Jumbotron shows Jackson Carter hauling ass toward the Penguins' net.

But then the play crumbles.

The Penguins' D-men swoop in, an intimidating force that drives Carter into the boards.

My heart leaps. The arena erupts into jeers and cheers and enthusiastic chanting for both teams.

"*Go!*" Charlie shouts, her nachos all but forgotten as she thrusts one hand in the air like she's angling to catch a steer. "Go, go, go!"

Zoe's not much better, especially as she used to work as a publicist for both the Blades and the Detroit Red Wings. "Find a way out of the pocket, Jax! Let's *go*!"

I don't watch Carter.

I can't.

I tear my gaze away from the Jumbotron, which is focused solely on Carter's plight to get the hell out of dodge.

Where is he?

I catch sight of Beaumont jumping into the fray, his big body towering over the Penguins' D-lineman as he works to get Carter free from the boards.

A hole opens.

I almost don't believe it; I almost don't believe it exists.

But it does, slight and small, and the puck squeaks out like a forgotten toy.

There he is.

My chest deflates with a holler and a happy shout as

Marshall hooks his stick around the puck. His powerful legs erase the distance from the players huddled around Carter to Pittsburgh's net where the goalie holds up his gloves in preparation.

Marshall doesn't hesitate.

Like a scene from a movie, he fakes a left and the goalie falls for the ploy in a rare show of naivety from a pro-hockey player.

That split-second is all Marshall needs.

He aims.

He shoots.

He scores.

Hat trick.

The end of the game buzzer rings forty-five seconds later. Marshall's three-goal performance isn't enough to pull the Blades to victory, but it proves one thing quite clearly: when Marshall Hunt wants something, he goes for it.

All these years, he's aimed for me.

Now it's time to prove that I can return the favor—I plan to score the guy. And for the first time in my life, I'm going all in.

10

HUNT

Given the fact that we lost tonight, you'd think that we would be a hell of a lot more pissed off. Yeah, Coach is stomping around like he wouldn't mind trading us all. Everyone else, though . . . we've accepted our fate.

The win wasn't in our cards tonight. Maybe if Andre hadn't decided to illegally elbow someone, he wouldn't have ended up in the sin bin for a second stint. One power play later, the Penguins had scored the one goal we hadn't been able to overcome.

Not even my epic goal during the final minutes on the clock could do the trick.

New game. New chances.

It's the motto I live by most days.

"Hunt, your phone just went off."

I pull my lightweight sweater over my head in a heartbeat, already reaching for where I left my phone on the bench. Henri Bordeaux, a left wing from Montreal, inches it close to me.

"Thanks, man," I mutter, already swiping my finger across the touch screen.

Gwen.

Just the sight of her name on my phone brings a ridiculous smile to my face.

"Your wifer?"

I lift my gaze to Bordeaux's open expression. "What?"

He dips his chin, pointing to my cell. "Your wifer. Isn't that what they call it?"

Beaumont snaps his locker shut to my right, dragging a ball cap onto his head in a smooth motion as he turns around. "Pretty sure he meant wifey. You know, what all the kids are calling their girls these days?"

"That's the stupidest shit I've ever heard," I mutter, only to crack a grin when Duke Harrison throws out, "That's what I said about that smizing shit. We're getting old."

I loop the strap of my duffel bag over my shoulder and across my chest. "Speak for yourself, old man. I'm ten years younger than you."

Harrison rubs his middle finger along the side of his face. "Don't forget that goalies have long life spans. Forwards, on the other hand? How do you like the prospect of retirement by the age of thirty?"

Like Cam Neely for the Bruins in the 90s or Mark Messier for the Edmonton Oilers, I'm what the NHL fondly calls a power forward. In layman's terms, I'm a center that kicks ass on the ice. In reality, Harrison's probably right—unless I pull a page out of Messier's Hall of Famer book and end up having a twenty-five-year long career. I wouldn't be opposed to that.

Still, I flash the veteran goalie the bird just to keep the joke going. There's been some talk that Harrison plans to retire this year. I really hope that's not the case. It's not often that you get along with every guy on a team, and this season's roster is top notch, all A-plus quality players. Beyond that, I consider these douchebags to be actual friends of mine. Brothers in uniform, if you will.

In all honesty, they're more family to me than I've ever had myself.

While my teammates rag each other about sagging balls and gray hair growing out of their ears, I swipe my phone again, hesitating only briefly before opening Gwen's text. You never know what you'll get with her—not that I'm complaining.

I didn't need to worry.

It's a photo of her leaning against my truck. She's decked out in a female Blades jersey that's trimmed tight at the waist, along with a Blades ball cap pulled down low. Her red hair is long and straight, and I'll be damned if I haven't been imagining it spread across my pillow for weeks now.

Years, really.

The caption of the photo reads, *Want to go on an adventure with me?*

Is that even a question?

Hell yes I do.

I clap my teammates on the shoulders, issuing an encouraging "we'll do better on the road this weekend" before I'm palming open the locker-room door and escaping into the dimly lit hallway.

If I had known turning Gwen down would light a fire under her ass to actually *see* me, I would have done it years ago. Six years ago, to be precise. But maybe life was supposed to happen this way—fate and all that other shit.

For a moment, I let myself consider the alternative: of Gwen and I getting together way back when. I wanted it then just as much as I do now. Doesn't mean it would have worked out. A three-year age gap is nothing once you're past college. But a three-year age difference while Gwen would have been diving into the workforce as I sat at a classroom desk? Yeah, maybe fate did play a heavy hand.

By the time I make it to the parking garage, I don't waste any more time. Feeling like some meathead out of a cheesy rom-com movie, I push my sleeves to my elbows and break into a light jog, ready to get my girl. My duffel bag slaps the outside of my right thigh as I cut over to where I left my truck.

There she is.

And there—

I slam to a stop, my bag swinging forward with the abrupt change in momentum.

No, she didn't.

Laughter floods my chest, and it sure as hell doesn't die down when Gwen rearranges her massive poster and lifts her chin to see me over the lightweight white cardboard.

"You didn't," I say, still struggling not to laugh.

She flashes me a bright grin, so genuinely pleased with herself that she looks like the kid who hasn't just stolen the candy, but the kid who's stolen everyone else's candy too. "I did," she confirms with a short nod. I can't make out her eyes, thanks to the Blades baseball hat that she's got on, but I sure as hell don't miss her dimples winking at me, nor the way she bounces from one foot to the other. "I wasn't sure if it was over the top."

"Oh, it is," I drawl, dragging my gaze down to where the words *Will u puck me 4 lyfe?* are scrawled in pink, glittery script. Cartoon-like rabbits fill in the white space, and they're all gripping pucks in their tiny little paws. The question mark is a misshapen hockey stick on drugs. And, hell, at least one of the rabbits is wearing a pink tutu, overlaid with more glitter.

It's awful.

There really isn't any other word for it.

My thumb hooks under my duffel's strap, and I lift it over my head and down by my side. "Your spelling needs some work."

Gwen glances down at her masterpiece. "That was the plan. I was hoping to distract you from my pitiful bunnies."

Stepping close to her, I trace one of the tutus, enjoying the way Gwen's gaze follows the path of my fingers. In a husky voice, I say, "Were you trying to tell me something?"

"Like what?"

"I don't know. Like maybe that you're the only puck bunny I'll ever want?"

The brim of her hat is shoved up with one finger, and then she's meeting my gaze head-on. "That's a given," she says with a small smile. "I'm turning a new leaf."

"Yeah?" I can't stop myself. I take another step closer to her. She retreats on instinct—I'm nearly double her size—and her back presses against the bed of my truck. "What sort of leaf are we talking here?"

With the poster stuck in between us, I can't feel her body. The poster crinkles as I lean into her, one hand going to the truck's tailgate, the other still holding onto my duffel bag at my side. Guileless blue eyes blink up at me, and the desire I see there nearly brings me to my knees.

"The leaf," I grunt, trying to remember where the hell this conversation started, as opposed to all the places I'd love for it to go.

Namely, some kind of flat surface.

I'm not picky.

Gwen swallows audibly. The shyness she's radiating is

not nearly the kickass publicist I've seen put my teammates in place after they've acted out of turn. *This* Gwen is for me, I know it—*only* me.

"The poster is a joke," she says, her fingers tightening on the flimsy poster-board. "I'm not looking to be a puck bunny, yours or anyone else's. I want to . . ." The poster inches upward, as though she's nervous to admit the truth.

"Tell me, Gwen." I swipe off her hat, and it clatters to the cement with hardly a sound. Neither of us move to grab it. I'm not interested in the hat. I need to hear what she has to say. "What is it?"

She shakes her head, and her red strands catch on her lip.

Fuck it.

My fingers brush that hair back, tucking it behind her ear before returning to her full mouth. "I've been dying to kiss you for years now," I growl, dropping my lips to the shell of her ear. "Ever since you sat down in front of me, wearing that short denim skirt. You've been temptation for me ever since."

Another swallow, but this time she tips back her head, exposing the column of her throat as though daring me to take a bite. And, fuck me, but I want to—I want to leave my mark, claim her as mine. A love bite that she'll work hard to cover up in public while tracing it with her fingers when she's alone. *Jesus.* "You drove me nuts. Every day for an entire semester, you pushed me to my limits." I meet her gaze, then add, "Did you want me?"

Her lips part on a sharply drawn breath at my question, and I wish she'd drop the damn poster and let me in close.

"I was dating your teammate," she says with a good dose of bitterness. "Mistake number one."

"Mistakes can be forgiven." I nudge her ear with my

nose, my tongue flicking out to tease her. That's all this will be—to get my fix until I can have her. All of her. Finally. "Tell me what you meant by turning over a new leaf."

"Just that I . . . I don't want to be a short-term girl. I've done it. I've been that girl for *years*. So no, I don't want to be the quintessential puck bunny who's down for a quick hookup and nothing else. I want more. I-I *deserve* more."

She does. She deserves everything.

I step back and reach down to grab my duffel and then her hat in one smooth move. Gwen's ridiculous poster is still plastered to her chest as she watches me carefully, as though uncertain of my next move.

"Take me on an adventure, Miss James."

Her smile is slow, definitely not as flashy as the one she gifted me with earlier when I first walked up, but it's no less powerful. No less mesmerizing.

"The girls picked me up today," she says. "I'll give you directions."

11

GWEN

"And here I was thinking you were bringing me back to Cheers."

"Not today," I murmur, taking the two pairs of skates from the attendant. "Have you ever skated in the Boston Commons?"

Marshall's pewter gaze darts to the ice rink behind me. Every year, the city decks out the gardens with a temporary rink. The trees are draped with vibrantly colored lights. Vendors line the pathways, offering everything from sugar cookies to hot chocolate to little holiday trinkets for purchase.

It's enchanting, and, until tonight, my experience with the festivities has been relegated to only what I've read online.

With a firm hand, Marshall takes both pairs of skates from me. "Can't say that I have. Anytime I play hockey, it's for a team. Don't think I've skated recreationally since my younger years."

I lift a brow. "Younger years?"

He tips his head back with a laugh, and the sound is

contagious, sexy-as-hell. "One of these days you'll get over the age thing." He gestures for me to take a seat at a bench near the open rink. "Just think, when we're old and gray, you'll be thankful I'm always younger and good-looking."

Stealing the smaller-sized skates from him, I slip off my boots and draw on one cream-colored skate. "You *are* pretty." I cast a quick glance his way to see if he caught my teasing comment.

His mouth flattens, just slightly, as he grunts, "I accept handsome, hot, sexy, and tear-off-my-panties-with-your-teeth-Marshall."

The last option sends the skate lace missing its appropriate hook. Because with his words comes a *very* hot visual of him tearing my underwear off with his teeth. Not that I'll admit to picturing him between my thighs—*yet*.

"You're pretty, Marshall," I repeat, eyes down on my lacing job. "Why deny it?"

His thigh presses against mine as he undoes his sneakers. "Makes me sound feminine."

"There's nothing feminine about you."

"Is that a compliment?"

"Depends on whether you'll let me tell you all the ways that you're pretty."

Marshall grins, his dimples indenting his cheeks as his blunt-tipped fingers string up his laces in the same amount of time it takes me to unzip my boot and cast it to the side. "How about this? You can tell me how pretty I am, but each time you do so, I have the option to remove a kiss from your tally."

I whistle low. "You're heartless."

"Evil, honey." He winks playfully. "Don't be mistaken."

Honey.

My heart stutters at the word. It feels . . . foreign, both off his tongue and also in general. I can't even recall the last time I was on the receiving end of an endearment. Manny's much too professional for any of that; calling me Teacup is the furthest he'll go. My mother—well, we'll save that for another day. As for the men I've . . . seen, endearments weren't a part of those arrangements. I withhold a snort. Honestly, not much besides *sex* was involved. Casual to the very end.

It suited me, then. Back when I tried with every fiber of my being to never let a man get close to my heart, to never be Adaline.

If only I'd realized that I didn't have to go to the extremes to disprove the saying, *like mother like daughter*.

No doubt I would have saved myself a world of internal heartache.

"Ready?"

My shoulders twitch at the sound of Marshall's husky baritone. Much like the night at Faneuil Hall, he's on his feet (or skates, rather), and holding out his hand for me to take.

"Should we put our shoes somewhere?" I ask, eyeing my boots. They aren't a favorite pair, but I'd rather not have to walk back to Marshall's truck in socks. "They've got to have lockers or some sort of storage nearby."

"Live a little."

My gaze shoots to his. "What?"

Marshall releases my hand to shove our footwear beneath the bench. "You promised me an adventure. This is the first step." With his knuckles, he edges our shoes farther beneath the bench. "Think positive and we'll be good."

His logic is so optimistic. "Have you always thought the best of society?"

"Nah."

He was in foster care, you dummy. Of course. And now I feel like a complete idiot. "Marshall, I—"

"It's in the past, Gwen. Now show me how well you skate."

The subject change is as subtle as an elephant rumbling along Boston's ritzy Newbury Street. Not that I should be surprised. We're still learning each other, trying to get beyond the outer shells we show the world. Everything else takes time.

Pushing to my feet, I give one last glance to our bench and then straighten my shoulders. Marshall is right. I promised him an adventure, and it's past time that he get one.

"I should probably let you know," I start as I penguin-walk over the narrow gravel pathway to where the rink awaits, "you may have to save me today. I'm not the best skater, but I figured you'd be willing to step in and make sure I don't land on my butt."

The blade of my left skate hits the ice, and I make a show of wobbling my knees and pinwheeling my arms.

I'm not disappointed.

I feel Marshall's big body swoop in behind me, his arms hooking under mine, catching me just as I would have face-planted on the ice.

His warm breath sends shivers down my spine as he skates us out of the path of traffic. "You okay?"

"Yes."

His forearms inadvertently squeeze my breasts together, thanks to our position, and it's with a gust of disappointment that I realize Marshall is setting me upright and then shifting back.

"I might fall again." *Put on a show, girl.* I straighten my knees—a skating no-no—and hold out my arms, palms facing down. "You should keep holding me."

Marshall gives me a slow onceover. "You won't."

My gaze jerks to his. "What?"

"Fall," he says, folding his arms over his big chest. "When did you learn how to skate?"

"I don't know what you're talking about."

Marshall pushes off his left leg and approaches me. When he's within arm's length, he surprises me with a finger to my waist. To an inexperienced skater, that one touch would rock their world and kill their balance.

Instinctively, I tighten my core and clench my thighs—I don't budge.

The wide grin on Marshall's face might as well be my alert system that I've given myself away.

Busted.

With a palm to his hard chest, I give him a little push to move him aside and then slide one skate in front of the other at a leisurely pace. I wait for him to catch up before admitting, "When Golden Lights Media hired me, I went all out."

"What do you mean?"

I shrug. "Literally, in every capacity I tried to make myself indispensable to my boss. Walter's a hard-ass but he's a fair hard-ass, if that makes sense. From the moment I started, it was pretty clear to me that he'd offered me the job because of my breasts."

Marshall's pace slows and I circle around to face him.

"Your . . . breasts?" His voice is low, dangerous, and entirely too sexy for my mental well-being.

I nod, avoiding eye contact by staring at the twinkling lights above us. "He spent the first three months talking to my chest. Stereotypical, right? I'm sure it won't be the last time I'm hired for the way I look and not for what skill sets I bring to the table. So, I sought to prove him wrong—to prove everyone wrong." Wishing that I had my gloves, I skim my hands up my sides and clamp down on my opposite elbows, hoping to stay warm. "It only took me a few weeks to realize that nearly ninety-percent of our clients were men. Which meant that if I thought Walter was bad, there was a good chance that he'd be the least of my problems soon enough."

Marshall circles me, his skates cutting in and out, crossing one over the other. His hands are tucked behind his head, gripping the back of his neck. He looks at ease, relaxed—if you don't notice his expression.

Mouth pulled into a tight line, he turns his face to the other skaters. Even in the shadowy night, with only the twinkling lights in the tree limbs above us, I note the tick in his jaw and his hard swallow. "What'd you do? You're obviously still there."

Theh.

If possible, his accent is even stronger than normal.

I reach out on his next pass by me, dropping my hand on his arm.

I'm not nearly strong enough to stop him, and I end up trailing him just a little, coasting. My palm slips down his arm until our fingers glide against each other. He twists his palm and clasps my hand.

Oh.

I fix my gaze on our hands, wondering if he'll let go, praying that he doesn't.

My heart is a wild stampede, a cacophony of words that don't belong in a single breath but have merged into one: *keepholdingon.*

I look up.

There's a smile on his face that wasn't there a moment ago.

"You planned this," I say, unable to stall the impressed awe in my voice.

He leans in, pulling me closer so that our hands brush his hip. "You started it the moment you pretended to be clueless about skating."

A girlish giggle escapes me. It sounds . . . I *want* to say that it sounds like the Old Gwen, that tinkling, awful laugh I used to give the men I wanted to sleep with. But it's not—it can't be. Because that other laugh was like nails on a chalkboard, even to my own ears, and this one is genuine, it's real.

Marshall ensures that.

He loops my hands around the back of his neck before releasing me to slip his palm over my shoulder, down my back, to just above my butt. We're chest-to-chest, thighs-to-thighs, while we move in tandem.

It's foreplay with clothes on.

The equivalent of grinding on ice—I won't lie, the atmosphere is a whole lot more romantic than a sweaty nightclub.

"You're slick, Hunt," I murmur, though I make no move to pull away.

"Slick *and* pretty," he retorts playfully. "I'll never let you forget it. Now finish the rest of your story."

When I shrug this time, my breasts push against his chest and we both suck in a sharp breath. Is it possible to be both in hell and heaven at the same time? *Focus, girl, you can do it.*

I tilt my chin to the right, so I can watch the families skate around us as Marshall leads me effortlessly like we're waltzing. "There's not much more to tell, honestly. I wanted to be taken seriously in the office. So, I studied our clients and tried to learn what they did professionally. Hockey. Golf. I've sat in on local court cases and I've learned a little something about nude drawings."

"Don't tell me you were the one who was nude?"

At Marshall's hopeful tone, I swat him in the chest with my free hand. My mouth opens to quip the old classic, "you wish," when he snags my wrist and brings my hand to his mouth.

He kisses my knuckles, and my legs wobble in a way that has nothing to do with the ice and everything to do with this man in front of me.

He kisses the beating pulse of my inner wrist, and I clutch his back, my nails biting into his sweater.

He slips my fingers into his hair, encouraging me to silently pull on the strands, and I feel my entire body quiver with lust.

"*Marshall.*"

His dark lashes flutter down, concealing his thoughts, and he's so damn handsome—and, yes, pretty boy model-like—that I'm tempted to yank his head down and do away with his no-kissing rule. I want to taste him. I want to know if my imagination has anything at all on the reality of Marshall Hunt.

"Finish your story."

I moan, not from lust but out of frustration. "I did what I set out to do when Walter hired me—I made myself irreplaceable. The company could come crashing down, but I'd come out on the other side unharmed. It was the first time in my entire life that I had the chance to be judged by my own merits and not my mother's, and there was no way I was going to let an opportunity like that slip away. And then, once my position was secure, I set about making changes."

"Like what?"

I glance up, momentarily distracted by the sight of my fingers playing with his hair. *My* fingers. *His* hair. Crazy. "I took on female clients, as many professional women as I could, no matter their field. Today, we're closer than ever to an equal playing field at Golden Lights. It's not perfect, not nearly as evenly balanced as I'd like it to be, but it'll get there. When I started, the figures sat at a nine-to-one ratio. Now, that number is closer to six-to-four. Perfect? No, not nearly, not yet."

Silence.

Pure, unforgiving silence.

I feel the heat prickling my already chilled ears, and my nose grows itchy with the need to laugh awkwardly.

I should have known. Really, I should have.

Why would Marshall, a pro-hockey player with endless opportunities at his fingertips, be impressed with what I'd accomplished? Never mind that; why would a guy of his caliber even care about—

"You're a damn intriguing contradiction, honey."

I nearly choke on my own spit, I'm so shocked. "What do you mean?"

"You." He shakes his head, and my hand falls to his shoulder, my thumb brushing the collar of his sweatshirt. "You show the world this icy exterior, this wall that no one but a very select few can breech, and then you blow everyone's perception of you out of the water by admitting to something like that."

My breath hitches. *Don't ask what you're thinking, don't do it.* I do it. "Everyone's perception, Marshall? Or also your perception?"

He slows us to a stop.

Wanting space, I try to pull away.

His hands lock around my elbows, and his hard voice

leaves me no choice but to meet his intense expression. "That's an unfair question and you know it. You've spent years pushing me away, Gwen. That ice you wear for everyone was a foot thick around me. So, yeah, I'm surprised."

He's right, damn him.

But just because I agree with him doesn't lessen the sting. "Then why chase me? Maybe I have my own reasons for pulling away, but why bother asking me out if you think I'm such a coldhearted bitch?"

"Because I don't. I never did."

I risk a peek up at his face.

Earnest, is my first thought. He looks so damned earnest as he watches me with narrowed gray eyes.

"I don't understand."

He blows out a deep breath. "You never noticed, but I took part in the same community service program that you did, back at Northeastern."

It suddenly feels hard to breathe. "You . . . *followed* me there?"

"Trust me, the truth isn't stalkerish at all." Massive shoulders lift in a nonchalant shrug. "Volunteering was mandatory if I wanted to stay on the hockey team. Most of the guys chose the soup kitchen. Others went for building houses. I chose something a little closer to home."

For a moment, the words escape me. All of them.

The only option is to stare at Marshall's handsome face, tracing his familiar features. Features I've seen on and off for six years but am only now letting myself memorize. The holiday lights above us go dark, no doubt the attendant alerting everyone that they're closing up shop for the night.

We'll have to return our skates and hope that our shoes haven't been stolen.

But my blades are rooted to the ice, my gaze rooted on Marshall's face.

"You chose to volunteer at a shelter for abused and battered women." The words come out slow, purposely even to conceal my surprise.

The newfound darkness has stripped my chance to make out the emotion in his eyes, leaving us both bare to the past.

When he speaks, his voice is low. "My father beat my mother. I don't remember much, since I was wicked young. I *do* remember him yelling at her, the sounds of his fists on her flesh." He coughs abruptly, and I can't help but wonder if he's trying to bury his emotions. "Anyway," he mutters, "when Coach told us to pick a cause, that was mine. It was the least that I could do after . . . everything."

Now the words flood on back. So many thoughts, questions, hitting me all at once. But the most pressing one escapes: "Did she leave him?"

The question is nosy and insensitive, but after witnessing the verbal abuse my mother's husbands handed her on a silver platter, and the truly horrible instances of physical abuse I dealt with at the shelter, it is the one question that I need answered.

"Later, I think. I wasn't there to find out."

Memories of his upbringing hitting the tabloids fill in what he doesn't—namely, his years spent in foster care.

My heart aches for that little boy who witnessed such violence; it aches for the young man who took it upon himself to volunteer at a shelter with women who were, no doubt, mirror images of his mother from his memories; and it aches for him now, too, as he stands so strong before me, opening up in a way I don't suspect is normal for him.

"Marshall, I—"

He cuts me off with a gentle hand to my face, cupping my jaw and brushing his thumb over my bottom lip in that way of his that is becoming increasingly familiar. "In any case," he murmurs, his gray eyes watching my mouth, "I've always known you were more than what you showed to the world. It's long past time that you let that woman out to play."

Still cupping my face, he bends down and my lungs seize with hope that, *yes*, this is that moment. Right now, he's finally going to kiss me. My head tilts back and my lashes flutter shut and I sigh his name in a way I've never done for another man. It's happening. *Oh my God, yes*—

His lips collide with my forehead.

My eyes spring open.

"Soon," he promises, and then lets me go.

I draw my arms around my belly, forcing a smile to my face to hide my acute disappointment.

Soon is not nearly soon enough.

12

HUNT

We're dragging tonight.

We all know it.

The crowd knows it, and, since we're playing in Toronto, the crowd is eating up every lousy play we make.

Coach Hall knows it.

He fires into us before the third period, and none of us are immune.

"You all trying to lose?" he bellows, a formidable voice in a not-quite formidable body. His face is red, his hands jab at the air as though he wishes it was our eyes, and he's been reaching for the crescendo for the last five minutes. "Beaumont, if I have to fucking tell you one more time to *not* go after their center, I will literally shove you into the penalty box myself. The guy's a pussy and he cries wolf if you touch him—don't fucking touch him!"

Andre's head hangs as he stares down at the cement between his skates. I don't blame him—Toronto's center *is* a pussy, and the minute he sees Beaumont coming, the douchebag is already curling up in the fetal position and calling foul play.

"Hunt!"

I don't jump at the sound of my name, though my balls threaten to pull a duck-and-run into my body for protection.

"Yeah, Coach?"

"Where the hell is your head tonight?" Coach growls, prowling the space in front of us like a caged lion. "You leave your shit back in Boston. Are you *trying* to miss every fucking shot tonight?"

He's right that my head isn't in the game.

It hasn't been in the game for days now, not since I opened up to Gwen and tore at all my old wounds. It wasn't pity that she'd looked at me with. No, Gwen decimated me with one knowing glance, as though she understood *fully* what I'd been through as a kid.

No one did.

Except for Dave, and I was still paying my debt to him for that even now.

"I'll get my head out of my ass, Coach."

It's a promise I keep.

I know what's riding on this game—the ever-hanging threat that if I don't play hard enough, if I don't play smart enough, I'll find myself back on the farm team, playing on a minor league level.

I'm as well-known for my ability to pull hat tricks out of my magic hat as I am for *bringing* my hat trick, or so that's what ESPN called it a few months ago.

Agility.

Dogged determination.

Unparalleled skill.

The "hat trick," according to ESPN.

Tonight, I'm relying on my bullheaded focus and skill because the agility is AWOL.

My teeth crash together, despite my mouthpiece, as I'm

bulldozed into the boards, my helmet clipping against the Plexiglas.

Fuck.

Vision blurring from the force of impact, I meet the wide-eyed gaze of a little kid. He's wearing a Toronto jersey and a matching Maple Leafs ball cap. His hands dive into a monster-sized bowl of popcorn.

Meanwhile, I've got a massive two-hundred-fifty-pound asshole practically humping my back as we both fight for ownership of the puck.

"Having a hard time today?" Toronto's D-man grunts behind me.

I eye the puck, driving for it. "You still jerking off to my picture at night, Tompson?"

"Fuck you."

"I already do every night in your dreams."

I barely allow myself a sigh of relief as I manage to shoot a pass to Carter. I can breathe when the game is over—or when I'm dead.

Carter scores, tying up the score at 2-2.

The rest of the period is a matter of getting the job done.

The Air Canada Centre isn't our house, but by the time we wrap up with another goal at .15 seconds left in the game (assisted by me), we treat it like it is.

Our house, our rules, our win.

Not that Coach praises our turn-around post-game. He barks at the media—clearly still ticked off that we dangled our cocks for two periods instead of playing *real* hockey—and has us packed up and on our way to the airport hotel within the hour.

Across the aisle in the bus, Harrison props up one arm on the back of the seat in front of him. "I want a steak, a call with Charlie, and my bed—not necessarily in that order."

Carter, seated in the row ahead of The Mountain, twists around to look at us. "I'm feelin' the need to drop cash on the best steak this city has to offer."

Harrison trades a side-eye glance with me, then says to our captain, "You owe me from last time. I fed your ass *and* paid your bill. Since I don't sleep with you, I'm feeling the need to collect on steak tonight."

"Done." Carter holds up his phone. "Let Sir Google tell us where to go, and I'll cover you, princess. Think of it as your Christmas gift."

"Since when did Santa turn into a slow-talkin' Texan?"

As the two of them bicker like old ladies and make plans to feast like kings, I tap my phone.

A text is waiting for me from Gwen.

The woman is burrowing under my skin, more than she ever has before. I don't mind it. I crave the contact with her in a way I've never craved anything in my life.

You should have kissed her the other night, you dumbass.

I should have.

Fear had stopped me.

Fear that she'd wake up and realize she's way better off without a kid from Southie. Better off without the sort of baggage I carry around behind the good humor and go-lucky attitude.

Lately, I haven't been feeling like that Marshall Hunt—the playboy version of myself.

I swipe my thumb across the glass phone screen, hungrily seeking out the text from a woman who pushes for the real me, and never shies away when he appears darker, sharper than the playboy mirage.

Awesome game! You had me at the edge of my seat. Xoxo

I stare hard at those X's and O's, wondering if she's popped them in just to be friendly.

Thought Coach was gonna blow a gasket, I type back.

Seconds later, my phone vibrates against my thigh. *He just can't handle your greatness.*

Pretty sure that was *not* what Coach Hall was thinking tonight.

I lean into the aisle, and sure enough, Coach is seated at the front of the bus, peering back at the lot of us with a pissed-off expression on his face. I wouldn't put it past him to be planning all the ways he plans to torture us during our next practice.

Next time you see him, do me a favor and don't tell him that. For me. Xoxo

"You blowin' kisses at someone, Hunt?"

Fuck.

Beaumont shoves me over on the bench, so that my hip comes into contact with the side of the bus. He folds his hands over his stomach, long legs stretched out into the aisle.

"Do you have a death wish?" I grunt, turning my phone over on my thigh. "Nothing good ever comes from snooping."

Beaumont won't be distracted. "Who were you talking to?"

"Your wifer."

His mouth curls into a smirk. "Don't pull a Henri Bordeaux, man. Also, if you were talking to Zoe, I hope you understand that I'd have to castrate you."

"Is that an offer?"

He dips his head. "A promise."

"Well, in that case then..."

"Asshole." With a punch to my arm, Andre laughs. "Really, though, you talking to Gwen?"

"Is that a problem?"

My phone vibrates, and I'm desperate to see what she says.

"Nah." Beaumont shakes his head, crossing his arms over his chest. "Not a problem. Just wondering how it's all going. Any complaints?"

Other than the fact that I haven't kissed her yet?

Not a one.

"We're testing the waters," I finally answer, taking the safe route.

"You haven't kissed her yet?"

Christ. Am I that easy to read? I rake my fingers through my hair. "We're . . . getting there."

"I'd say to let me know how it goes, but I'm sure I'll hear it through the grapevine, otherwise known as my fiancée."

I laugh because it seems expected of me, but the damn bastard doesn't move the rest of the way back to the hotel. Each time I try to sneak a peek at my phone, Beaumont starts up conversation again.

Is it wrong that I want to muffle him? The man doesn't talk to any of us for a straight year, and the love of one woman turns him into Chatty Kathy 2.0.

When we clamber off the bus a short time later, I can't grab my duffel quick enough. Harrison waves at me, shouting that he's going to grab steak and to not wait up. The Mountain and I usually camp out as roommates together when we're on the road.

I'm not above hoping Harrison goes to an all-you-can-eat steak buffet.

I wait until I'm out of the elevator and on my floor to call Gwen.

She answers on the second ring, her voice breathy and feminine. "Hello?"

I angle the door to my hotel room open with a shuffle of

my keys and a shoulder against the wood. "You go running?" I ask, flicking on the lights and setting my bag down in the entryway.

"What?" The word is a squeak, and I grin at my reflection as I start stripping off the suit we're forced to wear at away games.

The tie is the first to go, followed by the jacket. I toss both over a chair.

"You sound wicked out of breath." I toe off my shoes and then drop my slacks, adding them to the growing pile on the chair. "Were you working out?"

There's a pause, and then some shuffling. "I . . . um, did you see my text?"

My shirt is the next to go. "Not yet. Beaumont was hovering like a stage-five clinger. What did you say?"

"Ah . . ."

At her hesitancy, alarm bells go off in my head. "Hold on."

Pulling the phone away from my ear, I sit on the edge of my bed and open my messages. Two taps later and my cock is as hard as a fucking rock.

"Gwen?"

A pause. Then, "Yes, Marshall?"

I swallow, hard. My gaze lifts to the mirror. I'm a gym rat, something I've never really given much thought to besides the obvious: working out is my escape. It's an extension of releasing my emotions into physical activity. On a professional level, it's a necessary fact of life if I want to stay at the top of my game on the ice.

Right now, I'd kill to see Gwen's reaction to my almost-naked body.

I try to see myself through her eyes—big biceps, muscular thighs, broad triceps, ridged abs. Tattoos line my arms, down to my wrists. My cock thrusts up, the crown peeking out above the waistband of my black briefs. Eyes squeezing shut, I force my free hand to the bed, even though I'm dying to give myself a little relief.

"Are you still thinking of me?" I rasp, wishing that she were here in this hotel room with me. *Next time*, I tell myself.

"I probably shouldn't have sent that," Gwen says. "I don't know what I was thinking."

"You miss me."

"Well, yes."

My hand lands on my thigh because I'm a glutton for punishment. I wish it were her hand. "How many cocktails did you have before you sent that text?"

"One," she whispers. "Liquid courage while I watched your game at home."

One cocktail and the woman is bold enough to tell me that she wants to feel me between her legs sometime in the next half-century. I don't know whether to laugh at her forwardness that's so typically *Gwen*, or to groan because I'm hundreds of miles away from even fulfilling that fantasy.

In that moment, I make a decision. It's as bold as her text, bolder still, but the ache in my balls and that breathy note in her voice isn't doing me any favors. Harrison is gone for at least another few hours, definitely enough time to . . .

"End the call, honey."

"What?"

"I'm going to video chat you. End the call."

Her voice hits a high note. "Is that a good idea?"

"It's the best damn idea I've ever had."

She ends the call.

I shove my briefs down the length of my legs. With steady fingers, I tap an app on my phone and pull up Gwen's contact info. My own hesitation spans mere seconds—is this the right move? Does sexting ruin everything I've been working toward with her?

In the next second, I realize that I don't care.

Not right now, when my hard-on is desperate for her touch.

Not right now, when I'm dying to see her stroke the hot folds between her legs.

I need this.

I tap CALL and wait. And wait. And then the screen is a mash-up of muted colors and red hair.

And skin.

Holy hell, she's not wearing a shirt.

"That's a greeting," I rasp, thanking God when my voice doesn't crack like a teenage boy's.

"I"—the camera shifts upward to show her beautiful face—"I didn't realize the angle I was holding the phone."

Just like that, her wry tone eases my nerves. "Sure you didn't." Her red hair drapes over one shoulder, shielding all the good things from view. "Do you have a mirror?"

Her lips part. "Yeah, why?"

Go big or go home.

In more relevant terms, get naked or get off the phone.

I tap the little camera-reversal icon, waiting for the phone's recalibration.

Her gasp coincides with *all* of me showing up on her screen. "*Oh.*"

Grinning, I say, "Yeah, *oh*. I want to see you, Gwen. I've been waiting for years to see you. I can't say that I'm all too pleased that this is the way we're gonna break down this barrier, but I'll take it."

"Hold on."

Her phone shimmies and shakes as she puts it down— on the bed, maybe? There's the sound of something being dragged across the floor, a graphic four-letter curse that makes me grin, and then I'm looking at her face again.

Then it's not just her face.

It's all of her: her painted toenails, her trim ankles, her slim thighs, her hand cupping between her thighs, a narrow waist, and heavy breasts. Her red hair hangs loose, untucked this time around, framing her face and dragging my attention up to her nervous expression.

"We don't have to do this." I'll die from blue balls if we don't, but I'm not down for this unless we both want it. "Change the camera around, honey. Let me see your face. It was a stupid idea. We'll forget about it, all right?"

"Tell me what to do."

My cock twitches at the softly issued command.

"You sure about this?"

"I want you, Marshall." Her legs spread wide and my mouth goes dry. "Now tell me what to do."

There's a good chance I'll die today. Forget the blue balls —I'll be gone long before that happens. Holy hell, I need water.

No, I just need *her*.

"Tuck your hair behind your ears."

She laughs, a touch awkwardly. "That's where you want to start?"

"I want to make sure I can see your beautiful face the entire time. Humor me."

Holding the phone with one hand, she does as I ask with the other. She bites her lower lip, teasing me from hundreds of miles away. "Next?"

Did I ever think her nervous? Clearly, I'm the only one with a rock in my throat that I can't swallow down, no matter how hard I try.

I draw in a deep breath. "I want to know how heavy your

tits are, honey. Yeah, cover them just like that. Tweak your nipple for me, yeah, that's a good girl . . ."

With her hand on her breast, her core is left unshielded.

And I want. I want so bad that I'm almost unaware of my hand gripping the base of my cock until I'm slowly pumping up and down, twisting my palm at the head, hard, just the way I like it.

"You're . . . bigger than I expected."

My gaze flits from her fingers to her face in the small screen. "What'd you expect?"

The corner of her mouth lifts. "A pretty cock," she whispers, licking her lips, "to match your pretty face."

If I were there with her now, I'd have her flat on her back for that comment. "You know how I feel about being called pretty."

With one last squeeze of her breast, Gwen slips her hand down her stomach and then skirts to the side, landing on her inner thigh and taking my heart right along with her. "What are you going to do about it?" It's a blatant taunt. "You're so very far away, Marshall."

For *that* comment, I'd have her on her back and my tongue driving into the very center of her.

Since that's not an option . . . "Touch your clit, Gwen. Now."

She flutters her lashes. "Is that your punishment? Making me feel good?"

Christ, she's feisty when she's horny.

I love it.

"You should be thankful I don't actually have any chains in my basement for you."

She throws me off course with her next question: "How badly do you want me to touch myself?"

"Bad."

"Bad enough that you'll throw out your rule about no kissing? We can skip everything else when you get back, Marshall, but I want my first kiss from you. I want to stop fantasizing about all the different ways you might taste and finally know for myself. I want that connection with you."

Her words are as much a turn-on to my body as they are to my heart. "The kiss is yours," I say, my gaze fixed on her flushed face. "When I see you, you'll have it."

She answers by dragging one foot up onto the bed, leaning onto her elbow, completely exposing herself to the mirror, and to me, before touching her clit, just as I'd asked.

I'm not prepared for the eroticism of the sight.

I'm not prepared for the way my tight strokes on my cock pick up speed.

I'm not prepared for the demands that spill from my mouth—I've always been dominant in the bedroom, but I've never been much of a dirty-talker. Hell, I generally leave the talking at the door.

But the sight of Gwen circling her clit with two fingers apparently seizes that side of me from the depths of my soul and yanks the poor bastard into the real world.

"God, yes," I growl, noting the way her toes curl and the camera shakes, ever so slightly. "Taste yourself, Gwen. Tell me what you taste like."

Her breathing is quick and loud, even over the chat line.

I don't have to ask twice.

She sinks those two fingers into her heat, pumping once, before lifting them to her mouth for a single swipe of her tongue.

I groan, loudly, curses diving off my tongue. "Tell me, honey."

"Sweet," she says softly. "I taste sweet."

"Good to know. The minute I see you, I plan to discover that for myself."

My words must strike a chord of want in her because those two sweet fingers of hers return to her core, slipping inside and driving me insane. I never would have thought six years ago that my first sexual encounter with Gwen James would take place in a hotel room with her in a different country.

Then again, I never would have thought that just the sight of her, with my imagination filling in all of the missing blanks, would be enough to make me orgasm, either.

I was wrong on both counts.

My groans mingle with her whimpers.

My grip is so tight, so desperate to mimic the feel of her smaller hands, that my orgasm isn't far off.

"I need you to come before me." My eyes eagerly track the way her fingers slick up her folds and land on her clit again. "Do you hear me, Gwen?"

Her head tips back against the bed. She's completely lost to the sensations of her body climbing to the point of no return. I still hear her wry, "always a gentleman," remark.

"A gentleman wouldn't think about you swallowing every last drop as you sucked him dry, honey." My voice grows uneven. "A gentleman wouldn't . . . he wouldn't want you to sit on his face as he made you come with just his tongue."

"Oh, my God."

Her pressure slackens, eases, then increases in tempo.

The realization that she likes me talking dirty to her is like a shock to my spine. Far be it from me not to give her everything that she wants.

"A gentleman wouldn't demand you come . . . and expect you to do so on his command."

"*Marshall.*" My name on her lips is part-reprimand, part-whimper.

I watch as her thighs twitch with the force of her orgasm, and it's all I need. I thrust twice more into my hand, making sure that the camera is angled so she can see exactly what she does to me. With a groan, I squeeze the tip of my cock as my balls jack up. Hot jets of my come land on my stomach.

Fuck it.

Seriously, just . . . fuck it.

"Marshall?"

I meet Gwen's gaze in the camera, not shocked to find that she's now zoomed into her face.

I'd do the same if I had the energy or the strength.

Between the game and this (unexpected) sex session, I'm all kinds of depleted.

But, holy hell, this is by far the hottest sexual experience of my life, regardless of whether or not Gwen's back in Boston and I'm in Canada. I would never want this moment with anyone else, either—just Gwen, *only* Gwen.

"Yeah, honey?" I ask after a moment.

Her blue eyes narrow though she's smiling. "You better not strip any of my kisses from the tally because of this."

I flop back onto the bed, reversing the camera so she can see my face and upper chest. "Don't worry. I've just decided to give you a holiday bonus. I'm tacking on an extra twelve, one for every night of Christmas."

13

GWEN

"Why are you smiling like that?"

My hands close over a package of lean meat and I plop it into the carriage. "Smiling like what?" I ask Zoe.

She circles her finger in my direction, and I have the random thought that she's feeling her antennae at me. Like she's trying to figure me out. I snag another package of meat from the display, purposely giving my best friend my back so she can't do her magical-reading skills.

It doesn't work.

"You got laid last night!"

The butcher behind the glass-display counter gives me a creepy grin and an even creepier once-over. "Lucky man."

So awkward. With a stiff smile—grimace? It's more of a grimace—I turn the carriage away from the meat section of Stop & Shop and head toward an empty aisle. Zoe trails behind me happily, her high heels clipping across the shiny linoleum tiles.

"Can we not?" I mutter, throwing a canister of bread crumbs into the mix. In an attempt to make my mother happy after the whole Ty debacle, I decided to throw her a little dinner for tonight. Just her, me, and Manuel. When I clued her in this morning, she put up a small fuss about having chefs who can do the cooking for us—but ultimately caved when I mentioned that it'd give her the time to get a load off her shoulders and vent.

I don't know what it says about my company that the prospect of a bitch fest was the enticement Adaline needed to spend time with me.

I push the sobering thought away. It's neither here nor there—end of the day, she agreed to suffer through a dinner with me, and I suppose that's all I can be grateful for.

With light fingers, Zoe snatches a small potato chip bag from a display at the end of the aisle and tears it open like a savage. At my lifted brow, she shrugs. "What? Mere mortals eat as they go, Gwen. Save the bag and pay later at the register." She shoves a chip into her mouth. "Anyway, you can't get out of this. You're looking at me like I'm crazy and yet you can't stop smiling—you had sex. Was it with someone new? Andre and the team are getting back from Toronto today, so it couldn't have been with Hunt."

My cheeks burn with the memory of what Marshall and I did last night—or rather, what we didn't do. I'd like to pretend that we were just two lonely people who agreed to a little mutual self-satisfaction, but that seems woefully inaccurate to describe my most vivid sexual experience.

Regardless of whether we were in two different countries or not, Marshall gave me an orgasm I'll never forget.

Exactly the reason you woke up this morning and took care of business . . . again.

"Not someone new."

"Hunt, then?" Zoe asks, crunching away. "Who knew the two of you would develop some sort of telepathic sex system?" She waves her free hand in the air, as though she's showing off a billboard. "Sign me up. It's a lonely world when Andre is on the road."

"We didn't . . ." Stopping in the noodle section, I eye my options and buy myself time before answering. Fettuccini or lasagna. Unbidden, a visual of cooking for Marshall pops into my head and I shove it away. *Don't get ahead of yourself.* "It was like . . ."

Popping another chip into her mouth, Zoe watches me like a hawk. "Yes . . . ?"

My gaze darts from one end of the aisle to the other. Spotting an elderly lady on the far end, at least ten feet away, I lower my voice. "We had video chat sex, okay?"

Her chip bag releases a strangled-sounding *pop! pop!* as though she's squeezed it too tightly. "Like Skype? FaceTime? Facebook?"

"Does it matter which platform it happened on?" I don't know whether to laugh or poke her in the ribs for being ridiculous.

"Not really," Zoe tells me, "but it does help set the scene for the sexy times."

"Well, then!"

The elderly lady I'd spotted earlier smacks her carriage into mine as she angles past us in the narrow aisle. Behind a pair of wire-rimmed glasses, her blue eyes turn into slits. "Heathens," she mutters. "Your generation has no common decency. You take up the aisle space, you steal the handicapped parking spaces without consideration for anyone else. You talk about—"

"Sex?" Zoe offers up, crunching away on her chips like this is the best form of entertainment she's had in months. "Hey, Gwenny, did Hunt spank you, by any chance?"

So much for keeping this between us. To support the

cause, I nevertheless swallow down my embarrassment and fake a casual smile. "Only once. I guess I haven't been a bad enough girl for anything more."

The woman's lips part and, with a shake of her head, she gives a hand-shove to my cart before marching down the rest of the aisle and turning the corner.

For a moment, Zoe and I stand in silence.

Then, "You think she hasn't gotten laid in years?"

I cover a laugh with my hand. "I was thinking that she might have some pent-up aggression toward anyone under the age of eighty."

"Heathens," Zoe agrees with a sage nod, "the lot of us."

We both erupt into laughter, and I wrap my arm around my best friend's shoulders to touch the side of my head to her shoulder. For a girl who never allowed herself to have true friends, the last year has been something of an awakening for me.

I don't have blood sisters, but Zoe and Charlie fill a hole in my heart I never even realized I'd been missing.

Zoe demands I open my mouth for a chip to, and I quote, "Prove that you are a plebeian like the rest of us."

I'm fully aware that not everyone grew up the way I did with butlers and chefs and a mother who couldn't be bothered with my existence.

To be honest, I wouldn't recommend my childhood to anyone either.

As we turn the corner, Zoe latches back onto our earlier conversation with barracuda-like claws. "So," she says, "you, Hunt, sex."

"Facetime sex."

"Ah." Zoe winks at me. "So it *was* FaceTime. A-plus quality and all that."

"You're insane."

"Not as insane as you. You and Hunt went from deciding that no sex was happening at all, and then you got down and dirty while he was away at a game."

When she puts it that way, I totally am insane. Marshall and I have always had chemistry—in some capacity or another—but I've never let myself dwell too long on it. What good would it do when I didn't have plans to sleep with him? But the way we were last night . . . the way he looked with his hand wrapped around his cock, every lingering protest in me died.

Hearing him order me to come, to stroke myself for him . . . it did it for me. Marshall pushed me over the edge with nothing but the deep timbre of his voice and the visual of his hard body.

In a whisper, I carve up my heart and spill it all to my best friend. "I worry I'm going to be in over my head soon, Zo. What if it's all part of a plan or something?" Insecurities rise up—particularly those that deal with wondering if I'm even good enough for a guy like Marshall. "What if he's just giving me a taste of my own medicine after all these years? Like, she fucked with me and now I'm going to mess with her emotions in return."

We step in line at the nearest register, and I push the carriage up to the conveyor belt.

"I'd kick his ass," Zoe tells me, and then gives me a little nudge.

I follow the direction of her gaze, only to swallow hard at the sight of Marshall on a *Sports Illustrated* cover. Since I'm not his publicist—he opted to sign with Harris Publicity during his farm team days—I had no idea that he'd been chosen to represent the month of December.

I skim the cover, taking in the headline: Marshall Hunt Brings Heat To The Ice. And then, directly below: No Other

Player Has Scored As Many Hat Tricks In A Single Season. Will The Streak Continue? Hunt Explains How Hockey Is More Than Just A Test Of Physical Strength.

In nothing but his navy-blue uniform pants, Marshall rests his hockey stick across the back of his shoulders. His upper body is a work of art—rippling muscles, tattooed arms, smooth, tan skin with a dusting of hair on his chest that narrows into a thin happy trail.

Last night, I had the chance to see where that trail led, and it was heaven.

"Ma'am, are you ready?"

Without giving myself the chance to decide otherwise, I set the glossy magazine on the belt and then begin unloading the groceries.

Zoe bumps her hip with mine. "I'm gonna take it that the, you know, was good then?"

My thighs involuntarily clench together at the memory of Marshall telling me to taste myself. "I've literally never had better."

I just hope I haven't set myself up for heartbreak.

14

GWEN

*F*ive hours later, I'm in hell.
"The lasagna is overcooked."

My mother pushes her plate away like she's worried something might launch out of the meat sauce and smack her in the face.

Fun fact, the lasagna is *not* overcooked. No one else at the table has said so. Not Manuel. Not Carli, my mother's chef who was wrangled into this dinner by, you guessed it, my mother herself. And not even Steven, my mom's new boyfriend.

Yeah, *boyfriend*.

The divorce hasn't even gone through yet and she's already making up for lost time.

Fortunately for the rest of us, he's not a complete jerk like her string of exes.

With a slight grimace, Steven downs half his gin and tonic. "Addie, the lasagna is fine." He looks to me with a reassuring nod. "I'm a bit of a lasagna connoisseur—if this bad boy had a problem, I'd mention it."

I'm not sure he would but I appreciate the sentiment. "Thanks, Steven."

Seeking out my glass of wine, I tip it back and wonder why the hell I thought this would be a great idea.

When will I get it through my head that Adaline will always find something wrong with what I do?

As much as the weight of defeat settles on my shoulders, I refuse to give into it. At the end of the day, *I* paid for this meal, *I* spent hours pulling it all together, from the flower bouquet on the table to the California red that everyone—aside from Steven—is drinking like there's no tomorrow.

I smile like I'm on the red carpet, wide and fake and showing off so many teeth *Crest* just might hire me for a new toothpaste commercial. "How was everyone's day? Manny?" Manuel's eyes go wide after being called on and he flashes me a thumbs-up. When it comes to my mother, Manuel O'Carlo turns as timid as a rabbit. I get it—not only does she cut his paycheck, but she has the opportunity to make his life hell. Right. Grabbing the wine bottle off the table, I offer it to Carli. "More wine?"

"Fill the bitch up. I need it, bad."

The words are low and throaty and clearly meant only for me, but Adaline's voice rings out like a shotgun. "What did you say, Carli?"

"I said, umm . . ." Brown panicked eyes flick from me to my mother and back again.

"Dessert!" If possible, my smile grows wider. *And more fake.* "She wants dessert. Which I have. The dessert, I mean. Plenty of dessert." Oh God, I need to shut up. "Blueberry pie, anyone?"

Manny hangs his head, and I'm surprised he doesn't bury his face in his palms and laugh out loud. His shoulders shake with mirth, and it's enough movement, thanks to his elbows on the table, to send his wine glass teetering over.

Onto my mother's pristine white tablecloth.

And all over her pale, yellow dress.

Oh . . . *shit*.

"*Manuel.*"

His name seeps out from my mother in a hiss that would rival Angelina Jolie as Maleficent. It's not pretty, trust me, and it sure isn't sweet. For his part, my mother's butler cringes and leaps up from the table, muttering something about grabbing towels.

He makes his escape in seconds, leaving the rest of us behind to deal with my mother's impending outrage. When he catches my eye and winks just before he exits the room, I don't know whether to applaud his outlandish maneuver or throw the damn wine bottle at the back of his head.

The timid mouse just earned his claws.

Stephen swipes at his longish brown hair. "Babe, you're fine. It's just a little wine."

Nope, wrong words. Totally wrong words.

My mother's chin jerks back. "Just a *little* wine? This dress is *Burberry*."

Stephen's dark eyes swing in my direction, wide and confused. "Did she mean blueberry?"

"*Burberry*." Adaline snaps a white hand napkin off the table and dabs at the skirt of her dress. "I said Burberry."

"Right." Stephen pauses, and for the length of time it takes him to exhale, I swear that my heart stops beating. Then, "Gwen, would you be a doll and cut me some of that blueberry pie?"

Do you remember those cartoons where the steam billows out from their ears? Just before shit goes down and everyone takes cover from an out-of-nowhere explosion?

That's how I feel when my mother drops her palms to the table and rises to her feet.

"This dinner is over." She points an accusing finger at me. "Fire Manuel."

What? My stomach twists with instant guilt. This is all my fault. All of it. If I hadn't thought this stupid dinner was a good idea . . . if I hadn't thought for one single second that my mother needed me, that I could make her feel better . . . Nausea throws my belly into *tipsy-topsy* central, and the lasagna threatens to pull a Second Coming.

Deep breath. Inhale.

"Mom, it was an accident. Everyone has them. You, me, *everyone*."

Her shoulders draw up indignantly. "Fire him. I'll have him replaced tomorrow."

How in the world did one dinner go so wrong? I look down at the wine bottle gripped to my chest, and then meet Carli's gaze. She twists her chin away, cutting eye contact, leaving me to deal with all of this *alone*.

Like always.

Bitterness rises to the forefront, and my fingers tighten on the glass bottle. "Manuel has been with us since I was a kid. You can't—"

Adaline's mouth firms. "I can and I will. Everyone is replaceable, Gwen. We've discussed this. Your employees, your men, your friends. *Everyone*."

Including me? I almost voice the words that have lingered in my head for longer than I'd like to admit.

Stephen beats me to it.

"Um, hey there? Babe?" He holds up a finger, twirling it in a *yoo-hoo* motion. "Not replaceable over here."

My mother stares at him. "I met you yesterday."

He shifts uncomfortably in his seat. "Yeah, well, it was

quite the meeting, if you know what I mean." When he winks again, the urge to vomit returns tenfold.

Beside me, Carli makes a gagging sound and then steals the wine from my grasp. She doesn't bother with a glass this time. Pushing away from the table, she salutes me, tells my mother good night, and then promptly strolls from the room —all the while bringing the wine bottle to her mouth and tossing back the dry red.

My mother is not amused. Blue eyes flashing with barely concealed fury, she grinds out, "You don't know Burberry," as though the biggest deal breaker of the night is the fact that her date is ignorant to the world of British fashion designers.

Apparently, even my mother has limits when it comes to what she'll put up with.

Stephen drags his tongue across his bottom lip. "Nah, I don't. You got me there." He turns to me. "But I *would* love a slice of that blueberry pie. Whaddaya say, Gwen? Get an old man a slice?"

I'd like to pretend that I had the foresight to see my mother reaching for her plate of "overcooked" lasagna. But I don't—Adaline might be dramatic, but I never once thought she was certifiably insane.

Not until the plate goes flying and the lasagna collides with a nasty *splat!* against Stephen's shirt. Red sauce splatters everywhere. It coats the white tablecloth like oozing blood. It sails through the air, sharing its meat love with the area rug, the original hardwood floors, the pale green walls.

If classical music were playing—and the lasagna had made its last descent in slow motion—the whole scene would be like something out of a movie.

But if this was a movie, Stephen would stand up like a

normal human being, call my mother a crazy bitch, and storm the hell out of here.

Nope, I have the oh-so-lovely good fortune of watching my mother and Stephen glance at each other through all of the mayhem and fall in love like some sort of screwed-up Lady-and-the-Tramp replay over a shared plate of pasta.

"Fuck me," Stephen mutters, "but you are so damn hot when you get all angry like that, Addie."

My mother doesn't even spare me a glance as she saunters around the head of the table, hips swaying with pure exaggeration. "I want to lick that sauce right off you."

His arms go wide. "I'm all yours, babe."

"You definitely are." She hooks one finger into the collar of his shirt, and he goes without prompting, trailing behind her like a lost puppy.

"Leave me the Burberry pie, Gwen!" is the only goodnight I receive as they disappear around the corner.

There's no way I'm leaving the Burberry pie or blueberry pie or *any* pie after that showdown. I collapse into my seat and stare at what remains of the dinner I hoped would bring my mom and I closer.

Simply put, it looks like a murder scene.

And if we're being all metaphorical here, that's exactly how my relationship with my mom feels right now.

Without giving myself the chance to second-guess everything, I reach into my cardigan pocket for my phone. There's a missed text from Charlie asking how the dinner went, and I send her a quick message promising to offer a recap tomorrow—with wine.

I try to ignore the way my heart rate picks up speed as I thumb down to Marshall's contact and hit CALL. My butt scoots a little farther down in the chair as I listen to the ringtone and play with my discarded dinner napkin.

Maybe he's not around?

He could be at practice. Maybe he's in transit from Toronto?

I'm so lost in my thoughts that the sound of his smooth voice over the phone sends a jolt through me.

"Hey, you."

Okay, maybe it's just me, but I've watched enough TV to know that those two little words said by a sexy guy are kryptonite to a female's piece of mind. Beneath the table, I kick off my stilettos and fold my feet under me on the seat.

"Hey." I eye the dining table. "I have a random question for you."

"Shoot."

I love how straightforward he is. I take a deep breath. "Have you ever wondered what it's like to swim in lasagna?"

Marshall doesn't even miss a beat. "It's been awhile since I left my lasagna-swimming days behind. But they were strong, once upon a time."

I nod, even though he can't see me, and try to ignore the warmth spreading through my veins. His good humor is contagious, and I know it was the right move to call him. *Why haven't I done this before?* Knotting the napkin into a ball, I say, "I'm swimming in it right now."

Through the receiver, I hear masculine voices in the background. I wonder if they're still at the airport, in transit back from Toronto. There's the sound of a door clicking shut and then all that remains is the sound of his voice—which is heavy with mischief. "Tell me you at least drenched yourself in Parmesan cheese."

And just like that, I grin. I can't even help it. Tipping my head back against the chair, I allow myself to imagine Marshall here with me, and that vision is . . . well, to be honest, it's lovely. "And ricotta," I say, trying to hold back a laugh, "it wouldn't be lasagna without ricotta too."

"Damn, aren't you my kind of woman?"

Yes, I want to tell him, *yes I am*. The admission tangles on my tongue but all that slips out into existence is a very quiet, "I want to be."

There's a small pause. It's long enough to throw my heart rate into triple-time and set off a stampede of *what were you thinking?!* thoughts. I know that he *claimed* to want my heart, but maybe he feels differently now that I'm actively opening up to him? Maybe he's spent the last six years putting me on this pedestal of his own making ... only to realize now that I'm not all he thought I was.

I laugh awkwardly, a choked sound that sounds miserable even to my own ears.

There's nothing quite like a bout of self-examination while you wait for your crush to speak to make you feel on top of the world—*not*.

I wonder how much worse it would get if I asked Marshall to never let me go, Rose-Jack style.

So bad.

"Gwen."

I swallow. "Yes?"

"What's the likelihood of you climbing out of your lasagna pool and meeting me tonight?"

The daughter part of me—the one so desperate for a slice of affection from my mother—is determined to stay here and clean this place right up. Make her realize that although she'll never, ever, put me first, I do my best to make her a priority.

Before tonight, I would have turned down Marshall's proposal and made the magic happen.

Tonight, after watching Adaline send away both her

butler and chef while keeping her new boy toy close, I think it's time to put *me* first. For once.

Eyeing the sauce-painted walls, I toss the napkin on the table and stand. "I have Burberry pie."

"What?"

Oops. "I mean, blueberry pie. I have blueberry pie."

"I'm not a man who turns down pie," he tells me, voice low, "and I'm not the type of guy who reneges on a promise. I owe you a kiss, Gwen, and I hope you're ready to collect."

Oh. *Oh.*

I don't have the chance to formulate a witty rejoinder.

His laugh is husky, sexy, and it's all too easy to picture him thumbing the belt loop of his jeans just before he strips off his shirt to show me the goods. "I'll text you directions to my house, in case you don't remember where I'm at." He pauses. "Don't forget the pie, honey. I'm feeling hungry in more ways than one."

15

GWEN

THREE YEARS EARLIER...

*H*eads swivel in my direction the moment I enter Write's Funeral Home over in East Cambridge.

I don't recognize a single soul, and the truth of that nearly pulls a laugh from my unsmiling lips.

Here I am for my father's funeral and none of his friends recognize me and I sure as hell don't recognize any of them. Maybe if I hadn't just retouched my blond roots with more red hair dye, I'd be greeted with hugs instead of blank stares ...

Or maybe you should just accept the fact that you and your father never had a relationship.

Tugging my cardigan tighter around my shoulders, I stop to sign the guest book. The names listed there don't ring a bell:

Greer Smith, Norwood, Massachusetts.

Viktor Choctov, Fall River, Massachusetts.

Sam Gilton, Nashua, New Hampshire.

I grip the pen in my left hand and press the ballpoint to the lined sheets of paper. In another universe, today would go differently. My mother would be here at my side, and I'd be surrounded by family as opposed to complete strangers. I'd stand up at the front of the funeral home by my father's open casket with my uncle and cousins, and even though my heart would feel scraped raw after losing my dad, I would know, at least, that I wasn't alone.

Unfortunately, alternate realities aren't a thing in my world and the only truth I have is that I am Mark James's daughter. A daughter he hasn't seen in ten years, and a daughter who has enough regrets to make even a sinner feel angelic.

Feeling the sting of tears behind my eyes, I scrawl my name beneath Mr. Gilton of Nashua.

Gwen James, Boston, Massachusetts, daughter of Mark.

As though I need further proof that I do, in fact, belong in this funeral home to pay my respects like everyone else.

On impulse, I write my mother's name just below mine.

She'll never know, and seeing her name there appeases some level of guilt inside me.

At least this way, we can all pretend Adaline isn't completely selfish.

No one turns to greet me as I skirt around groups of people reminiscing about my father.

"Such a good guy," one man says, "you'd never know from the way he worked his classroom and the ice rink that he'd been sick for over a year now."

I don't know what it says about me that I didn't even know my dad was sick until my Uncle Bob called me with the news of my dad's passing. Guilt thrives in my soul, relentless and domineering. It takes everything in me not to turn around and hightail it back to my car.

Don't ever bail.

Strangely enough, it's my father's last words to Adaline before their divorce was finalized that propel me forward.

Like a shield, I tug on my cardigan again, wrapping my arms around my middle as I step into the back room.

I spot Bob over by the casket, shaking hands with a broad-shouldered man whose shaggy brown hair is a touch too long to be remotely fashionable. A leather jacket encases his torso, despite the fact that it feels like a million degrees in here. He claps my uncle on the shoulder, issuing a farewell if I'm guessing right, and then turns around.

Faces me.

And no matter the fact that we're surrounded by twenty-plus people in a small, heated room, I feel like I've been submerged into the icy waters of Boston Harbor in the middle of February.

What is Marshall Hunt doing here?

He approaches with slow, measured steps, as though giving me time to acclimate to his presence in a space that doesn't belong to him. Not that it belongs to me, either, really.

My gaze latches onto Bob, and I can't help but wonder if Marshall knew my dad. But how?

I don't have the chance to give it any further thought because in the next breath, he's standing before me. Tall. Broad. Handsome in that pretty-boy model way of his that I remember so acutely.

"Gwen."

It's all he says, and there's got to be something wrong with me because that's the moment I choose to lose it.

A sob peels from my soul, and it should be loud and noisy the way it feels clanging around in my chest but it's not. The sound of my heart breaking for a man I never had the opportunity to know is silent and steady, just like our relationship over the years. Pushed into nonexistence because my mother saw fit to keep us separated, and by the time I'd reached adulthood, Mark James was done playing the games of his ex-wife and a daughter he barely knew.

"Come with me." Marshall tangles his hand with mine, leading me from the room and down a hallway. I should put up some sort of protest—I never let a man take control—but perhaps it's the shock of seeing Marshall, someone I haven't seen since college, that keeps me quiet.

He pauses outside a doorway, gives a rap of his knuckles against the wood. When there's no reply, he pushes the door open and pulls me inside. "You need air," he says, releasing my hand to go to the windows.

I swallow past the lump in my throat. "You could have brought me outside."

I expect to hear his quiet, familiar laugh, but the only sound is the creaking of the window scraping past chipped paint as he hauls it up and into place. "I could have," he finally says, "but I figured you'd rather have a moment to yourself where you're not being stared at by everyone your father knew and you didn't."

"You know me too well."

The words slip out before I have the chance to stall them, and Marshall gives a slow shake of his head. "Nah, but I wish I did."

My fingers twitch at my sides, and I step forward. "Marshall, I—"

He holds up a hand. "Gwen, that's not why I brought you in here."

"Then why did you?"

"Honestly?"

I nod.

"You looked like you needed a hug from someone who cared." His voice is like velvet, a soft caress that reminds me of hot summer nights and languid hours spent curled in a lover's embrace. "Let me be there for you."

Let me be there for you.

The tears threaten again, itching my nose and burning my eyes, and I tilt my face up to the ceiling. Over the years, I've grown an impenetrable outer shell. I've worked hard to show the world that I'm not a woman on the verge of shattering on the inside.

No one sees the hurt.

No one suspects the insecurities.

No one but Marshall Hunt, a guy too young for me who can't be on my radar. I know my track record with men, the way I'm only in it for the sex and nothing more, the way I'm more likely to have a one-night stand with a random stranger than give a guy I know the chance for a relationship.

I would ruin a man like Marshall, and I would hate myself even more than I already do.

But when his pewter eyes meet mine, silently commanding that I give in and accept what he's offering, I can't say no.

He reads me without a spoken *yes*. Strong arms envelop me, circling my waist and pulling me up against the hard planes of his chest. I catch the scent of his cologne and —*who am I?*—nuzzle my nose against his pecs.

"I've got you," he rumbles, running a hand over my hair. "I've got you, Gwen."

I squeeze my eyes shut, fighting the stream of inevitable tears. There's no doubt about it—I don't deserve a guy like Marshall. But for the span of a breath, I allow myself to wonder what it would be like to have him, to wake up each morning and know that he's in my corner. To come home each night to a hug just like this one, and a man who would move mountains to see me happy. To love and be loved, for once, in return.

And then I push the wisp of imagination away.

If I've learned nothing else over the years, it's that there's no point in hoping. Life will always bite you in the ass with reality—and it always hurts like a bitch.

16

HUNT

"You owe us steak."

Hands clutching my steering wheel, I send a quick, *get-the-fuck-out-of-my-car* glare at Harrison and Beaumont. "Yeah, I heard you two the first time—thirty minutes ago. Get out of my truck."

When Gwen called, we were at a Brazilian steakhouse after landing at Logan International Airport from our game against Toronto. No matter the day of the week, Gwen James trumps steak. Always.

Andre leans forward in the back seat, dropping his elbows to the center console and somehow—miraculously—shoving his massive shoulders between the two front seats. "Harrison," he draws out in a sing-song tone that makes me want to punch him, "we can't fault him. His fair lady has finally called. He's ready to make a fool of himself and come in two seconds flat. If anything, we should be giving *him* steak. He's going to need it when he embarrasses himself."

Teeth clenched, I mutter, "I hate you assholes."

"You don't." Duke pats me on the shoulder in an *aren't-you-special* kind of way. "But you do owe me a steak."

I furrow my brow, frustration getting the best of me. "You had steak last night with Jackson in Toronto."

"It was mediocre. Can't compare to good Boston steak. The fact that you made us leave *after* we already put in our order has got to be illegal somewhere."

I've already pointed out that they could have easily taken an Uber home from the North End, but I secretly think they wanted to spend the drive back to Beaumont's house just giving me shit. If I were in their position, I'd probably do the same. But since *I'm* the one on a time constraint, they've got to go.

"Got it," I grunt, flicking the locks in my truck so they'll get the hint. *Click, click, click.* "Now get the hell out of my truck so I can beat Gwen back to my house."

Beaumont's brows shoot inward as his phone goes off. "Give me a sec," he says, raising one finger up. My head drops back and I stare at the ceiling of my truck. Six years after meeting Gwen James and I *finally* get my shot with her, and there's a solid chance it's going to be blown to smithereens because my teammates are the worst jerks on the planet who don't realize that trash-talk can be toned down off the ice.

"Hey baby," Andre practically coos into the phone. On the ice, Andre is King Sin Bin, aka the toughest son of a gun there is in the NHL. Around us, his teammates, he still toes the line of perpetual bastard—it's in his DNA. Around his fiancée, Zoe, he's nothing but a pile of mush. "Oh, yeah," he goes on, glancing out the window to their shared Colonial-style house, "we're sitting in the driveway . . . Nah, we're just having a little talk with Hunt here about sex . . . Yes, with

Gwen. Yeah . . . yeah"—he taps me on the shoulder and I glance back—"Zo wants to talk to you."

Jesus Christ.

I motion for the phone but Beaumont only pulls it away from his ear and taps on the screen.

"Hello?" Zoe's sweet voice comes in loud and tinny. "Hunt?"

Someone just put me out of my misery. "I'm here, Zoe."

Next to me, Harrison chuckles quietly before drawing out his own phone and tapping away.

"Oh, hey!" If I squint hard enough, I can see Zoe standing in the window of her living room waving at me. The curtain is pulled wide and her shadow is illuminated by the living-room light behind her. "Listen, I'm so glad you've decided to give my girl a chance. She really likes you."

"That's . . ." *Good*, I finish in my head. But "good" doesn't even begin to cover how I'm feeling right now. Fucking anxious does a better job of it, and, even more appropriate—I feel shocked that Zoe knows something like that. Gwen is notoriously tight-lipped when it comes to her emotions, but I do think I'm slowly knocking down those steel walls around her.

Finally.

"Hello?"

My hands inadvertently squeeze the steering wheel at the newcomer's voice—Charlie Denton's voice.

I jerk my gaze to my teammate. Harrison only shrugs and palms his phone to his opposite hand. "I thought she'd feel left out if we didn't include her. She's known Gwen the longest."

"That's right!" Charlie says, and I have a feeling she's pointing at the phone. "I have known her the longest, and I think we can all agree that our Gwenny has come a long way, and if you break her heart I will break your dick, Hunt."

Well, things just escalated quickly.

Straightening in my seat, I bite out, "I have no plans to break her heart."

"We're honestly more worried he'll forget how to have sex he's so excited."

There is only one thing keeping me from punching Andre and it's the fact that we have ladies present. "I think I'll be okay, guys. Now can you please, for the love all things holy, get the fu—"

"Wear a condom," Charlie tells me, followed by Zoe piping up, "She's on birth control because of lady issues but best not to get sloppy on the first go-round. Strap up, Hunt."

"Out."

My two teammates erupt into laughter as they grab their duffel bags by their feet.

"We're being dismissed," Harrison tells his girl as he pops his door open. "I think Hunt is on the verge of coming undone."

"I see what you did there," Charlie answers with a robust laugh. "Is he red in the face?"

Harrison pulls his duffel strap over his head and then eyes me. "Red as a damn fire truck."

I'm going to murder them all.

I honk my horn, not even caring who I might be disturbing in the neighborhood. "Out! I have places to go, people to—"

"Bang?" I hear Zoe shout from Beaumont's phone. It's possible I'm also hearing an echo, considering the fact that she's standing less than fifty feet away. "You better make it an amazing banging experience, Hunt. I know where you sleep and Gwen deserves the best."

With another obnoxious honk of my horn, my teammates slam their doors shut and then scatter onto Beaumont's front lawn. I turn up the radio volume to drown out their laughter as I peel out of the driveway.

I can't get back to my house quickly enough.

17

HUNT

By the time I pull up in front of my house, Gwen's already waiting.

Seated on my front stoop with what I can only assume is the blueberry pie resting on her lap, she looks young and nervous and lonely.

Exactly as she'd looked at her father's funeral three years ago.

I try not to think of that day often—not because I don't miss Mark James but because I'll never forget how I held Gwen in my arms and comforted her, wiped away her tears, and all over a man she barely knew.

A man who'd influenced my life in more ways than one.

Until that moment, I'd never made the connection between Mark James, a man who'd taken me under his wing and showed me that I had a future in hockey, and the girl who'd turned me inside out in college.

If there were any photos of Gwen in Mark's house, they weren't in the areas company visited. His desk at my high school was similarly bare of personal items. In passing, he sometimes mentioned a daughter, but never could I have put the two and two together until I'd turned around from paying my respects and saw her standing there, tears welling in her eyes and uncertainty slouching her shoulders.

In one moment, Gwen James had rendered me speechless all over again.

That day, I offered her all the comfort I could—and she never asked me why I was there or how I knew her father. I need to tell her at some point, but the worry has always lingered that I'll make her feel even more shitty about the situation with her dad. That a guy like me had considered her father one of his greatest mentors . . . when she hadn't even seen the man in years.

Sometimes, I can't help but feel as though she'd rather not know of my connection to her father since she's never once brought it up.

With a deep breath, I shove my fingers through my hair and then climb out of my truck, slinging my duffel bag over my shoulder after grabbing it from the back seat.

Her smile is slight, unsure, and it takes everything in me not to lift her up and stamp a hard kiss on her mouth. After years of waiting, though, I'm not claiming my first kiss on my doorstep.

"Sorry I'm late." When I step directly in front of her, I offer my hand and hide a grin when she accepts the offer to help her up. "A few mutual friends of ours are the reason for the holdup." I unlock the front door and push it open, then step to the side so Gwen can enter first. "Seems as though you have some fairy godmothers looking out for you."

She scrunches her nose, and it's cute as hell. The minute we step inside, she shrugs out of her trench coat and slips it over one of the hooks by the front door. With her red hair down around her shoulders and her cream-colored dress snug in all the right places, she's also the sexiest woman I've ever seen. Then I notice a stain by her armpit, and I quirk a brow. "You weren't kidding about the lasagna swimming, were you?"

"What?" Jolted out of the moment, she stares down at her dress and releases a soft sigh. "I thought I escaped unscathed." She fingers the stain and then lets her hand fall to her side. "My mother had an accident."

"Sounds saucy." I wink at her, and she rewards me with a chuckle.

"You have no idea," she says with a shake of her head. "My mom is . . . I don't even know how to best describe her."

Knowing now that Mark's ex-wife is Gwen's mother, it all makes sense. Mark's choice words about his ex-wife tended to stay in the colored, four-lettered variety. From what I gathered, The Former Mrs. James was (and is) a little temperamental.

And that's putting it lightly.

"You don't have to talk about it," I tell Gwen as we move into my kitchen. I flick the lights on and nod my head toward the counter, so she can put the pie down. "Not if you don't want to, I mean."

Gwen sets the pie on the counter and then lingers there, hands on the rounded lip as her shoulders draw up by her ears. "Do you have someone in your life that you don't particularly like but you still can't help yourself—you want to make them proud?"

Knowing it'll make her grin, I hold up my hands, spreading them wide. "You may not have noticed, honey, but my coach isn't the most likeable fellow."

"Hall?" She turns around and presses her butt to the counter so she can meet my gaze. "He's a total sweetheart. I've never had an issue with him."

"To *you*, maybe." It's not exactly P.C., but I go for the truth anyway. "Anyone with a dick is usually on his shit list."

She brings her thumb to her mouth and nibbles on the pad. My own dick rises to the occasion, wanting to be included in the conversation. *Go down, man. Not your turn.*

"*Anyway*," I mutter, moving past her to open the cabinets. I pull down two plates, grab utensils, and set them on the marble kitchen island that's more like its own separate continent, it's so big. Whoever owned this house before me either had a Napoleonic complex or was a mammoth—there's no in between. "Tell me what happened with your mom. Then I'll make you feel better with pie and wine."

"And kisses?"

I whip around at her sassily issued question. With her arms bent just so, and her hands perched on the counter behind her, her breasts are thrust forward. Her dress is demure, with a conservative neckline and a slim line that cuts off at her knees. But the look in her blue eyes is anything but demure and it takes every inch of my self-control not to toss the pie to the floor and hike her up onto the counter. The things I'd do to her...

My eyes screw shut as I struggle to even out my breathing. "We'll get there, trust me."

"Tonight?"

Opening my eyes, I find myself with my hands on her hips and pressing my hard-on against her belly. She's inches shorter than me, even in her heels, and she tips her head back to brush her lips to the underside of my jaw.

At the sensation of her lips coasting over my skin, I almost say *fuck it* and take what I want. Pull up her dress. Pop her up on the counter. Strip off her underwear and pump into her slick heat.

It'd be easy to do that.

But we started on this path because I wanted to be sure she was in this for the right reasons—listening to her talk about her mom, showing that I care about more than what's between her legs... that matters to me.

My control snaps when she loops an arm around me, her palm resting on my back.

I nip her to put her in place—a gentle bite to her earlobe that pulls a yip from her mouth and has her dragging her nails down my back. "Be good," I whisper as I move my mouth lower, to the sensitive spot where her neck and shoulder meet, "or I'll be forced to up the stakes."

Her head lolls to the side. "Sure, whatever—*oh!*"

I tug down her dress, just enough to press a kiss to her collarbone. "Whatever, what?" Another kiss, this one just above the swell of her breast. "I've waited a long time for this, honey, and I'll be damned if I don't make the moment exactly how I've envisioned it all these years."

Her fingers dance around to my front to hang onto me by the belt loops of my jeans. "Are there rose petals involved?" she asks in a sly voice.

"No." My voice isn't sly—it's an honest-to-God rumble that sounds deep even to my own ears. "No rose petals."

"Candles?"

"I think I've got a lighter somewhere."

"No rose petals," she mutters, her fingers sinking into my hair, "no candles. What in the world have you been thinking of all these years?"

Hell, it's going to sound stupid. I ignore the rapid tempo of my heart and pull back, letting her dress go so that can I cup her face. Pulling a deep breath into my lungs, I go for broke. "We're going to pretend this is the best idea you've ever heard."

She turns her face just far enough so she can press a kiss to my palm. "I'm good at pretending—for a price."

She wouldn't be Gwen James if she didn't challenge me every step of the way.

And I wouldn't be me—the NHL's best power forward—if I didn't take risks every day in my career.

"Deal accepted," I tell her.

She blinks up at me. "You don't even know what the price is."

I shrug. "Considering the topic of conversation, I figure I'm going to like it no matter what."

"I could suggest bondage," she says, throwing it out there like she's brought something scandalous into the conversation. "Tie you up or whatever."

Laughter floods my chest, and I move my hand to the nape of her neck. My thumb brushes the shell of her ear and I don't miss the way she shivers and her lids flutter shut. Which makes it the perfect time to admit: "Honey, I'm not scared of a little bondage. So long as I'm tied up to the bed and you're riding my face, I've got no complaints."

18

GWEN

Pop!

There goes an image of me grinding on Marshall's face, and let me tell you, it's what fantasies are made of.

The man of the hour just throws back his head and laughs at what I assume is my *oh-yes* expression. I don't know how he manages to have such tan skin all year around, especially since it's just days before Christmas. Mild winter or not, I'm the equivalent of a milk carton and he's just . . . masculine perfection. His tattooed arms bind me to him, and his broad chest grazes mine. I've never met a man with a chest as powerful and as hard as Marshall's, and I wouldn't be surprised if he works out even more than what the Blades require of him.

"Have you, um . . ." I wave my hand in his general direction, not even knowing how to finish off that sentence. "I guess what I'm trying to say is . . ." Once again, the words don't come and I'm left floundering like a besotted idiot.

Marshall's gray eyes warm as he glances down at me.

"You'd be my first, Gwenny, and I'd be more than willing to let you pop my bondage cherry."

Pop his . . .

Cheeks flushing, I roll my eyes and give a push to his chest. "You're ridiculous."

"Nah," he says, letting me go. From the way he eyes me as I sashay out of his embrace, I'd venture to say every foot I put between us is one that he regrets. "You can be too serious at times," he adds, "and I'm making it my responsibility to lighten you up. Aren't you glad you got with a younger man?"

It's a sore spot and he knows it. But, strangely enough, it's been days since I've thought about our difference in age. Back in college, the gap seemed insurmountable.

Standing here with him now, I can't help but take in my surroundings. It goes without saying that Marshall has made something for himself. For a man who grew up in the system, he has more opportunities at his fingertips than I ever will. Call me crazy, but that makes me happy—he deserves every bit of good that comes his way.

As for his house, the Tudor-style home is massive. The wood-paneling details throughout the entryway and kitchen are beautiful and not so heavy-handed that it looks like something out of the seventies. And I won't lie—from the moment I stepped into the house, my jaw did a little drop at the sight of all the stonework. The kitchen is completely new with big appliances and an even bigger kitchen island.

I guess it makes sense because Marshall is no small man —not in height and definitely not in the downstairs department.

I flush at the memory of his erection pressed against me. I'd been half a second away from dropping to my knees, peeling open his jeans, and worshipping his cock in the best way possible.

Taking a turn around the kitchen, I flash him a smile and then drop onto one of the stools at the island. "I'm beginning to like this younger thing. It means that you should have more stamina for certain activities."

"*Should*?" he repeats, and I can't help but laugh at his defensive tone. "Stamina isn't something you'll ever have to worry about with me."

"Do I have to worry about you stealing all of the pie?"

He glances down to where he's hugging the dessert to his chest like contraband. "Have I mentioned that I enjoy pie?" He looks up at me through thick lashes, and his mouth turns up in a half-smile. "Grab the plates, honey. We're going to watch a movie."

"Are we?"

"Yup. It's all part of my kissing plans." He cuts me a dark look that I don't believe for a hot-second. "Don't make fun of me, but back in college I used to think about taking you to the movies all the time. We'd sit up in the back row—"

"Only naughty things happen in the back row." I follow behind him with our plates and utensils while he grabs the wine from a fancy cooler next to the refrigerator. We take a hallway leading out of the kitchen, away from the front of the house. "I don't think I've partaken in that sort of thing since high school."

"Exactly." With his elbow, he flicks on a light at the end of the hallway, and I'm halfway not surprised that he owns an in-house movie theater. There are three rows of black leather La-Z--Boys, and I count nine seats total. Classic red walls complete the space, as well as the largest TV I've ever seen outside of an actual theater.

He gestures for me to take my seat in the back row —*naturally*—and I do so with a soft laugh. Marshall has clearly thought this whole thing out. Who am I to ruin his fantasy?

I take the back-left seat. "Tell me the rest of your fantasy, and don't leave out a thing."

"I never leave out the details," he rumbles. "I'm not that sort of guy." Bringing the pie and the wine to a wooden sideboard to our left, he snags the plates and utensils and doles out two slices. "I hope you're okay with drinking straight from the bottle?" Gray eyes twinkle at me in challenge. "It's part of the fantasy."

"We can be heathens together."

His grin is slow and panty-meltingly sexy. If I weren't so determined to follow his fantasy to a T, I'd strip off my underwear and throw them across the room.

Get the show on early and all that.

Patience has never been a virtue of mine.

Marshall returns with our pie and the wine bottle, then makes a quick detour to shut off the lights. When he settles in beside me, the space feels immediately smaller. His left leg presses into mine, and our elbows do a little dance as we stake our claim.

His elbow to the back of the arm rest—mine to the front.

It's like a tango a couple only makes once in their life, and I hide a smile by digging into my blueberry pie.

For a night that started out in nightmare status...this is everything I needed to feel better, to feel *right*. With Marshall, I belong, and I wish it hadn't taken me years to realize that.

"What do you want to watch?"

His palm falls to my thigh with the question, and right

then, that's when I realize why he wanted our first kiss to be like this.

It's a throwback to our youth when first kisses were secreted in the back of a theater. When you waited, in hope, for your date to make the first move. An arm around your shoulders. A hand to the thigh. A kiss that starts light and easy before you're hauled onto a masculine lap and grinding down like the soundtrack to the movie is something straight from a nightclub.

I cover Marshall's hand with mine, and it's so much less than what I want to do in this moment. Squeezing his fingers, I hope he gets the message loud and clear: *I can't wait to take this step with you*.

With his pewter gaze on me, he flips his hand over, palm up, so that we're holding hands.

Swoon.

Seriously, I'm feeling a little lightheaded right now.

"Movie, Gwen?" he prompts, a little knowing smile tugging at his lips. "I've got Netflix."

Is he asking me a question right now? I look down at our entwined fingers. Yup, my heart is beating a mile a minute and all I know is that I want this moment to last forever. I don't think I've ever—not ever—anticipated a man's kiss like I do Marshall's.

Considering the fact that I've already seen him naked, too . . . I feel like that says a lot.

"Um, honestly I can go with whatever."

"Horror?" He thumbs the controller in his opposite hand and turns the TV on. The instant lighting casts his handsome face in a glow, highlighting his strong jawline and his perfectly sloped nose. With a squeeze of my hand, he adds, "I like the idea of you wanting to jump into my lap."

Before I have the chance to process the words, I say, "I don't think you'll need a movie to guarantee that."

Again he laughs, the sound rich and throaty, and again I feel swept away on a fantasy that didn't belong to me though it's now one I cling to with both hands. Or with one hand—the other is gripping my fork and half stabbing my pie.

"Sounds good to me."

Marshall selects a movie, and, as the opening soundtrack kicks in, I do myself a favor and focus on the pie. Better than staring at him like a crazy lady.

The film opens with a woman screaming—she's blonde, always the first ones to go in movies like these—and being chased by a guy with a chainsaw.

Classic.

I dig into my pie with gusto, chowing down as fast as I can go.

Marshall leans over to whisper, "You swallowin' over there?"

If his intention was to make me think about getting on my knees before him, then he did his job well. I choke on the pie and he shoves the wine bottle at me with the order to "drink."

I don't think it has the same effect as drinking water in times like these, but I pull down the wine anyway. "I'm good. All set." I set the bottle at my feet and finish off the pie, and then put that to the side, as well.

Step One, done.

After all, I need my hands empty if I want to snuggle up against Marshall, right? And I can't do that if I'm nursing my pie all night.

I turn slightly, just far enough that my crossed legs brush his and my breasts are now shamelessly rubbing up against his arm.

Marshall makes a coughing sound.

"You okay?"

"Yup," he grunts.

And then he flips the script on me.

19

HUNT

Gwen has no idea how much she's playing with fire right now.

Without giving her warning, I set my pie on the seat next to me and then tug her legs over mine so that she's curled up against me. The hem of her perfectly respectable dress rides up, exposing lush skin from her knees to just below her pussy.

And then I clamp my hands down on her thighs where I begin to knead her muscles.

I keep my eyes on the shitty movie the whole time, unwilling to give away how much she's affecting me right now.

Because she is.

My cock is pounding at my zipper, demanding to put on a performance, and that's a surprise all on its own because my head is pounding so loudly I'm surprised I've got enough blood to gravitate to two different hemispheres in my body.

"I think we skipped the awkward, do-you-hold-me stage," Gwen squeaks. Her moan when I rub a particular knot in her leg proves that she doesn't give a shit how many stages we skip.

She wants this.

I want this.

It's only a matter of time before we give in.

"We're playing the adult version." I slip my hand up high on her leg, teasing her with the possibility of making contact with ground zero, before I trail back down to her knee. At her little growl of displeasure, I laugh. "Don't tell me you don't got any patience, Gwenny." I press my head to the back of the seat and look her way. "What's the fun if there's not a little anticipation?"

If she wants to stab me with my fork, she's going to have to crawl across my lap—and she won't hear a complaint from me.

With a little huff, she turns back to the TV and pretends to ignore me.

I could never ignore her.

For the next twenty minutes, I set out to make Gwen pant.

Yes, pant. It's all part of the fantasy—the one where she realizes I'm the one for her, the one where she'll do anything just to have the chance to strip off my clothes and crash her mouth down onto mine.

After years of working for her, I still want her to come to me—in the best way possible.

I massage her calves, her legs. I trace the lines of her stiletto until she's flexing her foot and turning it inward, giving me more space to play. When the movie turns particularly gory, I make a point of playing with Gwen's hair and pressing small kisses along the length of her neck.

And with each minute that passes, her control falters and then cracks and then disappears completely.

She clutches my forearm as though she's determined to get my hand where she wants it most—right between her legs. She rubs her legs alongside mine, until her dress is around her hips and I've got the most fantastic view of her white panties. She presses her hand to my lower abdomen and then flicks open the brass button of my jeans.

I like it when my Gwen is bold.

And I'll reward her for it.

"C'mere." My voice sounds like it's been scraped raw, but she doesn't question it. She leans in as somebody gets the axe on the screen in front of us, and I grip her chin between my thumb and index finger. One swipe of her tongue along her bottom lip and I almost come in my pants. *Jesus.* Shaking my head to get back into the game, I allow my thumb to catch the moisture left behind.

Her breath shudders over my thumb, and then she surprises me by sinking her teeth into my flesh—a sexy nip that cracks my own control.

"Oops," she murmurs. Her blue eyes flash with humor as she soothes the sting with her tongue. "Got ahead of myself there."

Everything in me stills. This is the Gwen I've always wanted at my side—snarky and kind and funny. I drop my eyes to her lips. We've played enough.

Does it matter if she kisses me first when it's clear she wants me with every fiber of her being? In my arms, she's an open book whose pages are begging to be loved.

I move my hand to her thigh. Higher, until my thumb is playing with the waistband of her underwear and I'm hearing the sweetest sounds spill from her mouth.

"I'm going to kiss you now."

Her eyes go wide and she licks her lips. "Yes."

That's all she says but the one word captures everything we're both experiencing.

Finally, after six fucking years, *yes*.

20

GWEN

*I*f I ever had any doubts, Marshall buries them the moment his lips claim mine.

This is what I've been missing. This heat, the way he angles my head and silently commands me to give everything back to him and then do it all over again.

Marshall kisses like how he plays hockey—hard, smooth, and powerful.

I can feel that power coiled under my hands when I clasp his shoulders and hang on tight.

I feel it when his big hand clutches my thigh. I'm not a stick and my butt has been known to test every pair of jeans that I own, but Marshall's palm spans the width of my thigh and when he squeezes... oh, my God.

Literally, that's all I have for you.

Oh. My. God.

I think it when he skims his hand down my leg, wraps it around my ankle, and then positions the sole of my shoe on his knee.

I think it when I realize that he's just put me on open

display. My panties are wet and I've never been more thankful for dim lights in my life.

His kiss devours me, demanding entrance. I give it to him freely and am praised with the smooth stroke of his tongue against my own. Hard, needy, raw—and then the kiss turns languid, like we have all the time in the world to make up for the lost years where I was stupid and stubborn and a million other things I don't care to think about right now.

He tears his mouth from mine to place a kiss to the leaping pulse just below my jaw. "Do you have any idea how much I craved this?" he demands in a gravel-pitched voice. "Do you have any idea how much I wanted to know the taste of your lips? The way you felt under my fingers?"

At the contact of his fingers brushing my inner thigh, I'm not ashamed to say that I act like a complete hussy. I drop my knee to the seat in front of us, giving Marshall ample room should he want it.

And, oh boy, does he.

He cups the apex of my thighs, rubbing the heel of his palm in tight little circles against my clit.

Oh. My. God.

Marshall groans. "Fuck, I can already feel how wet you are for me."

His name escapes me on a gasp, and I plant my elbow down on the armrest, leveraging myself upward so that I can see everything. I need to see him just as I need to feel him, and when he presses a single finger over my core, I nearly snap.

Please.

I don't even realize that I've spoken out loud until Marshall is lifting my chin with his opposite hand, so that I have no choice but to meet his gaze. "Please, what?" Eyes narrowed, he looks exactly how I've seen him on the ice—he's looking to score.

And I plan to let him.

Blunt fingers brush aside my underwear.

"Please, what, Gwen?" I feel the heat of his palm so close to where I need his touch. It makes me desperate, needy, and I lift my hips in the hope to close the difference and satisfy the ache between my legs.

"*Marshall.*"

His name is a plea and a prayer. He doesn't answer the call—not the way I expect him to, anyway.

"Answer the question." His free hand coasts up my body, brushing the tips of my breasts, and then curls around the back of my neck. "What do you want, Gwen? Do you want me to tear your panties right off you?" He doesn't play fair, choosing that moment to sink a finger inside me.

My toes curl in my stilettos as I throw my head back against the headrest. I don't know if I can do this. The sensations sparking through me are sharp, poignant, nothing like I've ever felt before. Every nerve is too sensitive; every breath I take too loud and too jagged.

Marshall's thumb makes contact with my clit, eliciting a whimper from my lips.

"Is this what you want?" he asks roughly, playing my body like an instrument only he knows. "Or maybe it's that you want something else completely?"

I feel his absence immediately. His hand pulls away from my core, and his other disappears from the back of my head. And then all I feel are his big hands at my hips, dragging me up onto the armrest that separates our two seats. I plant a hand on the back of the chair to stabilize my weight.

"Feet here," he commands, and then proceeds to move me exactly how he wants me.

Hips tilted forward, one foot digging into the cushioned seat—I worry that my sharp heel will puncture the leather but Marshall doesn't say a word about it. His seats, his rules. His—

Shripppp!

My mouth falls open. "You just ripped my underwear."

Marshall grins wickedly. "Guilty."

Like a white flag of surrender, he holds the fabric up and then tosses it over his shoulder.

Well, then.

"This is your fantasy?" I ask, trying my best not to tremble under the weight of his stare. My dress is hiked up to my stomach, and I don't even want to contemplate the reality of how I look right now. Messy hair, smudged lipstick, I'm sure. But Marshall studies me like he's never seen anyone more beautiful, and I . . . melt.

Literally.

My legs fall wide and I reach for him, silently demanding a kiss.

An unnamed emotion dances across his face as he meets me in the middle. His hands cup my face and mine go to his chest. He tastes like pie and sex, and there has never been a more singular flavor I wish I could bottle up and keep forever.

"This is my fantasy," he whispers against my mouth.

He drops to his knees and his hands go to my thighs.

"As is this."

The first brush of his lips against my clit is enough to make me see the colors of the rainbow. I make the most ridiculous sounds, and even if I wanted to, there's no chance that I could stifle the whimpers and the moans.

His tongue traces a line downward, thrusting inside me without preamble. His groan echoes in my ears as I watch him. Eyes shut, he feasts on me like I'm the best meal he's ever tasted—the one that has been kept from him for so long that he's starving, almost unforgiving in his caresses.

My cries mingle with his groans, and it's with a burst of embarrassment that I realize I'm practically humping his mouth.

I'd like to pretend that it's because I haven't had sex in almost a year.

But really, it's the fact that I have never felt more loved than I do in this moment.

I palm his muscular shoulder. "Sex."

How eloquent. I mentally smack myself in the forehead.

"What I meant to say is, please sex now."

Because that's any better?

Marshall chuckles against me, gives another swirl of his tongue in the most delicious way, and sits back. "Is this your fantasy or mine?"

His tone is nonchalant but there's no mistaking the hunger in his gray eyes.

"Does it matter?" I ask, yanking on his shoulders so he'll stand. When he does, my fingers go to the zipper of his jeans and I tug downward. Simultaneously, he makes quick work of his belt like we're in a rush to the finish line, then shoves his jeans down the length of his powerful legs.

I know that I saw him on our video chat, but . . . wowza.

Who says wowza?

Obviously, when faced with the godliness of Marshall Hunt's body, I do.

Wowza, wowza, wowza.

Andddd now all I can think about is Marsha, Marsha, Marsha.

"What's so funny?" Marshall asks. "It's bad form to laugh at a guy when he's half-naked."

That cuts my laughter real quick. I eye his shirt. "I wouldn't be opposed to *all* naked."

He gestures to my body. "After you, honey."

He won't hear a protest out of me. I fumble with the zipper of my dress, and tug that bad boy down, down, down until I'm shimmying out of the material completely and tossing it to the side. My bra is off in seconds.

I should be a lot more nervous than I am—but I just can't find it in myself to be that way with Marshall, a guy who's wanted me for years.

A guy, if I'm pushing for honesty, that I've secretly wanted in return.

I nod at him. "Your turn."

In that hot-guy way, he hooks his shirt up and over his head. Every inch that's revealed is ripped and gorgeous. Chiseled abs and rock-hard pecs. Huge biceps, and tattoos that line the length of his arms.

And, knowing that it'll get to him, I murmur, "You're so pretty, Marshall."

He reacts as I expect him to—with a low-seated growl that sends wisps of excitement down my spine. Strong arms haul me upward, and then he's dropping me onto the seat in front of us so that I sit on its cushioned back.

Marshall shoves his briefs down his legs, and his cock springs forth unapologetically. It's big, just as I remember, with a thick crown.

I can't help myself.

"Your cock's even prettier," I whisper, with a waggle of my brows just to show I'm teasing.

"The only pretty one around here is you," he growls. His fingers find my heated flesh, thrusting inside and then hitting my G-spot. All in one go. Either Marshall is a bedroom genius or he simply knows how to work me to the very edge. "I'm going to fuck you until the only word you remember is my name."

Um, yes please.

"Any last words?"

I grin, just a little evilly, as I tug his head down to whisper in his ear: "I hope I'm half as pretty as you when this is all over."

He enters me a second later with a deep-seated thrust. He's big, bigger than I expected. Or maybe it's that it's been so long for me. My hands find his arms and my nails bite into his skin and it feels so damn good that I don't know whether to cry or tell him to get moving.

"Fuck," he groans, his forehead pressed to mine, "a condom. I forgot—"

I've never been without one despite the fact that I've been on birth control since my teens. The men I've slept with . . . I refused to give them access to that last part of me. Having me without barriers wasn't part of that dynamic. With Marshall, it's different. With him, he asked for my heart—and I want to give him more than just that. I want him to have my trust, as well.

I kiss his cheek, stubbled with a five o'clock shadow. "I'm on the pill," I say, wishing there was a less clinical way to put it, "and clean."

"Same here." His arms grow tighter around me. "Are you sure?"

I can tell it's taking him every ounce of control to remain still.

My answering nod is jerky. "I'm good."

He lifts his head to meet my gaze. "If you're not now," he murmurs, "you will be."

As his hips pull back, his mouth finds mine. I will never get over kissing Marshall, not today or tomorrow or ten years from now. He pours every bit of emotion into his kiss. Right now, I taste his worry that he's hurt me, his need to dominate, his desire to see me lose control.

When he thrusts forward the next time, my mouth parts on a gasp. Yes, yes, *right there*. Fingers grip my sides, holding me still, and then he changes the angle and I'm done for. With each pump of his hips, he slides against my clit.

The pressure heightens as his hips churn faster.

I lift my gaze to take in his handsome features. Tension lines his expression and his gray eyes burn bright with lust. Marshall is a king taking what's his . . . and, in this moment, I'm his queen.

"*More.*" The cry is ripped from my soul, and I don't even know what I'm asking for. More of his hard cock? More of our chemistry, which is off the charts wild? More of his affection?

Whatever I'm asking for, he gives it.

His hips slam into mine, hard and fast.

As promised from that night in Faneuil Hall, I come all over his cock, my head tipped back as his lips press feathery light kisses to my chin and my neck and my forehead. His orgasm follows seconds later, and he shouts my name like I belong to him.

"Holy shit."

I don't know which one of us says it. Maybe both of us.

With my forehead against his damp chest, I say, "Pretty sure if we had sex like that at an actual theater, we'd be arrested."

"The perks of having your own theater." He pauses, the silence drawing out until all I hear is our ragged breathing. "Not gonna lie, honey, you've ruined me. I don't even think my legs are going to hold me up for another second."

If he feels all wobbly the way I do, I don't blame him. I

pat his shoulder. "Sit your Jell-O legs down and take me with you."

He wraps his arms around me and hoists me up into his embrace, bridal-style. He makes a move to sit, mutters "fucking armrest," and then shifts over to the next seat.

I snuggle against his chest, my arms wrapped around his neck, as I inhale his scent and wonder if it'd be weird to ask for a shirt. Not to wear, just to . . . keep. Okay, yeah, that's weird.

Marshall collapses as gently as possible with me in his arms.

I hear the distinct sound of metal clattering to the floor, and then—

"Fuck. Me."

I jerk back to stare at him, only to find that his eyes are wide with panic.

"What?" I poke him in the chest. "What's wrong?"

His gaze clashes with mine. "The pie."

Um . . . "It was tasty, right?"

He blinks. Once. Twice. Thrice. "The pie"—he swallows audibly—"is underneath me."

No. I lean to the side, blink a few times, and wish that our shadows weren't throwing the entire seat into darkness. I glance back up at him. "Are you sure you're sitting on the pie?"

His tongue sweeps over his bottom lip. "*Yup.* I'm going to need you to get up, Gwen. And to also never mention this again."

"But—"

His gaze zeroes in on me, as though daring me to challenge him on this.

So I do.

"But how will we ever tell anyone about our first kiss then? It's all part of the fantasy, after all."

"All part of the . . ." he trails off, and I don't have time to register the fact he's pulled me up into his arms and plopped me down in his place until I hear a very loud *squishhhh*. Oh. My. God. He swallows my shriek with a kiss and a full-belly laugh.

"Don't worry," he whispers in my ear, "I'll be sure to lick you all clean."

21

HUNT

I wake to the sound of my phone ringing—and a warm body snuggled up against my chest.

Gwen stretches and shoves her butt against my crotch. Even in sleep, she's a temptress I can't live without. More than that, she's a woman I want by my side for the rest of my life. Everything about her calls to me in a way that I can't necessarily dictate into words—and the thought alone brings to mind the studies I've seen online that circle the question: why do you love a person?

Always, the interviewee's answer came back to attributes: she's gorgeous, his smile, their laugh. Or maybe, even, *he understands me* or *she makes me happy*.

That's how I feel about Gwen. It's so much harder to give definition to the wonderment I feel when we grin at each other or the sense of completion that envelops me when she says my name like I'm the only one in the world who can give her what she needs.

Those studies had the right of it. Tonight, I knew with every fiber of my being that Gwen fits me in every way—but if I had to give bullet-point reasons why, I'd have only one answer. She just does.

I slip my hand over her curves and momentarily lose myself in the memories of this evening.

It's pretty hard to believe that this moment is my reality. After years of hoping that she'd look at me as something more than the guy from her Accounting class, I finally got my taste of her. Hell, I got a lot more than I bargained for.

I think back to the moment when I realized I'd been balls deep in my slice of blueberry pie. With any other woman, no doubt I would have found myself getting the hell out of dodge as quickly as possible.

With Gwen, I couldn't help but laugh.

And then promptly get her dirty, too.

I'd enjoyed the shower we'd taken together. The way she'd begged for me to take her against the shower wall, with her leg looped around my hips as I powered into her.

My phone starts up again, and with a heavy sigh, I roll over to snatch it off the bedside table. If it's Beaumont or Harrison calling to ask how the "banging" went, they're about to become dead men walking.

Voice rusty with sleep, I mutter, "Hunt."

"Bro."

Fuck me. Pushing the covers off, I cast a glance at Gwen sleeping peacefully in my bed. I've dreamt of this moment over and over again, and having Dave call me in the middle of the night is not how I envisioned it ending. Nope, I was totally hoping for another round before she left for work in the morning. Maybe some breakfast—pancakes, eggs, the whole nine yards.

With one hand, I grab my sweats off the floor and pull them up my legs. I don't speak until I've shut the door behind me. "What do you want, Dave?"

"I'm in trouble, bro. Big fucking trouble."

Fan-fucking-tastic.

Taking the stairs down to the kitchen, I flip the lights and sit my ass down on one of my stools. "How much money we talkin'?"

"More than I've got handy," he mutters. "I need you here, man. I need my family."

I won't lie, not even to myself. I want to believe my brother. I want to believe that he actually needs me for something more than a Benjamin Franklin whenever it suits him. Call it the little brother syndrome; hell if I know.

"It's late," I say instead because even if I want to feel needed, I don't trust Dave. I haven't trusted him in years. "I've got practice in the morning and if I show up looking like shit, that's my ass on the line."

I don't mention the fact that if I bomb on the ice that means Dave's money supplier could end up traded or, worse, jobless. I figure he can read between the—

"You really going to put fucking *hockey* above your own blood, bro?" I hear him spit, literally, just before he adds, "I knew I couldn't rely on you. My own fucking flesh and blood. What'd they do to you in foster care, bro? Did they teach you to turn your back on the only person who's watched out for you all these years?"

My hands ball into fists. I know where he's going with this—it's where he always goes. It's the one thing he's got over my head and he knows it.

Feeling as though I might crack, I tip my face to the ceiling and count to five. Swallow down my helpless rage and then bite out, "Where are you?"

"Brockton."

I let out a merciless laugh. Of course. Because where else would my brother be than at an illegal fighting ring?

"You want directions, bro?" Dave asks in a clear attempt to push me to the edge and watch me teeter to my death.

"Fuck you."

I hear his chuckle just before I hang up the phone. It's time like these when I wish we still used old telephone receivers. The kind you could hang up with a semblance of violence. If I do that shit now, I'll be shattering my screen and be even more pissed than I already am.

I force myself to breathe, slowly allowing my curled fist to unfurl. The thought of driving to Brockton right now has me wanting to throw something. But as always, the guilt is there waiting, just waiting, for me to remember that without Dave I'm completely alone.

Are you, though?

My focus drifts to Gwen. She may have a fucked-up mother, from what she told me earlier and from what I recall from her dad, but the truth of my existence would horrify her. Tempting as it is to climb those stairs and tell her everything, Dave isn't her problem—he's exclusively mine, and there's not a chance in hell that I want him tainting her with his negativity.

I tap my phone against my leg, then push off the stool to yank open one of the kitchen drawers.

Fifteen minutes later, I'm on the highway heading south to Brockton. I left a note on top of Gwen's phone, letting her know I'd hit the gym for my regular, early morning workout, and that our night together meant everything to me.

I'm banking on the fact she won't see it until later in the morning so the note will ring true. Mentioning an emergency of any kind would invite questions, and that's just not what I need right now. Gwen's a whole lot better off without getting on Dave's radar. I can only imagine what sort of shit he'd pull, and just the thought alone has my blood boiling.

By the time I pull off at the Brockton exit, I'm torn between wanting to nail Dave in the face at my first opportunity and worrying that this time he really screwed up. Sometimes, there's only so much money can do.

I flick on my high beams as I pull onto a back road. Dave's been on this track for a while—but he's been coming to the same place for years now and I know exactly where to direct my truck. When he first started, I'd been in middle school and still filled with hope that my big brother wanted to watch out for me.

I squirreled away money for months, doing odd and end jobs until I could afford the cab ride down here from Southie. That night, I watched from the blacked-out bleachers as my brother pummeled opponent after opponent.

He'd been dead-ass drunk on his feet, and it's a miracle no one popped him in such a way that his neck didn't snap. I'd sat there idolizing Dave like an idiot, but it wasn't until he'd stepped off the makeshift stage and traded in his winnings for a baggie of coke that I realized Dave only looked out for himself.

Jail or not, criminal or not, Dave Hunt was a bastard.

I pull in next to a Ford-150, my eyes already locked onto the warehouse before me. Without looking away, I pop open the center console for my checkbook—because I sure as hell don't have plans to carry cash into a place like that. I don't make a point of carrying thousands of dollars on me. When I left the house, I also brought my gun. I hesitate over it now.

The guys Dave fights aren't exactly Boston's classiest men. What they want is money. What Dave wants is money. And money I'll give him.

I slam the center console shut and climb out of my truck.

As I close the distance to the warehouse's side door—the

one the fighters enter through—I decide no more. If Dave fucks up after this? He's on his own. I refuse to be strung along by my dick of a brother for the rest of my life just because our mother gave birth to us both.

My teammates—guys like Beaumont and Harrison and Henri Bordeaux—those men are my brothers. Sometimes, blood literally means shit.

Since this is the side entrance, there's no bouncer at the door collecting covers. I try the handle, half-expecting it to be locked, and then pull it wide. Duck my head as I enter the warehouse.

Come to a dead halt when I realize that there isn't any music playing or announcers talking smack. I swing my gaze to the left and then to the right but come up blank. The warehouse is empty.

Fingers itching for the gun I left in my truck, I focus on keeping my body loose. Nothing Dave does is ever an accident, and if he called me here . . . well, the worst thing I can do is whirl around and beat feet back to the door.

Time to go for casual, laid-back Marshall Hunt.

Despite the tension tightening my muscles, I call out, "You guys jacking off back there or something?"

There's no response, not that I expected there to be.

I stroll toward the corded-off fighting ring. "People always say that hockey is a gay-ass sport, but wrestling? Boxing? You guys are way worse. I bet you all get hard-ons the minute you nail someone's ass to the ground."

Growing up, I had no one to watch over me. Southie was brutal back then—brutal and deadly. I learned to watch my own six, just as I learned how to use a gun at the age of eleven. It was partly due to survival . . . and a little bit because I refused to be the only kid who didn't know how to protect himself.

Mark James taught me differently. He convinced me that street hockey would get me nowhere, and each time I jammed up the sewers and cracked the fire hydrants open in the middle of winter, I was striking up another point toward landing my ass in jail.

"Take these, kid," he'd muttered when I first met him, throwing me a pair of hockey gloves. "I'm running practice for the high schoolers today. Get your ass there and I might let you collect their towels afterward."

No matter how many years it's been since my Southie days, it's hard to forget the need for survival. I pull it on now like a cloak, waiting for Dave to pop up, preparing for the worst.

Seconds bleed into the next, minutes seeping together, until I accept the fact that Dave ghosted.

At least my wallet won't be going on a diet tonight.

I move back toward the side entrance, full-on ready to get back to Gwen, and yank on the door.

It doesn't budge.

The fuckers locked it from the outside and there's not even a deadbolt to flick open.

Dammit.

"Stay fucking calm," I order myself, trying to pull on my memory for another exit. It's been years since I took the cab here, and I don't know the warehouse well enough to get myself out.

I twist around, searching the dark space for a red, blinking exit sign. It occurs to me that operators of an illegal fighting ring wouldn't be concerned with proper safety precautions.

When I find Dave, I'm going to pummel his face in so hard, he's not going to be able to eat right for months.

Adrenaline hammers at me as I slip away from the side

door. Even if I have to break a window, I'm getting the hell out of here and heading home to Gwen.

One glance upward proves that plan is total crap—the warehouse does have windows. Problem is, they're a good twenty feet up. I'm big, but not that big.

I turn the corner toward what I think might be the front of the building. My hands coast along the wall, keeping myself oriented in the pitch-black room.

I hear the running of footsteps before I see their shadowed silhouettes on the opposite wall.

It's not enough time, no matter how skilled I am or fast.

One second I'm bringing my fists up, ready to glance off a blow, and in the next I'm on the ground thanks to an unseen trip wire.

22

HUNT

Like the sadistic bastards they are, they strap me to a chair in the ring.

Dave waltzes around me, high as a fucking kite. "So glad you could join us, bro," he says now, pointing to his four conspirators. "We're so glad you could make it."

I don't say a word, not even to snidely point out that he's repeating himself. It'd probably go right over his head.

Quietly, I watch as my silence sends my brother into a small flounder. He cuts a quick glance to his buddies, and for the first time I have to wonder if he's not the top dude around here. From the reports I've picked up over the years, I'd always been under the impression that Dave ran shit.

He wins, always.

Now, I'm not too sure about the dynamics in the group.

"Did you bring the cash?" Dave prods as he approaches. A tick comes to life in his forehead, and he does a quick swipe of his forearm just under his nostrils. "I told the guys you were bringing cash."

"How much cash?" asks the bald guy in the corner. I size him up: six foot, two-hundred, thick around the middle. I'm a bigger match, but the fact that my wrists are tied is proving a difficult thing to manage.

I think of the knife strapped to my calf—utterly useless while my wrists are tied.

My notorious slow-growing temper spikes. "Is this how you guys celebrate the holidays?" I raise my brows, daring them to do something besides stand there. "Do you idiots get your rocks off on tying people up so you can, what, fuck them?"

The bald one mutters something under his breath. "It's not going to work."

I hold my breath, waiting.

Dave sighs like I've personally done him wrong. "You've lost your touch, bro. You can't best us. You know that, right? You can't trick us into untying you just like you can't fool us into thinking you didn't come here armed." He drops to his haunches and yanks up the hem of my pants. A *tsk-tsk* sound escapes him as he removes the knife and tosses it to the side, where it slides across the smooth flooring and nose-dives off the ledge into the arena area below. "You went into your big fucking world with hockey and you left this all behind."

At that, my brother widens his arms as though demanding I take notice of our surroundings.

Then he leans in. "You don't know how to survive here anymore, bro."

His arm reels back and I know what's coming just before it does—my brother's fist hand-delivers a right-hook that whips my head to the side. Stars burst like mini-fireworks in my vision and I taste the distinct tinny flavor of blood on my tongue.

"Untie him."

Dave steps back as the bald man sweeps in close. The

rope-ties around my wrists tighten before loosening, and then he's forcing me upward, regardless of the fact that my ankles have been tied too.

I catch myself before I stumble, ignoring the pain in my face and focusing instead on staying on my feet. I have no doubt I could get off the remaining ties in seconds, but—

"Zip-ties," Dave cuts in with a nasty grin. "The rope was just for your wrists." He points to his head. "Survival, right?"

Just like that, my temper snaps. "Fuck you, Dave. If you think for a goddamned second that I'm going to give you a dime after pulling this shit, you're delusional."

Dave only snaps his fingers.

A second later, a bright light flashes in front of my face.

Jesus, did they take a *photo* of me?

"Thanks, Evan," Dave says.

"No problem, boss," one of the other guys says. He holds up his phone with a victorious wave.

I'm not so dumb that I don't understand why they did it.

"Delete the photo, Dave." My heart ramps up speed, and I take a step toward him—only to fall to my hands and knees, thanks to the zip-ties.

My older brother steps up next to me, giving a little kick to my right elbow so it gives in. "I don't think I will, bro." His voice takes on an almost whimsical quality. "Thing is, Marshall, that photo is pretty good evidence. And it's worth way more than you'll ever give me. What do you think the press will say about the Blades' star forward?" He sinks down so we're face to face. "You think they'll want you after knowing you've been doing some underground fighting of your own? Add some drugs into the mix, and you can kiss your career good-bye."

A ringing starts in my ears, loud and oppressive.

I'll take my lick where I can—I snap his jaw back with

an uppercut he's not expecting. Dave falls to his side, cupping his jaw and laughing like he's just seen the funniest thing ever.

"You're fucking dead to me, Dave."

My brother pushes himself to his feet. "You're wrong, bro. I've been dead since I got locked in jail after *you* tried to kill Dad." He opens his arms wide. "Welcome to the club, Marshall. Enjoy your last few days of being the celebrity everyone loves before your new secret life hits the tabloids."

Memories of that night assault me, blurred by my youth and all the years that have separated me from the moment I picked up that kitchen knife and struck my father in the upper thigh. An eight-year-old kid doesn't have the strength to do any lasting damage, let alone cause enough blood loss for my old man to end up in ICU.

"You can't pass the blame all onto me." My knees scrabble on the padded flooring as I try to haul my body upward. "I was protecting Mom," I grind out, mouth dry, head pounding, "and I remember—"

"That I tried to finish what you failed to do? Yeah, I did that. But you struck first, and *I* got slammed with the charge." His bleary blue eyes twinkle with masochistic humor. "You'll get what's coming to you though. I'll make sure of it."

With a finger wave at his cronies, Dave and his band of douchebags climb under the ringside ropes and then jump down to the arena area. He swoops down and picks up my knife, giving it a side-to-side wiggle that has me seeing red.

"I'll leave this by the side door for you, bro, although I hate to think I'll miss you crawling your ass toward it. Consider it my token of goodwill."

23

GWEN

Of all my clients at Golden Lights Media, Holly Carter might be my favorite.

The blonde sports photographer is Texan to her very core, despite being born in Louisiana, and having an appointment with her is as close as I get to breaking open the champagne and having a girls' day at work.

"How are you liking the new office?" I ask her as I pour us two rounds of lemonade—sans alcohol. "Did the renovations work out the way you wanted them to?"

Holly's red-painted lips widen in a strained smile. "Girl, you have no idea. Working out of my house has been . . . rough."

I don't want to prod but I get the feeling she wants to unload. Setting my desktop computer to sleep mode, I take a sip of my lemonade and then place the glass back on my desk. "Things aren't getting any better with Jackson?"

Holly's husband is Jackson Carter, the captain for the Boston Blades. I've met him on a few occasions—Golden Lights represents him but he's assigned to one of the other publicists—and he's always been nice from what I've seen.

My client shrugs and then sinks a little lower in her seat. "God, I don't know, Gwen. It's not like he did anything wrong and I know I haven't either. It's just . . . sometimes people grow apart. That's us."

Her accent thickens as she speaks and it's clear she's getting upset. If I had booze in this office, I'd pour her more than just the lemonade. All I can do is push my glass across the desk and offer it to her with a nod. "Pretend there's vodka in it."

This time, her grin is all the way genuine. "You're the best, you know that?"

I don't think that's true but I certainly try to be the best at anything I take on. "I know you don't have much family here," I say, wondering if I'm overstepping boundaries, "but if you wanted to just get away for a little, you're more than welcome to hang out with me for Christmas. It'll just be me, myself, and I."

Adaline hasn't contacted me since the lasagna night incident, and I spoke to Manuel briefly to clue him in that while *I* would never fire him, it might be in his best interest to apologize before showing back up to work. Turns out, the wine-tipping incident was Manny's last hurrah. The minute he walked out of my mother's house that night, he'd decided he was never returning. While I applauded him, I wished I could find that similar backbone.

I won't be heading over to my mother's house for the holidays—I never do—but I'm sure I'll find myself keying open the front door at some point or another to try, once again, with my mother.

Or maybe you'll spend the day with Marshall?

The thought sends butterflies fluttering into motion in my belly. I don't want to get my hopes up but maybe, just maybe, he'll want to get together and spend Christmas Day watching more movies and snuggling.

"I appreciate the offer, Gwen, I do, but—"

My phone ringing cuts Holly off. Shit. I wipe my hands across my skirt and yank my phone out of my drawer. "I'm sorry," I mutter, "let me just make sure this isn't a client. We had an . . . *issue* this morning involving a panda bear and the zoo's curator."

Holly waves me off with a smile. "Do what you have to do. I'll drink my fake-vodka cocktail."

I could hug her.

Whirling away, I give the unknown number flashing across the screen a cursory glance before answering the call and stepping into the hallway. I gently shut the door. "Hello? This is Gwen."

"Hey, you."

That voice.

We've spoken via text since our "fantasy night," a few days ago, but we haven't had time to catch up with our mismatched schedules. I press my back to my door and feel the smile inching across my face. "What's with the unknown number?"

Marshall's husky laugh is like music to my ears. "Would you believe me if I said Harrison's fat ass broke it?"

The idea of The Mountain sitting on Marshall's phone and snapping it in half is hilarious, and I find myself giggling along. "Is that really what happened?"

He pauses, for effect, I think, and then goes on. "Nah. Unfortunately, I was at the gym this morning and accidentally dropped my dumbbell right on the damn thing. It sounds a lot better when I blame Duke for it though."

"Don't tell me you were thinking of me naked and *then* dropped the weight," I tease. It's not so out of the realm of possibility. I *may* have sent him a photo of me last night before I climbed into bed.

Maybe.

In my defense, the photo didn't even constitute as a nipple shot seeing as it was collarbone and up. But my hair had been wet and my face makeup free, and clothes or not, I'd let him come to his own conclusion. Like any guy, he'd chosen to believe I was snapping photos of myself in my birthday suit.

"You caught me," he tells me now. "In the future, give a guy a little warning before you do something like that."

"I should give *any* guy a warning before naked-time or only you?"

I don't know what makes me say that, and Marshall doesn't let the comment sit for longer than a moment.

"Me." I can almost imagine his narrowed pewter eyes, his broad shoulders . . . "There's no one else in this equation but the two of us."

"I know."

"Good. Listen, I'm just leaving an appointment with my publicist and I want to see you."

Sneaking a quick glance back at the door behind me, I state the obvious, "I'm at work."

"I'll come and wait for you." There's the sound of an engine kicking on, and then the radio blares loudly before being silenced. "Give Walter the chance to see what he missed out on all those years ago."

I laugh even as I silently admit how true it is. My boss skipped over Marshall when he was on the farm team, choosing to believe that the Blades' top draft pick would ultimately be traded elsewhere before being pulled onto the first line. Marshall shocked everyone by proving them wrong—and my boss is fully aware that he missed out on a client who could have earned him a good chunk of change.

"Why don't you give me an hour and I'll meet you."

"My house? I'll cook us some dinner." Marshall pauses. Then, "Don't wear panties."

There must be something in the rule book about not blushing and thinking about your guy naked while at work. I do a quick look around to make sure the hall is blessedly empty. "It's December and cold out."

"All the reason to let me warm you up when you get here, honey."

Damn man, I think, when I hear the dial tone on the other end of the phone. He totally backed me into a corner on that one, and he *knows* I don't like to back down from a challenge. Feeling altogether way too flustered to return to a meeting, I smooth my skirt and reenter my office.

Holly's on her phone, legs crossed, with our lemonades empty at her elbow. She glances up at me with a half-smile. "Who was that? The panda bear guy?"

I shiver at the reminder of my morning. No one, and I repeat no one, should ever wonder what happens when a panda tries to hump one of the head staff at a zoo . . . while having it all caught on camera and then uploaded to every social media site in existence.

There are a lot of things I've covered up over the years and squashed into nothingness—but the humping panda is going to prove tricky, even for me.

Taking my seat, I plop my phone back into the drawer after setting it on silent. "It was nobody."

Holly gives me a droll glance. "I heard you mention the word naked, twice."

I freeze. Did I say it twice? No more than once, right? Squirming at having been caught, I tap-tap-tap on my keyboard, bringing the computer back to life. "I, uh, may have been trying to tell a client they shouldn't strip naked and run around the mall like that."

"*Mhmm*." Holly taps her glass with her nails. "You know, Gwen, although my husband and I are on the outs, I do still hear the gossip."

"Oh?" This doesn't sound good.

"Yes, ma'am." Holly waits until I've turned to look at her before wrapping up my present of humiliation and sticking the bow on top. "It turns out that just about everyone knows you and Marshall Hunt are a thing."

Are we a *thing*?

I've never really been in a thing with anyone before. My past relationships have all been short-term stints, emotionless, and boring.

This thing—so, yes, I guess it is a thing—with Marshall fits under none of those categories. "I, um"—I fidget some more—"we may be doing . . . something."

In his movie theater, in his shower, in his bed.

We've done a lot of somethings and I definitely want to do more.

Holly smiles, and it's so sweet and sincere that I can't help but return it. "I hope it works out for y'all." She offers a little shrug, then twirls the glass round and round. "Jackson and I . . . well, anyway, I like you and I like Hunt. Keep that one on lockdown, girl."

I think of Marshall walking away from me at Zoe's engagement party. I never want to feel that level of despair again. This *thing* with Marshall is special, and I'm ready to hold on with two hands and never let go.

"That's the goal," I finally tell my client. "Trust me, that's the goal."

24

GWEN

Panties or no panties.

It's a tough decision. We've got three days until Christmas, and let's just say that Boston has decided to spread its holiday cheer with snow, icy temperatures, and no hope in sight for anything above eighteen degrees.

I give Marshall's house a quick look from where I've parked my car in his driveway. He's not standing by the windows or anything like that, but I know, without a doubt, which option he'd want me to go with.

No panties it is.

Pulling up my skirt, I thank God that Marshall lives in a quiet neighborhood without a lot of drive-by noise. Or neighbors, for that matter. All the houses are separated by a good acre, and so I go about my panty-dropping business without the fear that someone might stroll up to the window and see me flashing my naked goods to the world.

I slip my underwear over my heels and then stuff the fabric in my purse.

Okay, showtime.

All right, *almost* showtime.

Marshall's driveway is a sheet of black ice—not appropriate for stilettos.

Like a baby deer learning to walk, I pick my way up the sloping path, cursing my shoes for being pretty but so utterly worthless.

"Having trouble down there?"

I glance up to see Marshall approaching. Dressed in faded jeans, a Blades hoodie, and a backward ball cap, he's so damn good-looking it almost hurts. I point to my shoes, feeling a little pathetic when I call back, "Kate Spade clearly doesn't know what it's like to hike up a driveway in these babies. They aren't ice-proof."

His mouth quirks in a crooked grin. "Aren't you glad you've got your own hockey player, then?"

Big hands land on my butt the moment he steps near, and the next thing I know, I'm being boosted into the air and then clutched tight to his chest.

"*Oh!*"

Cold air hits my bare girl parts, and this time my shout is a little more of a shrill shriek.

Oh My God.

So, so cold. Why did I agree to no panties? Because it is *cold*, really, really cold, and I can't help but wonder if things can, you know, freeze down there? Like how guys always talk about their nuts hibernating in their stomachs and their dicks shriveling? Does the equivalent happen to women?

Frozen vagina.

I can't say that I recommend it.

"You okay?" Marshall peers down at me like he's uncertain if I'm going to leap from his arms and throw myself back down his driveway. "You seem a little . . ." He presses his lips to my forehead like he's checking my temperature.

If I weren't so worried about my vagina freezing, I'd stop to think about how sweet the gesture is.

He shifts my weight as we near the door, and my skirt rides up a little higher.

Naturally, he gets a handful of my butt and that's when it hits him.

"Gwen?"

"Yes, Marshall?" I bite down on my teeth to keep them from chattering.

I watch his Adam's apple slide down the length of his throat. "Are you wearing underwear right now?"

"*Nope.*"

"Gotcha."

Bouncing me higher against his chest, he bolts for his front door, his feet thudding against the frozen concrete.

"Oh my God, we're going to fall!" I cry out, clutching his sweatshirt in a vicelike grip. "Slow down!"

"Not a chance in hell," he growls. "You're not wearing—"

His weight teeters, which means that *my* weight teeters, and I have a vision of his knees buckling and us rolling back down the driveway in some R-rated version of Jack and Jill climbing the hill.

"Marshall," I warn.

"Gwen," he returns, stepping onto his front stoop and pushing open the door. He doesn't set me down until he's locked everything up.

Then he carefully takes my purse and sets it to the side. With two big palms to my shoulders, he backs me up against the door. "Time to warm you up, honey."

His fingers push up my skirt as he drops to his knees. With a gentle tug, he encourages me to lift my leg over his shoulder. I do, although I can't help but announce, "My deal."

"What deal?" He looks up at me through long, dark lashes. He leans forward, and then he covers my clit with his mouth.

Wowza.

It's as good this time as it was in his movie theater. I thread my fingers through his hair, unable to stop from releasing a moan when he swirls his tongue in tight little circles that has me seeing stars.

I shed my coat, throwing it to the floor beside him. "My deal," I repeat, trying for the life of me to remember what it is. With his mouth working me to the point of no return, I don't even remember my own name. "It was . . . *oh,* yes, yes right *there.*" His thumb dips into my wet heat, then takes the place of his mouth when he sits back to watch me.

"Your deal?" he prompts again.

Dammit, I'd *remember* it if he wasn't doing all that warming-up business.

Not that I'm really complaining because Marshall has magical hands and a mouth that's equally as magical.

"Fantasy kisses," I finally stutter out when he thrusts two fingers inside me, just the way I'd once shown him I like it. "You had your fantasy first kiss . . . I want . . . oh my God, Marshall, *yes.*"

He pushes me over the edge, chuckling against me when I tug on his hair and shout his name at the top of my lungs.

I just . . . did we really . . .

I shake my head, trying to clear it. "I think I have a fever."

With a sexy laugh, Marshall gives me one last swipe of his tongue before straightening to his full height. "You don't have a fever, Gwen."

"I'm seeing stars."

He winks at me playfully. "I'll take responsibility for that one."

"My legs are like Jell-O."

"Be glad we don't have any blueberry pie around."

We burst into laughter, and I can't stop myself from stroking his face. He's got a lingering bruise and a cut lip along the right side of his face. Although it's faded somewhat, I can't imagine it felt good when he was on the receiving end. "Rough practice?" I ask.

"What?"

"Your bruise. You guys haven't had a game since Toronto so I was thinking..."

"Oh." He grabs my hand and presses a kiss to the center of my palm. "Yeah. Bordeaux got me. High stick."

I frown. "Must have been a very high stick."

Rubbing the back of his neck, Marshall's expression goes blank. "That's Bordeaux for you. Can't trust those Canadians."

"Beaumont is Canadian and he's your best friend."

Marshall touches his forehead to mine. "Like I said, can't trust those Canadians. Now, come with me. I have something for you."

As I follow Marshall, my hand clasped in his, I can't shake off the worry that he's not telling me something. I might be riding on the aftereffects of an orgasm, but still...

He twists around and gives me a bright smile. "I missed you."

Or maybe I'm just crazy. That smile doesn't kick off any alarm bells. I smile back. "I missed you, too."

25

HUNT

I should tell Gwen everything right now.

I slam the oven door a little harder than necessary considering *it* wasn't the one to punch me and fuck up my life.

"Are you hangry?" Gwen asks from the kitchen island, completely oblivious to my inner turmoil.

How the hell do you tell someone you care about that their entire perception of you is a lie?

I visited my publicist today and brought both my agent and lawyer along with me. I'm not an idiot. If shit hits the roof with Dave, my career would be over if the Blades had no idea what was going on.

That's what Dave wants. He wants to watch me crumble until I'm dragging my sorry ass back to Southie and knocking on his door, begging for scraps.

Fuck that.

Fessing up to people you admire and respect that you've been inadvertently enabling your coke-addicted brother for the last few years? There's no other words to say except that it sucked, and it sucked a lot.

There were no moves to suspend me, for which I was incredibly grateful, but there's still the small, minor detail that . . . Dave has disappeared. His phone hits a dead-end each time I call, and I've visited his apartment twice now with my lawyer—nada.

Even the landlord mentioned that Dave just up and left a few weeks ago.

Which means he's been planning his takedown for longer than I was even aware, sometime between my last visit at the start of the month and the night down in Brockton.

With no paper trail to follow, all we can do is wait. My publicist is ready to contain backlash, but there's no point in airing my dirty laundry to the public if Dave only plans to hold his blackmail over my head for the rest of my life.

I pull down plates from the cabinets, along with glasses for some wine.

On the ice, hockey is a controlled environment. Sure, random shit happens. People break rules whether intentionally or not. People get elbows to the face and we've all tripped our opponents with our sticks.

It happens.

But even with its randomness, hockey is a game of rules and regulations.

Real life doesn't always reflect the same moral codes or ethics—at least, douchebags like my brother don't. It takes everything in me not to sink into the memories of that night. Some people claim that tragedy acts like a highlighter, illuminating every moment until each second is bold and vivid and so damn slow that you worry you'll never escape its brutal wrath.

The night that I stabbed my father, I was only eight years old. I remember little, aside from the blood staining my hands, purple bruises blooming on my mother's face, and a kitchen knife protruding from my father's leg.

Everything else is a black abyss of tears, my mother sobbing to the police, and my brother standing off to the side, watching with a look of glee on his face and covered in blood.

I feel Gwen's hand to my shoulder like a balm to my nerves, just before she slides her arms around my waist and snuggles against my back. "Something's wrong," she whispers, "you're way too quiet."

"Maybe I just wanted to cook you a nice meal?"

With a small upturn of her nose, Gwen lets me get away with the lie. We sit at the table and drink our wine and chow down on the baked chicken I prepared for us, along with the roasted vegetables.

Gwen expertly smooths over my awkwardness by telling me about her day. "The poor curator," she says, shaking her head as she stabs a slice of chicken off her plate, "there he was just bringing the panda's food and then *bam*."

"Butt stuff," I tease, feeling my mood lighten with the hilarity of the story. "What a way to get initiated."

I'm treated to Gwen's husky laughter. "Poor panda is more like it."

My brows shoot up. "Poor *panda*? First it was the poor curator and now you're swapping loyalties?"

She gives a delicate shrug. "I mean, the panda was probably lonely."

"Buy him a panda blow-up doll. Problem solved."

Gwen rolls her eyes but her smile is so bright and lovely, and it's all for me. "Only a guy would ever suggest that."

"That's because women are worried about the panda when, in reality, it's the poor curator who's getting reamed."

She wrinkles her nose at that, and it's so damn cute that

I catch her hand and kiss the fluttering pulse at her inner wrist. Being able to touch her whenever I so please . . . fuck, it feels good. No, it feels *right*. No matter what sort of shit Dave pulls, I'm not willing to give Gwen up—what we have is too special.

I refill her wine glass and then do the same to mine. "Have you heard from your mom at all?"

Her shoulders droop and she stares at the Chardonnay like it might have all the answers to her questions. "No. I should probably call her—scratch that, I *know* I should. But I feel like I've just reached my breaking point, you know?" She takes a sip of the wine, then rotates her wrist, allowing the Napa Valley blend to gently swirl in the bowl of the glass. "It's weird, I guess. You can know someone your entire life and still not understand why they do the things they do."

Gwen's astute observation hits way too close to home. Have I ever understood Dave's motivations? Not really—unless they truly boil down to anger and jealousy only. It's no way to live, and over the years . . . well, I guess I've been holding out hope that Dave's been operating with something more than just revenge on his mind.

Considering he tied you to a chair, probably not the case.

I tip my wineglass to my lips and down it in one go.

"You had me thinking about something the other day," I say, setting the glass down on the marble and pushing onto my feet.

Gwen's blue eyes follow me. "You mean, you can think about something else besides your penis?"

Laughter climbs my throat. "Minx."

She lifts her hands. "Just asking a question for womankind everywhere."

"Yeah, well, how does womankind feel about my penis?"

My cock strains against my jeans when she trails her gaze down my chest to my crotch. "We like him, a lot." Her mouth tilts upward. "He's just so damn pretty."

I didn't think it was possible to fall in love with a woman over talk about dicks. Hell, it'd almost be preferable if that *weren't* the case. But with her blue eyes shining with mischief and her wineglass still clasped in one hand, I know that there will never be another woman who matches me like Gwen does.

In some subconscious way, I've known that for years. It's why I only ever involved myself in superficial relationships where the "deepest" we got was just burrowing under the covers. From the start, Gwen has captivated me like no one else—showing, in return, that I'm the right man for her has proved marginally harder.

With a finger to her chin, I angle her face to best receive my kiss. My lips slip over hers, soft and easy, and my palm moves to the back of her head. She moans against my mouth. I hear the *clink!* of her glass hitting the marble just before she turns fully in the stool so that she can rest her palms on my hips.

I try to imagine what we look like together—a tatted-up man with hard edges but with, according to her, pretty-boy model looks. A redhead with smooth, creamy skin and the kindest heart behind her steel exterior walls.

A guy from Southie. A woman from Boston's upper elite.

Romeo and Juliet, Boston-style.

I nip at her bottom lip and then pull back. Her skin is flushed, and I doubt I'm any better when I rasp, "I have something for you. Then, after that, be sure you have a plan for your fantasy kiss. I'm going to deliver on it, one-hundred percent."

I leave her sitting on that stool, her fingers pressed

against her lips, her legs spread because I'd taken my place between them. The urge to turn back around and make love to her on the kitchen island is strong.

But she deserves something from me first—it belonged to her father and now it should belong to her.

26

GWEN

Marshall reenters the kitchen with a small cardboard box and a blank expression on his face. Without a word, he pulls up the stool beside mine and sits down. He's lost his ball cap, and his brown hair looks like he's spent the last five minutes raking through it with his fingers.

Is he nervous?

I eye the closed box on his lap.

Should I be nervous?

Swallowing hard, I force the question that's begging to be spoken. "Is this a parting gift?"

Pewter eyes blink back at me. "Why the hell would you think that?"

"I-I don't know." But I do know. In the past, my relationships have always come to a close with some sort of trinket. Bracelets, necklaces, gift cards—yes, *gift cards*—and a host of other items have all been shoved into my hand as the man I was dating decided it was time to go on his way. The fact that all those men left doesn't bother me. Our arrangements were always temporary, at best. No, it was the fact that they felt inclined to give me a little "something" before they took off that made me feel cheap.

I'm not proud of the way I lived my life for so long. Even so, when a guy you've dated presses a gift card to The Cheesecake Factory into your hand on his way out the door, you grow accustomed to feeling . . . trashy.

"Gwen." Marshall's hand lands on my thigh and gives it a quick squeeze. "Look at me, honey."

I risk a peek up at his handsome face.

With his brown hair tousled beyond repair and his gray eyes practically searing me with their intensity, I know that whatever he says next is the real deal.

"I've wanted you for six years." The words are said softly but with a sharp edge. "There's no fucking way I'd walk away now, not when I finally have you where I want you."

"And where is that?"

He shakes his head with a small smile playing at his full lips. "In my home, Gwen." He pulls me forward to meet him with a palm to the back of my head. I go willingly, eager for another kiss, eager for another taste of this man who has turned my world upside down. "I have you under me, on top of me"—I slap his arm and he lets out a husky chuckle—"I have you eating the food I cooked for us and drinking my wine. I'm not willing to let that go . . . are you?"

My nails scrape the fabric of his jeans on their way to ground zero—the hard erection I see shoving mercilessly against his zipper. "No," I whisper against his mouth, "but I sure know what's involved in my fantasy kiss."

With a deep groan, he pushes me back onto my seat and shakes a cardboard box that's wider than the length of my forearm. "Not yet. After." When I fake a pout, he curses under his breath. "Fuck, you're temptation and a half, honey.

But we're doing this first." He shoves the box at me. "Open it."

The brown box gives me absolutely no inclination as to what could be inside, and so I give it a little shake and hope I'm not rattling something that's alive inside. I jerk my gaze up to Marshall's face. "Is it a puppy?"

His laugh is the stuff of sexual fantasies, it's so damn throaty. "It's not a puppy, Gwen. You think I'd put something adorable and fluffy in a box with no holes?"

"I just had to ask," I grumble, pulling the cardboard leafs open. I tilt the box toward me, palms sweaty with anticipation . . . "Thank you for the gloves?" I pluck one out and lift it this way and that. "Not exactly my size but I could do some damage in the rink?"

The hockey gloves are red, thick, and tattered. Maybe this is Marshall's way of saying he'd like for me to attend all of his hockey games? I wouldn't be opposed to it—I love watching him kick ass on the ice.

"No, they're—" Marshall heaves out a breath and then tugs the other glove out of the box before stealing my glove away. "These are the first hockey gloves I ever owned."

Oh.

I gently try to pry them out of his grasp. If they belonged to him, then I absolutely want them. This is way better than a T-shirt of his to keep, am I right? Not that I'd sleep with these gloves—they look a little worse for wear—but I'd set them upright on my bedside table so that I can see them each night before I hit the sack.

Warmth sluices through me, and I give the gloves a harder tug.

Marshall finally lets go with a sheepish smile. "Sorry, I'm a little sentimental toward them."

I set the box on the island and then curl my arms around the gloves in my lap. "Would you rather keep them?"

"No, I—" He shoves his fingers through his hair, messing up the strands even more. "Maybe it's better if I back up and tell the story."

Tilting my head, I note Marshall's high coloring. He's *nervous*. "Only tell me what you feel comfortable with."

"Yeah." He slicks his hands across his jeans, like he's nervous, and I'm so far deep in with him that I find the movement adorable. Yeah, I said it. Adorable. A word that no other person in the world would ever say to Marshall Hunt's face at the risk of being knocked down to the ground.

Inhaling deeply, he lets it out on a slow, even exhale. "From the age of eight onward, I grew up in the system. My foster parents—I hate to say that they didn't care about us kids. It's more like..." He purses his lips, as though trying to find the right word. "It's like they'd been bitten one too many times in the ass by life, the system, everything. There were seven of us kids and I was the youngest. I never knew what it was like to own anything. My clothes were handed down from the oldest boy to me, passing through four other kids before I slipped them on. Food was much the same. The oldest kids went first—they were always the hungriest."

I think back to my own childhood. Adaline may have been crazy and she may have had a revolving door of husbands waltzing through, but Carli always saw me fed. Manuel always ensured that I was safe.

My heart aches for the little boy who had nothing, and I reach out to squeeze Marshall's knee, offering silent encouragement.

His answering smile is fleeting. "As I got older, I started hanging with the wrong crowd. I desperately wanted to fit in. I wanted to *be* someone, other than the Gottim's youngest foster kid. My new friends taught me a variety of life skills most people will never know. We stole bikes from the kids at MIT, hopped on the back of firetrucks like they were our own cabbie service. Because we were small, we'd climb into people's backyards and swim in their pools during the summer. The way we saw it, everything belonged to us."

There are so many questions burning on the tip of my tongue, but I force myself to sit still and listen.

"We grew bolder, too. In the middle of winter, we'd stop up the sewage pipes in the neighborhood. Blast off the fire hydrant with a little work, and then let the street ice over. Our skates were stolen. We didn't have a real net. But every afternoon, we'd do it over and over again. That's when I met your dad."

Just like that, my body freezes and my brain immediately launches back to my father's funeral. How I'd seen Marshall standing next to my uncle. Then, later, him comforting me in a side room.

"I don't know whether your dad took pity on me or what, but he snagged me by the collar one day and dragged me off the ice. Shoved those gloves you're holding into my arms and told me that if I got my ass down to the high school after I was done behaving like an asshole, he'd maybe consider letting me practice with the team."

Would my dad say something like that? It pains me to admit that I don't know. My memories of him belong to infrequent lunch dates with my mother watching us both like a prison guard. I can probably count on both hands the number of times Mark James and I were ever in the same room together—Adaline saw to that.

I swallow my grief. "Were you in high school at the time?"

Marshall shakes his head. "No, middle school. But your

dad was the tenth-grade math teacher, along with being the high school's head hockey coach. For weeks, I'd show up and be relegated to picking up the team's towels. I carried those gloves around with me everywhere, convinced that one day he'd let me play. One day I'd own a hockey stick and pads and skates, and I'd make something of myself. Hockey was my way out of Southie, the only reason a school like Northeastern even looked at me."

My tongue feels swollen, thick. As much as I want to jump up and down, and point at Marshall's home and be all, "*look what you've accomplished,*" I can't help but feel remnants of the little girl who used to beg her mother for the chance to see her dad. I was told multiple times over that Mark James had no time for me, that he didn't care to see me. Knowing that he had time to take Marshall under his wing burns in a way that I wished it didn't.

Have I really changed at all if I can't find it in myself to put aside the pain?

I choke back a cry. I box up the little girl who so wanted love and was handed mistrust and judgment on a silver platter instead. And then I put her away—because I love Marshall, and if this is the moment where I'm forced to decide between wallowing in my own pain or comforting his, I will choose the latter each and every time.

Pressing the gloves together, I place them both in Marshall's lap. "You need to keep these," I whisper, hating the way my voice quivers with emotion. "My dad"—I suck in a deep breath—"he gave them to *you*, Marshall. They're yours."

He watches me with an inscrutable emotion, his gray eyes searching my face. "Put them on."

"What?" I let out a rough laugh. "I don't think . . . I mean, they're a little big for me."

"Humor me."

Not wanting to disappoint him, even though I feel mighty ridiculous as I do so, I tug on the right glove. My fingers don't even reach the tips and it looks like I'm playing dress-up. I meet Marshall's gaze; he only nods his head in a "keep going" gesture.

All right.

As I slip on the left, he begins to speak, his voice a deep rumble that warms me up and strips away the hurt: "I've had the gloves for years. I should have given them to you on the day of your father's funeral or right after that. I didn't, and I'll regret that forever. After you left, your uncle pulled me to the side to give me a box of your dad's belongings. I looked inside. All hockey stuff."

Inside the well-worn glove, my fingers brush against what feels like a sharp edge of paper. An envelope, maybe? Frowning, I strip off the other glove so that I can dig into the left one and pull the envelope out.

"I never really gave it much thought," Marshall goes on, and even though I've got my focus on the task at hand, I can feel him watching me. "The other day when you were talking about your mom and your relationship with her, I decided it was time to give you these. I found the box again, thinking that there might be something else in there for me to give to you, too. A trophy of your dad's, maybe. I don't know. I just didn't expect to find these."

I want to pretend that my fingers aren't trembling—that would be a lie.

Cracking the seal open on the yellowed envelope, my heart leaps to my throat as I widen the flaps. There are more envelopes, all much smaller with a RETURN TO SENDER stamp emblazoned across the front.

And they're all addressed to my childhood home.

27

HUNT

Gwen's beautiful face blanches when she opens the envelope—and I don't blame her.

I didn't open the envelope when I found it the other day; it would have been an invasion of privacy. Back in middle school, I remember Mark bitching about his ex-wife sending back every letter he wrote to his daughter. I wish I knew why he didn't just put down his foot and make shit happen, but you can't ask questions to the dead.

All I know is that when I finally noticed the thick envelope in the box Mark's brother had given to me, I suspected what they were, and that perhaps they'd unintentionally ended up in my box. Mark didn't know about my relationship with Gwen in college, and so it makes little sense that he would have given them to me with some ulterior motive. Call it a stroke of good luck or not, but I knew Gwen had to have them.

I watch her now, the way she's trying so hard to hold back the tears. Her shoulders shake with the smallest movements. She flips through the envelopes, not opening a single one but seemingly counting each and every time her father tried to reach out to her ... and every time her mother stood in the way.

"You look like you need a hug." My voice sounds as though I've swallowed a bucketful of nails. If she recognizes that I said the same words on the day of her father's funeral, she doesn't mention it.

But she does set the envelopes on the counter, along with the hockey gloves.

And then she's throwing herself into my arms.

I lock her close, binding her to me as I whisper into her hair. "I've got you, honey. I've got you."

Her sobs are quiet, her pain wrapped up so tight within her walls that the only way to tell she's crying is by the way her shoulders shake with each indrawn breath. For the next few minutes, I only hold her. I cradle her to me like she's the most precious thing I've ever held; I wrap her tight in my embrace, giving her every ounce of strength that I have, letting her know without words that I will keep us upright, that I won't let us fall.

Baring my childhood to her wasn't easy—particularly because I didn't tell her the one event that changed the course of my life forever. It's the reason that I ended up in foster care, the reason Dave went to jail, the reason he continues to blackmail me as though something that I did at eight years old should be counted against me for the rest of my days.

The honest truth is that I can't bear to see the affection in her eyes be replaced with disappointment—or worse, disgust.

I'll tell her soon.

I make the vow to myself, repeat it over and over again as she remains curled up against my chest.

When she pulls back, I run my thumb beneath her eyes,

catching moisture and dashing it away. "You okay?" It's a moronic question but it nevertheless needs to be asked.

"My fantasy kiss."

Traitorous bastard that he is, my cock rises to attention at the thought of kissing Gwen. *Be a decent human being and get your mind out of the gutter.* "Later," I mutter, even though my body is screaming *hell-fucking-yeah*. "I gave you a bit of a shock just now—"

Gwen pulls away from me just far enough to shove her red hair behind her ears. "I've always . . . how do I even say this?" Her hands curl into fists that she rests on my thighs. "You said once that you wanted something from me that no one else has ever had, my heart."

Heart thundering with nerves, I think back to that moment in Faneuil Hall. It feels like ages ago, years even, and yet it's only been a few weeks. With hesitance dogging my heels, I gently frame Gwen's face with my hand. "I did say that."

Her blue eyes burn bright, and I know without her admitting it directly, that I already have her heart. Licking her lips, she says, "I've always dreamt of kissing someone who loves me. T-that's my fantasy. Kissing someone who cares for me, who can see beyond—*oh!* Marshall, what are you doing?"

"I'm going to collect on that fantasy kiss," I tell her as I resettle her weight in my arms. And, yeah, maybe I'm a bit of a caveman because there's nothing I like more than holding Gwen, bridal-style.

"*Oh.*"

This time, her voice is full of wonder when she speaks and it sets off every bit of fire inside me.

I take the stairs to my bedroom two at a time. And I sure as hell don't stop until we're both naked and on my bed. My hands wander everywhere, over the slope of her breast as I suck her nipple into my mouth. Over the lengths of her smooth legs, massaging the muscles there until her legs are pushed wide. She's a sight for sore eyes.

I don't actually kiss her, not yet.

But I play—with my lips on her clit, my tongue in her pussy, my fingers tweaking her nipples into hard little peaks. I work her over and over again until she's shuddering against my mouth and demanding more than just my fingers and my tongue.

"Get on your knees," I tell her, "and then face the mirror."

She does as she's told, moving to the edge of the bed and lifting onto her knees. Her skin is blotchy with lust, a rainbow of peaches and pinks and reds. She's utterly gorgeous, and she's all mine.

"Two fingers, Gwen." I move behind her on the bed, my arms wrapping around her lean frame so that I can cup her breasts. Then I brush her hair back, so that I can kiss her neck. "Two fingers, just the way you like it."

With my free hand, I tug on her nipple, then roll it between my fingers. Her gasp is audible, and I feel the way her shoulders jerk under my mouth. I flick my gaze to the mirror just as she sinks two fingers inside her pussy. My cock twitches against her back, and I give it one single stroke to tide me off.

Not yet.

This moment, this fantasy, is for Gwen.

My voice rumbles throughout the room, dark and demanding. "Run your thumb over your clit."

Her hips spasm as she does, jerking forward as though chasing that elusive orgasm that I plan to give her. I watch as the pumps of her fingers turn frantic.

"Marshall," she whimpers, her blue eyes wide and on me as she watches us in the mirror. "I need you."

Fuck me, but I'll never get tired of hearing her say that.

My hand latches onto her wrist, stilling her motions. "My turn."

I shift her slightly, so that my feet are planted wide on the floor and she's straddling my hips, her pussy brushing the tip of my cock. I keep her facing the mirror because I want her to see everything—the way I'll rub her clit and tease her nipple, how I look behind her, how we look *together*.

"Take what you want, honey," I whisper against the smooth expanse of her back. "Everything that I am is yours."

When she sinks down onto my cock a second later, she is hands-down the most beautiful thing I've ever seen. Through the mirror, I watch her neck elongate as she throws her head back. Her tits bounce with each upward drag and downward thrust. Her flat belly tightens, her core working to keep herself moving in a hypnotic rhythm. And her pussy . . . Jesus Christ, but watching her take me, seeing the slip and slide of my cock moving in and out of her, is almost enough to send me over the edge.

I fist her hair in one hand, pulling her back just slightly, so that she's cradled against my chest.

And then I take over.

My hands grip her hips as I lift her up and bring her back down.

"*Yes*," she whimpers, "oh my God, yes."

It's the only encouragement I need. Her hands lock down on my forearms, using me as leverage to move even faster.

She cries out my name when I touch her clit and press down on the sensitive nub.

It's all she needs to tip over the edge. She comes, whispering my name, begging me to never stop.

Three more hard thrusts, and I follow her into the abyss. I roar out her name, and spill everything that I am within her.

A no-good kid from Southie with a dirty-talking mouth and an obsession with hockey.

"My legs," she whispers after a moment, "my legs are going to die."

"Was it worth it?" I change our positions, rolling her over onto her back so my body covers hers.

Her smile is beautiful. "*So* worth it."

I grin back down at her. "I saved the best for last."

"What's that?"

"This," I tell her, and then I lower my face to hers. Gwen meets me in the middle for a kiss that steals my soul. It's soft and languid, and nothing like the sex we just had—and it's just another reason to love this woman.

She sighs against my mouth. "Best fantasy kiss I've ever had."

"I know."

Her hands drift up my back. "You know the only thing that would make this better? Pie."

Laughter clogs my throat as I stare down at her. "I'm done with the pie. Hell, my *ass* is done with all things pie too."

Beautiful blue eyes meet mine. "I guess I'd be willing to trade the pie for another kiss."

I sink down into her, grazing my lips over hers. "Now, that I can do..."

28

HUNT

I'm hot tonight on the ice.

It's our last game before Christmas in two days, and TD Garden is full of holiday cheer.

And by that, I mean, the Tampa Bay Lightning fans are losing their shit after I nail the net with my second goal in the last period.

Carter grabs me around the neck and touches our helmets together. "That's what I'm talking about, Hunt," he shouts over the din in the arena, "that's what I'm fucking talking about!"

I don't know whether I'm riding on the euphoria of being with Gwen or the fact that me and my boys are taking names and kicking ass tonight, but I don't want it to stop.

It's games like these that remind me I'm on the right path, that I spent months collecting dirty towels for a reason before Mark James ever let me step foot on the ice.

Gwen's father taught me to respect the hard work hockey requires.

He also taught me to keep my head out of my ass and recognize that I won't always be the best.

Tonight, though, I am the best and I plan to milk it for all its worth.

Coach Hall calls us to the bench for the second line to take over. Our shift swap is fast, efficient, and the next thing I know, I'm guzzling Gatorade from the sidelines and watching my teammates defend our two-goal lead against Tampa Bay.

We'll have maybe one or two plays to get a breather, and like always, I do my best to keep my mind in the game.

"Hunt! Hunt!"

I'm used to hearing fans chant my name, and I'm not one of those pricks who won't pause for a half-second to appreciate that the people in this stadium are the reason I play hockey for a career.

I twist my head, glancing to my right toward the line of folks seated on the other side of the Plexiglas. The two dudes closest to the barrier bump arms and then point at me. Nothing new, even though I'd prefer it if they didn't look at me like I'm some weird-ass animal in a zoo.

Bringing my bottle up to my mouth again, I squeeze my hand to squirt out more energy drink. Time to get my head back in the game before I lose focus and shit hits the fan.

Persistent knocking on the Plexiglas has me looking at the dudes again, only this time they're holding a cell phone against the divider. My gaze catches the headline, and my stomach roils with nausea.

Fuck.

"Hunt!" Coach Hall from my left. "You're in!"

I can't stop looking at the article on the phone. He did it. My motherfucker of a brother turned that shit in like I'm nothing to him.

Fury burns in my veins as Hall shouts my name again. "Hunt! Get on the fucking ice!"

I don't remember skating back to my position. I don't remember making pass after pass at the net, to my teammates. I don't remember making an assist that wins the game or doing anything remotely worthy of landing on ESPN's top ten plays for the next morning.

Betrayal clouds my vision and there's nothing I can do to stop it.

By the time we make it to the locker-room, I'm already steamrolling toward my locker where all my shit is. My hands tear at my duffel bag as I search for my phone.

I need to call my lawyer, my agent, my publicist.

Dave Hunt has risen from the dead, and he's determined to drag me down into hell.

29

GWEN

"That one," I say, pointing to a beautiful mermaid-silhouette wedding gown on one of the mannequins. "That one is totally yours."

Next to me, Charlie sips the champagne Nina, the wedding consultant, brought us when we arrived for Zoe's appointment.

"I feel fancy," Charlie mutters out of the corner of her mouth. "Whenever Duke and I get married, I want only champagne at our wedding."

"I have a feeling that'll be sooner rather than later," Zoe says, sipping her own champagne while we wait for Nina to return with the next round of dresses. "Duke can barely keep his hands off you."

Charlie flicks back her blond hair with flair. "Do you know something I don't know?"

Zoe and I exchange looks over our friend's head. If we knew Morse code, our blinking would probably say something like this:

Do you know anything?
Nope. Do you?

Nada. Dammit, the men don't tell us anything.

I pat Charlie's knee. "I bet he's planning a proposal as we speak. I mean, realistically speaking, you two are definitely the couple who would wake up one morning and decide to go to the courthouse and get hitched."

Charlie grins into her champagne glass. "You know us so well."

I don't know why I do it, because it's certainly not the time or the place, but I nudge my friend in the arm. In a low voice, I murmur, "I'm sorry, you know. For how I was in college and then . . . everything with Duke when the two of you started dating."

She blinks back at me. Stunned, maybe? Tossing back the rest of her bubbly, she sets the glass on the table beside her. "Gwen, I forgave you a while ago. What brought this on now?"

Clearly, I'm getting sentimental in my old age.

I motion toward Zoe, who's standing on the little elevated platform in a dress she described as "*eh*" but nothing to write home about. If it takes her another forty-eight tries, I know I'd sit here and pound back champagne with Charlie until Zoe found the perfect gown. "I guess I'm just saying thank you—for not writing me off when you could have. For giving me the chance to prove to you that I'm not a total Regina George."

From the platform, Zoe laughs. "You kinda are a Regina, though."

"I hate you," I tell her, knowing she knows what I'm really trying to say: *You're the bestest friends ever, and I love you both to pieces.* "I've done a lot of soul-searching recently, and I realized . . . sometimes your family are the people you choose." I think of Charlie, Zoe, Manuel. "I don't know. Not to be sappy or anything like that, but I love you guys. That's all."

Charlie throws a hand to her forehead in a fake swoon. Not to be outdone, Zoe pretends to collapse on the platform, but considering she's wrapped up in a tight dress, she nearly stumbles and goes down face-first.

Laughter bubbles up within me. My girlfriends are sarcastic and ridiculous and I wouldn't have them any other way.

"Are we ready for the next round?" Nina asks, coming back into the massive dressing room with an armful of gowns. "I know we'll have the perfect one in the mix."

"You need something that's going to give Beaumont a hard-on the minute he sees you at the end of the aisle," Charlie announces with a flamboyant wink. She points at her crotch as though to further elaborate her point.

"Really?" I ask, settling back in my seat with my own champagne flute in hand. "I was thinking something romantic. Andre is always trying to make you swoon."

"Andre Beaumont?" Nina murmurs, and I can tell she's a Blades fan just by the high pitch of her voice. "Do you all know Marshall Hunt?"

I sit up a little straighter at the mention of Marshall.

Charlie lays a hand on my leg. *Down, girl*, that hand says. Over the last year, both Zoe and Charlie have learned to deal with puck bunnies galore. Me, on the other hand? I'm brand new at the game and am not enjoying the lick of jealousy weighing down my limbs.

"We do," Charlie says evenly. "He's a good friend of ours, as is his girlfriend."

Her words smooth my ruffled feathers—somewhat.

"Poor girl," the consultant tells us as she unlaces Zoe from her current dress and sweeps it off to the side. "I hate to be her when she realizes that her boyfriend is about to be kicked off the team. Terrible stuff. The Blades aren't going to be the same without him."

What in the world is she talking about?

I yank my phone out of my purse and switch off Airplane Mode. I'd sent Marshall a text earlier in the day to let him know I'd be out with the girls wedding shopping. My leg jiggles with nerves as the internet comes back to life on my phone.

Like a scroll out of a nightmare, text after text after text pops up on the screen.

All from Marshall.

I close them out, hand trembling, as I open the internet browser and type in his name.

Hit ENTER.

Deep breath.

One by one, articles flood the Google search.

Marshall Hunt Discovered in Illegal Fighting Ring in Brockton, MA: What Witnesses Are Saying.

NHL Star Marshall Hunt Caught Dealing Drugs: Will The Boston Blades Cut Him Now?

Uncovered Secrets: Boston Blades Forward Marshall Hunt Nearly Murders Father In Youth

My hand closes over my mouth. "I'm going to be sick."

Charlie snatches the phone from me, her gaze skimming the headlines. "You need to go to him."

"I-I . . ." I don't have any words to say. None at all.

"Ow!" Zoe shrieks, and it's not until I lift my eyes to her face that I realize she's trying to distract Nina. "Careful with that pin. I bleed like crazy. Trust me when I say you don't want this gown turning red."

"Charlie," I whisper frantically, "what do I do?"

With a hand to my face, she forces me to look at her. "Do

you remember when you were all upset about him turning you down? And Zoe asked if you would give Hunt your kidney if it ever came to pass?"

"Well, yeah. But what does this—"

My best friend taps me on the forehead. "*This* is the kidney moment, Gwen. Don't think the worst of him, not yet. Go, listen, be there for him."

She's right. She's so right.

I stand. "I have to go."

Charlie gives me a little slap on the ass. "Go get 'em, girl. Protect what's yours."

She's right, again. Marshall is mine and I'll be damned if I let someone bring him down. We'll figure it out. We'll tackle it together.

I just have to figure out where the hell he is first.

30

HUNT

*L*ike the rat he is, Dave decided to miraculously "appear" in my house when I got back from dealing with the Blades' head staff.

I knew I made the right decision in going to them when this shit all went down. The tabloids may be having a field day but my coaches, the authorities, and the NHL all know that it's a load of crap.

Best decision of my professional career? Turning on the recording app on my phone just before entering that warehouse in Brockton. When the cops showed up a few days later, asking for me to turn my cell phone in for evidence, I did so without question, even if I did have to lie about breaking it at the gym to Gwen.

If there's one thing my childhood taught me, it's always being prepared for the worst.

Optimism will get you far, but pessimism will ensure that you get out alive.

Not everyone has your best interests in mind, and Dave definitely doesn't have mine.

I stare at my older brother, waiting for him to speak first.

"You think you're so smart, bro," he spits out. He wavers in place, and I can smell the alcohol seeping out from his pores even from here. "You think"—he throws a hand on the kitchen island to keep himself steady—"that you know *everything*."

"I don't know everything." I let that sink in before adding, "But I know you, Dave. The way your mind works and the tricks you think are so stealthy."

He throws his head back and laughs, a gurgling sound emerging from his lips. "I hate you, you know." With shaky steps, he nears me, one hand trailing along the wall. "I hated you when we were kids, when Mom would shield you from our asshole father. Did she ever do that for me?" He points to his chest. "Fuck no she didn't. She left me to defend myself."

"You're seven years older, Dave." I don't retreat from his approach, choosing instead to hold my ground. "You were bigger than Mom. You don't think she would have done something for you, too, if she thought you couldn't protect yourself?"

"Nah," Dave says. He stumbles over his legs before using the wall to keep himself steady. "The reason she didn't bother with me was because I wasn't hers."

What?

My eyes go wide and my palms go slick. "What the fuck are you even talking about?"

"Exactly what I said, *bro*."

I shake my head. "No, you're obviously stoned. Not in your right fucking head." The detectives handling my case had slipped me their number in case Dave showed up. I put my hand into my pocket, wishing I had one of those old school phones with actual buttons. There's no way I'll be able to call the cops with Dave bearing down on me like a drunken ox.

Worst case scenario: I take him down and sit on his ass while I wait for the detectives to show up.

"Listen, Dave." I hold my hands up so he can see I'm not packing. "There were a lot of things our parents said while we were growing up. It doesn't mean that you weren't—"

"I was a stripper's son," my brother cuts in, "one that Dad apparently loved to fuck in those early years when him and Mom first got married. He made her take me in, and I fucking wish he hadn't."

"Dave, stop. Just think rationally for a second, would you?"

His head tilts to the side. "Was that the doorbell?"

"No." I put a hand to his shoulder. "Listen to me, Dave, regardless of whether or not you're Mom's—"

"That's definitely the doorbell, bro." He flashes me a nasty grin. "Expecting anyone?"

No. I'd told my teammates I needed space today. And there's no one else . . . oh, fuck. *Gwen.*

31

GWEN

You can do this, I tell myself when I'm in front of Marshall's door. *Be his kidney. Just knock casually.*

Is there any other kind of knocking?

In an attempt to bring a smile to his face, I bought us both hot chocolate from Starbucks. Charlie was right—until I hear the admission from him directly, I choose to believe in the Marshall I know. *That* man is a gentleman and would never, ever put his career at risk. As for the matter with his dad . . . I have to trust that not everything is as it seems. I'm the perfect example of that.

Shuffling the cups into one hand, I *casually* knock on the door and step back to wait.

Masculine voices echo from inside the house, and then there's silence.

I push out a breath and do a quick rearranging of the Styrofoam cups again, so that I've got one in each hand.

The door swings open, my heart catching in my throat, and then Marshall is standing there.

Fully clothed, a little tired around the eyes, but no less good-looking.

"Hi."

Really? That's all you could come up with? "Hi" is woefully inadequate for what I'm feeling right now. I want to throw myself at him, ask what I can do to help. Listen to him just as he listened to me about my family.

I guess "hi" will have to do for now.

Marshall's hand, still locked around the doorknob, shifts as he steps out onto the front stoop and eases the door shut behind him.

"Hello."

Was the door-closing a hint that I'm not allowed to come inside today? Awkward, definitely awkward. An awful thought hits me: what if he's changed his mind about us? I look down at the Starbucks cups and wonder if I've completely made a wrong judgment call here.

"Is that for me?" Marshall's fingers slip over mine and pull the hot chocolate from my grasp. "I wasn't expecting you."

I can't help it—my gaze flicks to the shut door. "I saw your missed texts, and I"—well, it's now or never—"caught wind of the news in the tabloids. I wanted to be here for you, if you needed me." I shift my weight to my other foot. "I probably should have called beforehand."

"Fuck. It's not like that, Gwen."

I'm not sure whether he can just read me like an open book or if my face has settled into the stereotypical suspicious-woman mode. Either way, the fact remains that he doesn't want me in his home when shit is spiraling down around him.

Clearly, he's prepared to comfort me but when the roles are reversed, he'd just rather be alone. Which is fine, just fine, great.

Oh, my God, I think I might cry.

"No worries." I flash him a bright, oh-so-fake smile. The Old Gwen smile, the fragile one that couldn't look more pained if I were battling it out with Mona Lisa. "I just wanted to stop by and offer you my kidney if you needed it." Holy cow, I need to shut up. "Well, we've said hi, so I'm going to be leaving now."

And flee to a place where I can lick my gaping wounds.

And stop talking about kidneys.

"Gwen," Marshall says firmly, catching my wrist before I can escape down the driveway. He releases my hand to run his fingers through his brown hair. "It's my brother."

I don't see the problem with that. Isn't it a good thing that he's still in contact with a family member considering everything? Except . . . "I didn't realize you had a brother." I can't quite hide the wary edge to my tone.

"It's not . . . It's complicated. We don't have a good relationship, and I'd rather you not meet—"

He doesn't have the chance to flesh out the rest of his explanation.

The door cranks open behind him and a big man steps out. He's older than Marshall, maybe even older than I am, if the age lines creasing near his eyes and around his mouth are any indication. A black shiner darkens one eye, and he's rocking a pretty serious-looking gash on his temple.

Their similarities end with their brown hair.

Marshall is warm where this man, his brother, radiates a frigid vibe that could compete with the Gwen of yesteryear. Marshall is tall and muscular, leanly cut for expert agility on the ice. His brother is broad with a bulging gut, his arms as thick as tree trunks.

He looks exactly like the sort of man my mother always warned me lived in *those* neighborhoods: otherwise known as the less affluent.

I'm not Adaline, however, and so I stick out my hand and offer a pleasant smile. "Hi there, I'm Gwen."

The man doesn't take my hand, leaving Marshall to curse under his breath. "Dave," he grinds out, "this is my older brother, Dave. He was just leaving."

My hand falls back to my side.

I have a feeling their holiday dinners are just as awkward as mine.

"I'm sorry for interrupting," I say, jerking a thumb over my shoulder. "I'll leave you both to it. Marshall, hopefully I'll see you soon?"

"You look familiar."

Dave's deep voice stops me, and I glance back, looking between the two brothers. "I represent a few of Marshall's teammates. Maybe you've seen me in photos with them?"

It doesn't happen often, but it does happen.

"Nah," Dave murmurs, pushing his brother aside. "Somewhere else." He taps his stubbled chin, then points at me. "Northeastern! Ain't that right, Marshall?"

"Dave, don't."

My gut, for whatever reason, tells me to run and to not look back.

I don't.

Instead, I meet Marshall's gaze. I wish that I hadn't. His gray eyes are bleak, bottomless in the defeat that I see there.

"I knew Marshall back then," I say slowly. "We were in class together."

Dave laughs, a bitter sound that rings in my ears. "Course you were. My little *bro* ensured that he got in—"

"*Dave*, shut the hell up. This isn't for you to—"

I lift a palm, cutting Marshall off, then look to his brother. "I want to hear what your brother has to say, Marshall."

The grin Dave gives me is all broken, yellow teeth. "You didn't know?" He swaggers close to me. "I guess my baby bro is wicked good at keeping secrets. I'm assuming he didn't tell you how he almost killed our father. Right"—his finger points to his thigh—"here. Got himself put in foster care for that one, am I right, baby bro?"

Marshall's hands clench at his sides, his shoulders heaving upward with a sharply drawn breath. "He was fucking hitting her, Dave."

Upon hearing it for a second time, I decide that I hate Dave's laugh. Hate it with every fiber of my being. It scratches like nails on a chalkboard, squeals like a potato-chip bag breaking open, rubs my nerve-endings raw.

Then he leans in, and I catch a whiff of body odor and booze. "I took the blame for that one when the cops showed up, even though I was innocent." He blinks, a terrifying grin pulling at his chapped lips. "Thanks to Marshall here, I had my ass in jail for quite a few years, considering that his bitch-ass mother refused to stand up for me. She said that I acted violently all the time, that I was also the one responsible for the bruises on her face. Marshall got to go off while I sat behind bars. But I think . . ." He touches my red hair, and it takes everything in me not to yank back. *Stand your ground, stand your ground.* "It's time that Marshall pays the price for a wrong he's committed. I tried once already but my baby bro thinks he's so smart. But this way . . . oh yeah, there'll be nothing he can do about it."

I don't see it coming.

Dave's back thuds against the door, swinging it wide open as the brothers tumble into the house.

"Stop!"

My shout does nothing as Marshall sheds his charming public persona.

Their bodies are a blur of swinging fists and hulking frames. *Be calm. Don't panic.* Dave barks out a string of four-letter words as Marshall rolls him over, and I leap back to jump out of the fray.

"You're a fuckin' asshole," Dave grunts, legs swinging up to hook around Marshall's waist.

In a moment of quick thinking, I glance down to my hot chocolate. Considering the frozen temperatures outside, it's more chocolate milk than anything remotely hot right now. Not nearly enough to stop over three hundred pounds of angry males, but desperate times and all that.

Marshall has his brother pinned to the ground when I toss the cup, aiming directly for the wall behind them.

Chocolate liquid goes everywhere, splattering their heads and clothes. It's startling enough that Marshall whips around, brown hair plastered to his face, his right eye already bruising from a balled fist.

"Stop. I don't care which one of you tells me what's going on. You two want to tag-team it? That's fine. But if this so-called *wrong* involves me, then I deserve to know."

I deserve to know, but that doesn't necessarily mean that I *want* to know.

Already I feel the strain in my heart, and there's a sickening sensation tugging at my gut, indicating that this moment will be my last with Marshall.

Rolling off his brother, Marshall lands on his ass and props his elbows on bent knees. "Get the hell out of here," he says to Dave. "You've done enough."

"I don't think I will."

Marshall's eyes narrow. "Don't play that game with me, *bro*. After the shit you've pulled, your ass is mine. One call to the cops and you're done for." He jerks his head toward the door. "Get the fuck out."

The threat must resonate because Dave lurches to his feet and flies out the door.

Leaving Marshall and I alone.

This is so *not* what I expected to happen today.

I clear my throat and avoid making eye contact. "What did your brother mean when he said that you made sure to get into class with me?"

His gray eyes meet mine ruefully. "The bet."

My stomach sinks, and my feet backpedal into the kitchen. "It was just Adam who was in on it, right?" I ask stupidly, thinking of my college ex-boyfriend. An ex who'd made it *very* clear that our relationship meant nothing when I caught him kissing another woman in the middle of my senior year. Even now, I can still hear the nasty note in his voice when he told me I was nothing more than a challenge—a girl like me would never, ever be the real deal for him.

A girl like me. He'd meant promiscuous, even though I'd been a virgin until him. If it weren't for a dare, he'd told me, he never would have given me a second look.

Marshall had stood next to me—we'd just finished one of our study sessions—an arm wrapped around my shoulders as though he could physically shield me from the hurtful words.

Except that, apparently, he'd been in on it all from the start.

Jaw clenching tightly, Marshall pushes to his feet. "The whole hockey team was in on the bet, not just your ex."

I can't breathe. Just like that, the air vacates my lungs and my vision recedes at the corners. "I don't . . . *why?*"

"Because your grandfather was Northeastern's primary donor. Because we were all a bunch of pricks who thought it'd be funny to take the virginity from Mr. Landon's granddaughter."

I never cry—but it seems that in front of Marshall, I'm making a habit of it.

I feel the heat of tears slip down my cheeks. I itch to wipe them away, to erase the vulnerability from my being, but I *want* Marshall to witness my pain. Yes, I may have talked a big game back in college, trying to fit in when I felt so much like an outsider. Adaline had ensured that I never made friends easily—*they'll stab you in the back; just look at what Monica did to me last year*.

Who would have imagined that Gwen James, the girl who wore diamond earrings and knew all the best makeup techniques, was nothing but a sheep in wolf's clothing? Yeah, the saying usually had it the other way around—not for me. I wasn't the girl who I showed to the world, though I tried my damned hardest to be.

"It wasn't funny."

It's all I say.

"I know."

It's all he says.

And then, "It was wrong on so many levels, Gwen. *Every* level. I didn't—I never planned to go through with it."

"Except that you clearly did, Marshall." I jerk my chin to the right, squeezing my eyes shut against the hurt in my chest. "Did you even need an Accounting class or did you sign up for it because you wanted to win your little bet?"

"Gwen, listen—"

I slash at the air with a flat palm, stopping him in his tracks when he tries to step closer. Disgust and a healthy dose of mistrust form into a ball of nausea in my stomach, twisting and twisting and twisting until my palms turn sweaty and my heart thumps furiously. "You let me believe that you fell for me," I say, my voice growing stronger with anger. "You sat behind me *every day* for a semester asking me out—and none of it was real." The laugh that escapes me is caustic and bitter, and in it, I hear traces of my mother. The thought alone is enough to make me snap. "You did a real good job of pretending to console me after Adam gave me the boot. No wonder you were so adamant that I dump him. Obviously, *you* were waiting in the wings to swoop in and take his place."

"Fuck the bet, Gwen!" Marshall storms forward, all masculine perfection, before abruptly twisting away. His muscular arms go up, his hands settling on the back of his neck. Two deep breaths expand his shoulders. "The bet may have been what landed me in the damn class, but it wasn't what made me want you. Seeing you three times a week was the highlight of that semester. I wanted to hear your voice call me out for trying to cheat off you. I wanted to see your skirt ride up your smooth skin. Seeing you kiss him drove me fucking insane, and not any of that had to do with the bet."

"I don't believe you."

"What?" Marshall's voice sounds as though it's been carved from granite, cold and infinitely hard.

I steel my heart against him. "I said that I don't believe you."

He's a goddamn rat-snake bastard, Gwenny, my mother would tell me right now. And even though I *know* that Marshall is like none of Adaline's ex-husbands, including my father, the words won't shake. They eat at my soul, twine up my legs like twisting vines, suffocating and all too familiar.

"Gwen," Marshall grinds out, his palms coming to face me like he's trying to calm a panicked animal, "we've come a wicked long way since college. A long fuckin' way." One of his big hands lands on his chest, right above his heart. "I messed up and I fully admit that. But you've got to trust me when I say that those were the actions of an insecure kid who wanted to fit in, and they sure as hell aren't the sort of thing I would do now or ever again."

But you've got to trust me.

Marshall's words ring exceedingly loud in my head, and it hurts—oh, it *hurts*—the way I feel so torn. My stomach turns to knots and my palms turn all slick, and all I can hear is Adaline whispering to me about shitty friends and cheating husbands and so much mistrust I could choke on it as though it's a physical manifestation.

And in the end, all I have is one resounding realization: "I can't do this."

Marshall's hopeful expression hardens, just as it did at Zoe's engagement party—and I almost laugh because hadn't I suspected that this would happen all along? Hadn't I known, even on the day of my father's funeral, that I would be the one to wreck Marshall Hunt?

"Are we over because of the damn bet?" he asks me, his chest rising and falling with shallow breaths.

My own breathing isn't that much better. "You should have told me about it long before today."

"Answer my question, Gwen." Gray eyes hone in on me, unwavering in their intensity. "Are you fucking breaking up with me because of shit from six years ago?"

No, I'm desperate to say, *I'm breaking up with you because I'm broken.*

Dramatic, maybe. Coming from anyone else, I'd readily call bullshit. But standing in my shoes as I am? I hear nothing but my mother talking about her shitty husbands, see nothing but the string of men who left me with a damn gift card and a pat on the shoulder.

"You asked me to trust you," I say, my voice raspy from spilled tears and the sobs threatening to burst out into the open, "and I did. You've pushed me to open up, to prove to you that I'm willing to give you my heart. When you asked me to dance at Zoe's engagement party, I said no because I've spent the last year working on myself. Trying to be a better me, a version of myself who trusts easily and lets down emotional walls."

My hand curls against my heart, as though I can possibly stop it from breaking. "I trusted you today when it would have been all too easy to believe what the tabloids reported. I came here for you, to show you how much I love you." Voice cracking with emotion, I add, "But when push comes to shove, I can't take the final step." *I'm too much of my mother.* "Somehow, I'll hurt you or you'll hurt me, and I *can't do it*."

I can't be my mother in her bed for days on end, crying after another husband files for a divorce.

I can't be the girl who sought affection from anyone and everyone, begging for scraps of love, and who didn't even know how to love herself.

I can't be the woman I am today, staring at a man like Marshall Hunt and breaking his heart because I'm terrified to let my icy armor melt for good.

"So you're going to run," Marshall says without heat. He doesn't shift closer, and his expression is blank and unreadable.

A tear slips over the crest of my cheek. I want to say no, to leap into his arms and snuggle in close, but if I can't trust him—if I can't trust *anyone*—then what good does that do, for either of us? And if a mention of a bet from six years ago sends my progress rewinding faster than I can blink, then I can't imagine I'm in a place to date anyone . . . not even Marshall.

"You aren't your mother"—my gaze flicks to Marshall's face as he speaks—"and you aren't your father. You know how to love, Gwen, and you know how to love hard. So I'm going to assume that if you walk out that door, then it's simply a case that you don't love me enough to stay."

His words burrow like a knife in my side, crippling in their sharpness.

And then I speak my utter truth, carving open my fears and letting them spill out: "I don't know if I love myself enough."

I don't think I'm good enough for you.
I don't think I'm worthy of your love or your trust.
Like mother, like daughter.

I brush past him, head down because I don't think I can bring myself to make eye contact.

His footsteps echo on the stone floor behind me. "Gwen—"

I don't turn around at the risk of crumpling in a heap.

"Love is fucking messy, Gwen," Marshall calls out to me as I step onto his front stoop. "It's messy and it's hard and there is no one else in this world that I would rather be in that mess with than you."

My chest heaves with a silent cry and I cup my hand over my mouth to reel it in and keep it on lockdown. I fumble for my key fob in my purse, yanking it out and blindly unlocking my car.

Marshall standing tall and proud in his driveway is the last thing I see before I peel away. I drive until I hit the nearest convenience store, and then I'm in the parking lot.

My hands on the steering wheel, my heart warring with my head.

I've done this to myself, and there is no one else I can blame for my heartbreak but me.

For my entire life, I have done everything in my power to be the opposite of Adaline.

But blond hair or red, divorced or never-been-wed, I am my mother's daughter. The mistrust she instilled in me from birth can't be beaten into submission—and I've lost the only man I've ever loved because of it.

I've never hated myself more.

32

GWEN

I don't know what I expect when I go to my mother's house on Christmas night.

An elf running around the mansion, at least.

A hug, at most.

What I get is an empty house and a note on the front door that reads: *Have gone out with Steven. Help yourself to leftovers.*

No signature, no flourish or a heart or even a smiley face.

"Why are you even surprised?" I mutter to myself as I stare at the note. The longer I stand there, the angrier I become. Ripping the damn thing off the door, I crumple the pink Post-It note into a ball and hurl it into my mother's dead Chrysanthemum bushes.

All around me, the houses along my mother's street are lit with Christmas lights and blow-up lawn decorations and so much holiday cheer that I feel like the Grinch in a pair of knee-high boots.

You miss Marshall.

I push away the thought, the self-pity and, more importantly, the self-disgust. With quick steps back to my car, I slide into the driver's seat and bring up my contact list on my phone. There's no doubt in my mind that this is a bad idea, but I do it anyway.

Clearly, I'm on a roll with bad decisions lately so I might as well keep them going.

Pressing CALL, I lean back and stare at my childhood home. And then I wait and I wait and I—

"I'm with my friends, Gwen," my mother says in greeting. "Did you need something?"

No *Merry Christmas* from Adaline, of course. No *I'm sorry I ditched you for dinner* or *Oops, I'm so sorry I fucked up your head so you can't even function like a normal adult in love.*

When my silence stretches too long, Adaline presses, "Gwen, I don't have all day. What do you need?"

"A mother."

I can almost picture her gripping the pearls around her neck. "Excuse me?"

"I'd rather not. I've let you get away with enough excuses over the years."

"Gwen Adaline James, if you have nothing nice to say to me then I will hang up this phone right now."

I haven't bothered to turn the car on, and the icy temperature permeates the car so that I see little puffs of air when I exhale. My body, on the other hand, is so heated with anger that I could light up this half of Weston and the other side of town would only see gulfs of flames reaching up above the treetops.

"I need a mother," I finally say after I've worked up the patience to not immediately spit fire into the phone. "I've always needed a mother and instead I had *you*."

"Well, I—"

I cut Adaline off without a second thought. "You who

taught me at a young age that women were spiteful and untrustworthy, that men would only ever want me for what's between my legs—and that I should give it to them. Whoever wanted it, whenever they wanted it."

"It's called marrying up," she says stiffly, her nose no doubt brushing the ceiling it's tipped so far back with indignity.

"No, it's called not having any self-worth."

"Watch your tone, Gwen."

"I will not watch my tone." The silence in the car thunders in my ears like the greatest deafening stampede there ever was. I have waited *years* for this moment, for the chance to speak my mind and, Christmas Day or not, I refuse to squander it. "You made sure that I didn't have a relationship with my dad," I add, thinking of the forty-two letters I opened this morning and read three times through. "You sent back his letters and let me believe he wanted nothing to do with me. How could you do that? How could you do that to your own daughter?"

If she's wondering how I discovered my dad's letters, she doesn't say so. Instead, with a decided chill in her voice, she murmurs, "Is that all?"

My ears pop, I'm grinding my teeth so furiously. "What do you mean, *is that all*?"

There's the sound of fingers tapping on something hard, and then: "It's a special night for me, Gwen, and I won't let you ruin it with your negativity. Now, as I said, is that all?"

I'd like to pretend that I answer with some modicum of civility. But Civilized Gwen took a hike around the time I broke both my heart and Marshall's, and all I say is, "Screw you, Adaline."

And then I hang up on her spluttering voice.

Dignified? Not one bit, but it sure does feel good.

For a moment, I hold onto the hope that she'll give me a call back and apologize for everything she's done and hasn't done for me. I hold onto that hope for about the length of time that it takes for my car's lights to shut off from disuse until I'm left in the darkness.

Alone.

Always, always alone.

You could have been with Marshall tonight.

If I hadn't been an idiot. If I hadn't carried a lifetime of trust issues and hightailed it the moment the road grew bumpy.

Before we'd even discussed what truly mattered—Dave and the accusations he'd leveled against Marshall.

For what feels like the fiftieth time, I scroll through my past texts with Marshall and stare at the one that I've left half-written: *You frighten me, you know. You frighten me to take a leap of faith into the unknown, where my only safety net is your arms. You frighten me with the realization that I have never trusted another human in my life not to hurt me. I strike out first—*

I stopped writing after that. It all felt like an excuse and I'm done with excuses.

The truth of the matter is, I panicked. I panicked and I ran, and the blame for our broken relationship can rest on my shoulders exclusively.

Movement in my rearview mirror catches my attention, and I squint at the mirror. Behind me, at the house across the street, the front door cracks open and light spills out onto the snow. Kids pile out of the house, one after another, as they dart into the front yard and start tossing snowballs at their siblings.

A couple stands in the doorway, arms wrapped around

each other's waists. No coats from what I can tell, just their combined body heat.

Without realizing quite what I'm about, I turn on my car and roll down my window so that I can listen even as I keep watching in the rearview mirror.

"I've got you!" one kid squeals. "Bam! Bam! Bam! Triple throw!"

"Not at the face, Toby," the mom warns loudly enough that I can hear both the censure and the humor in her voice. "Below the shoulders, remember?"

"Bam-bam!" Toby shouts, hurling more snowballs like he's on the pitcher's mound at Fenway Park. "I'm going to win!"

I watch as the couple twist their bodies so that their chests touch as their lips brush together in a kiss.

And I *yearn*. I yearn with everything that I am to know what that's like—to have a partner by your side and kids to laugh with, and someone to love unconditionally.

Loneliness seeps into my bones, whispering *hello* to the regret already residing there like they're old friends.

Take the leap of faith.

With cold, numb fingers, and my rapidly beating heart, I pull up his phone number and make my second call in the last hour. I wait and I wait and I wait, and then my pulse leaps when the phone clicks on and—

"Hello, this is Marcus."

Marcus? I pull the phone back to stare at the number, just to make sure I called the right one. "Hello?" I say. "I'm sorry, I think maybe I've got the wrong phone number? I'm looking for a Marshall?"

I hear molars grinding like the guy is chewing gum. "No Marshall here, lady. Listen, I got to go, okay? It's Christmas and I've got people over. Have a good one, yada yada yada."

There's an audible *click* as the call ends.

My gaze shoots back up to the rearview mirror only to find that the family has moved back into the warmth of the house and the door is shut.

Locking their love inside where it belongs.

Meanwhile, I'm sitting in my car on Christmas night with absolutely nowhere to go and no one to see. I don't want to bring down either Zoe or Charlie's holiday, and it's incredibly obvious that Marshall has moved his queen into place on the chessboard.

Actually, he's swiped all his chess pieces off the board and removed himself from the game.

The knowledge burns like hot coals under my feet.

My phone comes to life on my thigh. *Marshall*. I swipe it open without glancing at the Caller ID, giddy butterflies coming to life in my belly as I answer. "Marshall."

"Not Marshall," comes a female voice with a laugh.

Crap. Rolling up the window, I tuck my phone against my shoulder and then rub some warmth back into my fingers. "Holly. I'm so sorry. I thought . . . Well, it doesn't really matter what I thought. What can I do for you?"

There's a small pause before she replies. "Does the offer still stand to hang out today? I'm drinking alone at a bar and I'm not going to lie, it's mighty damn pathetic."

Part of me wants to ask where Jackson is if he's not with her, but it's none of my business. "Which bar?" I ask, already backing my car up out of my mother's driveway. "Any chance you could have a shot waiting for me?"

"How about a flight of shots?" She laughs into the phone, but the sound is tired and more than a little sad. "It sounds like you might need them just as much as I do."

I think of calling Marshall and some random guy named Marcus picking up. If that's not a sign then I don't know what it is. "You think one of those will cure a broken heart?"

"Not sure. But I'm down to give it a go if you are."

"Done."

Then I think of the couple standing over their suburban kingdom, watching their children play in the snow and the almost reverent way they held each other.

Marshall is the only man I've ever wanted—*loved*—with all of my being. I want it all with him: kids, the white picket fence, marriage. Not necessarily in that order.

Don't ever bail.

I bailed and I bailed hard, but that doesn't mean the game is over, right? Sometimes there's overtime. Sometimes there's a shoot-out. And sometimes I need to stop thinking about hockey references, even in my own head.

Foot to the brake, I slow the car as I pull up to a red stoplight. Feeling bolstered by my mental pep talk, I say, "I need a plan."

Holly's momentary silence is interspersed with her asking for another round of drinks. "Good thing you're a publicist. Planning is pretty much your job description, isn't it?"

For the first time since I walked away from Marshall, I grin. It's small and pathetic but it's mine and it's full of hope. "It's actually my middle name. But I'm bringing it up because I need your help."

"Of the cocktail variety?" she asks with just-there trepidation.

"Of the photography variety, which is *your* middle name."

"I'm drunk."

"Even better," I tell her. "Drunk planning gets way more

creative, and if I want to show Marshall that he should trust me again, I'm going to need something elaborate."

"Like John Cusack?"

Something tells me Marshall wouldn't be impressed with me holding a boom box over my head while playing "In Your Eyes" loud enough to wake his neighbors. Unless I was naked. Maybe.

"No," I say finally, "but I have an idea."

33

HUNT

"If you keep drinking hot chocolate at the rate you are, it's scientifically proven that you'll turn into an asshole who breaks his girl's heart," Beaumont tells me from across the plane aisle.

I'm pretty sure there's no evidence to back up that particular theory, and I don't bother to correct Andre on the fact that Gwen was the heartbreaker in this situation. Her pain is hers, however, and I'm not the sort of guy who goes running at the mouth and tells the entire world someone else's personal baggage. It's easier to let my best friend and the rest of my teammates believe that I'm Douchebag *Numero Uno*.

I haven't seen or spoken to Gwen in two weeks. Christmas and New Year's Eve went by without a word. I'd promised myself that I would give her the space she clearly needed—nothing good ever comes from pushing a person toward something they aren't ready for yet. But, damn, it's been hard to keep my distance. Even harder not to show up at her apartment and demand she see me. If I manage another twenty-four hours without reaching out to her, I'll consider it a win.

You could use the excuse that your phone was stolen.

Yeah, I could totally do that. Just a little text to let her know that if she needs me, she'll need my new number since my last phone was swiped from the locker-room after a game last week. A reporter, maybe, or someone from the cleaning crew. For what it's worth, it seems I have shit luck with phones lately, considering my first is still with the police department.

The only good news to happen since Gwen walked out of my life is that Dave and his crew were caught, thrown in jail, and my career is still rolling onward like nothing ever happened.

There's a reason I pay big bucks to my lawyer and publicist. Within a week of the tabloids circulating that I was one foot out of TD Garden, they changed their tune. Now, the magazines are discussing my childhood since it's all been aired to the public. According to my publicist, it was the best way to go about it. Since his plan worked, I gave him a massive Christmas bonus and told him that he's stuck with me for life.

But even knowing that my professional life is better than ever, it's been at the expense of my love life.

I drain the rest of my Starbucks hot chocolate, just to shut Beaumont up.

And yes, I'm aware that drinking hot chocolate from Starbucks makes me out to look like a lovesick idiot. Everyone knows I'm a diehard Dunkin Donuts fanatic.

"Hey guys," my best friend announces, "anyone wondering where America's most charming hockey player disappeared to? Pretty sure he died the night of my engagement party."

"Fuck you," I growl, dropping my hand to our makeshift table on our flight from Los Angeles back to Boston. We wrapped up our road games on a high note against the Kings, and overall kicked ass for three out of our four games. "Deal the cards already."

We're playing Go Fish like true adults, mainly because none of us feel like losing money tonight with poker. And poker's no fun without money riding on the line—according to Jackson Carter, anyway.

Beaumont shuffles the deck for longer than necessary before they disappear beneath his drop-down tray.

"What the hell are you doing?"

"Putting the cards where I know you aren't about to reach for them," he replies darkly.

"You wouldn't."

His hands come up, not a single card in sight. "You want to play cards, you're going to have to reach into my pants for them."

The guys all groan.

"Fuck you, Beaumont!" calls out Carter from two rows ahead. "I was up next, you asshole."

"Should we burn it?" Bordeaux asks from beside me. "I've got a lighter."

"Christ," Harrison mutters from on the other side of Beaumont, "no one is lighting Beaumont's dick on fire. You all want to see Zoe pissed off?"

Everyone shakes their heads—no one even bringing up the fact that a lighter on a plane is a bad idea—and the game plan ensues as to how to steal back our only form of entertainment.

Everyone, that is, aside from Andre Beaumont.

His black eyes track me, and I know he's trying to pick up my thoughts like some sort of Jedi master. Good luck to him. The last two weeks have been filled with only one thought—how the hell do you convince someone that they are worth everything in the world and more?

"You're a moron."

I glance up at my best friend. "Tell me something I don't know."

"You're a moron for even agreeing to that bet, and you're even more of a moron now for letting Gwen walk away."

"Newsflash," I snap, "I'm aware that I fucked up." Because I did fuck up—I *should* have told Gwen about the bet long ago. That goes without saying.

Bordeaux elbows me in the side. "Women say that: it's fine, it's okay." He waves a hand in the air. "They get over it, if they love you."

If they love you.

The words cut deep, nearly as deep as the memory of Gwen admitting that she had given me her heart before realizing she couldn't commit. As for the bet . . . I shove my fingers through my hair, tugging at the strands.

I was there when that asshole, Adam, told her that she'd been nothing but an easy lay. Although it hadn't been easy for him—Gwen didn't jump into bed with him for months. Then, when she finally had, Adam had informed the entire team of the "news." By that point, no one had cared.

The bet had started on a drunken lark at summer hockey camp.

By the end of fall semester, the only two people who gave a shit were Adam . . . and me. Not because I wanted to win the bet, but because I'd grown to consider Gwen a friend. A friend who I wanted to date, sure, and definitely a friend I wanted to see naked.

Witnessing the moment when Gwen saw Adam kissing another girl had been gut-wrenching. Witnessing the way

Adam turned to her and spouted out hurtful words about never wanting to date her, and how she'd only been good for "popping her cherry," had incited a rage in me that I hadn't felt in years.

The very next day, Adam walked into the locker-room with two black eyes, a cut lip, and the promise to never utter Gwen's name again.

All of that, none of that, would make things right with Gwen now.

I never told her any of it, not once in six years, and that's the problem.

I asked her for honesty; I didn't give it to her in return.

And on top of all that, she couldn't find it in herself to stick it out with me. It's like something out of a soap opera—except that it's my life.

Beaumont kicks me in the shin to gather my attention. "Go to her, man. Get on your knees if you have to. Beg. Do whatever you have to do to prove that you love her."

I don't have the chance to say anything before Harrison is piping in. "You love her. Don't even deny it. You've loved her for years. You going to be happy when she permanently leaves your sorry ass and finds love with someone that's not you?"

It sounds like my new version of hell—a special concoction whipped up just for me.

And even though I know that I should wait for her to make a move, if she ever does, sometimes the only person you can rely on to be bold is you.

I eye my friends. "Tell me what I need to do."

34

GWEN

Christmas ended with me and Holly needing an Uber to take our sorry butts home.

The good news? I think I have a new friend.

The even better news? I woke up the next morning with a sense of purpose.

The bad news? I haven't heard from Marshall, and each day that goes by makes me wonder if I screwed things up for good. Charlie and Zoe respected my wishes to stay out of it —their significant others are his teammates and best friends —and working through it all on my own proved to me one thing: I'm strong enough to handle anything that comes my way.

I spent New Year's Eve alone after deciding it was best to take some time away from my mom—maybe permanently. After our heated conversation on Christmas, I didn't have it in my heart to go another battling round with her. She'd made her decisions in life for whatever reasons suited her. Over and over again, she'd chosen men over me. Or her friends over me. Or, really, *anyone* over me.

Hard as it's been to find lately, I know my self-worth, and

begging for answers she'll never give me isn't worth my time or energy.

Marshall Hunt, however, is worth every bit of energy I've got housed in my five-foot-five frame.

Bracing my shoulder against my massive packages, I stab the elevator button up to my fourth-floor apartment. I need to call Holly as soon as I put everything down. I—*we've*—been waiting for my order for two weeks now to arrive in the mail.

The fact that no one even batted an eye when I picked up six, life-size cardboard cutouts at the post office proves one of two things. The first: Bostonians are jaded human beings, and nothing surprises them anymore. The second: they were too busy wondering where they could buy a life-size cutout of Marshall Hunt for themselves.

The thought of him alone sparks a need in me that I haven't been able to quiet since I fled his house before Christmas. And, just saying, but I'm fortunate that Google has Incognito mode because my search history in the last two weeks would make me out to look like some kind of weird stalker. Fun fact: Marshall has some of the sexiest GIFs on the internet right now. In case you were wondering.

Juggling my three Marshall's and three Gwen's, I wait for the doors to ping open before stepping onto my floor. With a shimmy and a prayer, I wrap my arms around my most prized possessions and shuffle my way down the empty hallway.

The doors are all decorated with wreaths and little garland-dressed trees by the welcome mats. Most of the tenants haven't taken down their holiday decorations, which can't be said for my door which is remarkably empty.

As usual.

"Almost there," I mutter as I waddle awkwardly, trying to

keep my legs from tangling with the mass clutched to my chest. Then I do another shimmy as I ungracefully unlock the door.

First step when I drop off my load inside? Call Holly.

Second: Stage the cutouts so they're all in place when she arrives to take their photographs.

Third: Ask Andre Beaumont for Marshall's new number.

One firm kick of my boot to the door later, and I shove it open with the back of Cardboard Marshall's handsome head.

It's time to make the magic happen and show Marshall *exactly* why he should give me another—

What.

The.

Hell.

The cardboard cutouts flail to the ground as my hold loosens from shock. I turn slowly, taking in the sight of my apartment transformed into some sort of winter wonderland retreat.

A decked-out Christmas tree sits in the corner of my living room, its red-and-white lights twinkling brightly. Beneath it are an assortment of presents. My TV has been exchanged for what looks to be an electric fireplace. The fake flames hiss and crackle as though the wood they're burning is real.

Garland and tinsel is strung throughout the room.

My gaze catches on the balloons dancing along the ceiling, along with signs boasting *HAPPY NEW YEAR!*

Looks like Zoe and Charlie were incredibly busy today—

My heart stops at the sight of his hard, athletic body strolling toward me down the hall. Jeans, socked feet, and a plain black T-shirt are accompanied by a red Santa hat perched jauntily on the top of his head.

"You did this?" My voice emerges rusty from shock. "All of this?"

Marshall points to his hat. "I had some help from a few of Santa's elves." Lips turning up in a small grin, he adds, "They bitched and moaned the entire time. I plan to lower their wages."

I don't even know what to say *or* how to feel.

"There are New Year's decorations," I say, as though that makes a difference.

"I know." From his pocket, he pulls out a kazoo and brings it to his lips. His cheeks suck inward as a loud squawk splits through the room. When he tosses it on the countertop, he says, "I had holiday plans for us, you know. I'd booked us a room at the Ritz and planned all these other holiday-themed activities. Clearly," he drawls, "none of that happened. So I thought I'd get creative here."

He approaches me silently, and that's when I remember my plan.

Oh, God.

I leap in front of the cutouts, careful not to stomp all over them. They didn't cost me a fortune but finding a company who could create them on special order *and* a deadline proved way more difficult. "How did you get in?" I ask, wringing my hands in front of me as he completely sidesteps me.

I shift to the side, blocking his sight . . . or *trying* to, anyway. The man is a whole lot bigger than I am.

He cocks his head slightly, leaning around me. "Two little reindeer showed me the way."

The wry remark would have made me grin, if I weren't so determined to follow my plan to a T. *You're not supposed to see it all yet!* I want to shout. My face heats with embarrassment and I do another shuffle-shuffle-shuffle when he plants his hands on my shoulders to hold me in place. "Which one had the red nose?" I ask, desperate to keep his attention on me.

With a husky chuckle, he murmurs, "Who do you think?"

"Charls?"

He drops his hands to his sides. "Literally. I found a stuffed red nose at the store late last night. It was half-broken and looking tired as hell. I'm guessing the store clerk missed it when they were taking all the holiday stuff off the shelves. I had all these plans to wear it for you today. Unfortunately, Charlie claimed it as payment. Told me I'd look better without it anyway."

He does look—

Marshall drops to his haunches and lifts one of the upside-down cutouts. Crap, crap, crap. It's just my luck that . . . "Is this me?"

I stare at the ceiling and pray for the Universe to send me a sign. "Ummm . . ." Or words. I'd also take words right about now.

Marshall tips the cutout over, so that Fake Marshall lands on his back, exposing all of his— "I'm naked."

Gulping audibly, I keep my gaze averted. *Do not make eye contact, do you hear? Do NOT look at him.* "You're not completely naked."

"You're right, I'm in Calvin Klein—" He breaks off with a startled but still sexy laugh. "This is from a shoot I did for them two years ago."

"Is it?" Another shuffle and I'm effectively standing over him, my poor brain working overtime on how to explain all of . . . *this*. It would be one thing if he saw the whole thing on display through *photography*, as I'd planned it out with Holly.

Not the cardboard cutouts in all of their . . . cardboard.

With firm hands, Marshall once again shifts me over. One by one, he lifts the cutouts until they stand tall and are resting against my wall. And with each cutout that he sets into place, my heart thuds a little harder and my hopes flit to life a little more aggressively.

When he's finished, he steps back, hands on his hips, mouth in a firm, uncompromising line.

"They're us," he murmurs in a voice laden with emotion.

I swallow, then fist my hands behind my back to keep from yanking them off the wall. *Don't ever bail.* "Yes. They are."

For a moment, we don't speak.

In the first cutout version of us, Marshall is in the blue navy suit he wore to Zoe and Andre's engagement party. I'm wearing the red dress that I donned that very same night. In the second cutout versions, Marshall is decked out in tight boxer briefs . . . and nothing else. He's right; I found a photo of him online from the shoot and opted to pretend copyrights didn't exist for only this instance. I figured Calvin Klein would understand and support my cause. As for my cutout, I allowed Holly to take a picture of me in a lacey bra and panties. I wore heels because, truth time, they made my butt look better.

"Gwen."

The way he utters my name is like a burst of sunshine after weeks of rain. I struggle to hold myself back, to keep from launching myself into his arms. "Is it too much?" I ask, striving for a confident tone even as the back of my neck itches with nerves. "It's probably too much."

Two steps bring him to the final cutout set, and he reaches out a hand to trace his fingers over Fake Gwen's face.

"You're in a wedding dress," he says, his smooth baritone breaking on the last word.

I clutch the back of my neck and shuffle my weight. "I, um, dragged Holly Carter to a local wedding gown shop so she could snap a few photos."

He points to the furry figure at the bottom of the white, flowing gown. "You brought a dog there?"

God, did someone twist the temperature up to steaming hot today? I clear my throat. Straighten my shoulders. "It's a stuffed toy, actually." Pausing, I force myself to continue. "I thought, maybe, one day we could get a dog. I've never had one. My mother wasn't a fan."

Glancing over his shoulder at me, gray eyes meet blue. Humor tugs at his lips. "I've never had one either. Although I've got to say, I'd always envisioned a golden retriever, maybe, or a bullmastiff. Not a . . ."

"Chihuahua?" I grin.

"I was going to say a puntable dog."

"Puntable isn't a word."

"It is when we're talking about yap-yap dogs," he says on the tail end of a husky laugh. "But I also didn't picture myself in a powder-blue tux for my wedding day either."

Heat stains my cheeks. "It's the only photo I could find for Holly from the internet. It's from—"

"I know where it's from, Gwen." Marshall faces me, hands in his pockets. Like always, I can't help but marvel at the powerful expanse of his chest and the breadth of his shoulders. He radiates control, strength, and—I hope—love. If I'm lucky. "What I want to know is, what did you plan to do with these? Keep them in the house? For fond memories we've created and memories we never had the chance to make?"

Here we go. I struggle for a deep breath, squaring my shoulders to get out the words I've rehearsed every morning and every night for two weeks. If this is the moment I have to show what I feel for him is real and that it's *lasting*, it has to be perfect.

But then he cuts me off: "Tell me something, Gwen. How did you feel when I walked away from you at the engagement party?"

Like I'd been stabbed in the heart. Swallowing past the lump in my throat, I wring my hands before me again. "As though I'd lost the one person who'd always been in my corner."

"Exactly." His expression grows somber, as though determined to make me see how serious he is. "The thing is, Gwen, that's how I felt when you walked away from me just the other day. Angry. Disappointed. Frustrated. All at myself, of course, but also at you, too."

The laugh I give sounds awkward and stilted, and I do my best to keep my gaze off the cutouts that now watch me mockingly. Especially the one of me in a wedding dress that's not mine and of Marshall in a tux he wore as a groomsman for a friend's wedding. "I'm fully aware that I'm responsible for—"

He lifts a hand. "Hear me out."

"Okay."

With a short nod, he rubs the back of his neck with one hand. "I've spent my life trying to escape my past, Gwen. You heard what Dave said the other day—my actions landed *him* in jail. And now the whole world knows that."

"No," I hastily say, "wait. You were trying to protect your mother, Marshall. I've read all the articles." Ah, crap. Maybe

I shouldn't have admitted that. But because it's already out in the open, there's no reason to pretend I haven't read everything and anything I could find on him in the last two weeks. "You can't—what happened wasn't your fault."

"She didn't want my help, I realize that now. She wanted out of that relationship and out of that house, and there was no better way to get a divorce than landing her husband in jail." His gray eyes go flat as he stares at the floor. "I don't want to claim that she used me or Dave to get what she wanted, but she saw an opportunity for escape and she took it. So, yes, I wanted to protect her. And, yeah, maybe Dave did actually feel an inkling to protect me or maybe he was just that pissed that he pushed me aside and wrapped his hands around that knife."

There are so many things I wish to say, but from the way a tick pulses in his jaw, I know he's not done. He needs to finish his story—and I need to let him, without interruption, however much it kills me to keep silent.

With a heavy exhale, he continues, "However it happened, my mom knew what she was doing when she called the cops and said that my father had beat her and then tried to strangle me." At my horrified gasp, Marshall flashes me a humorless grin. "She didn't lie about any of that. The knife was in my hand, but I didn't do anything with it until my father's hands wrapped around my neck. Striking out was survival and a childish hope that I could protect my mom. When I woke up from blacking out, Dave was covered in blood and my mother was whispering to the police that both my father and Dave had gone insane and attacked us. They both went to jail. She got out of the life she'd always hated, and I went into the system."

Another nod, this one short and clipped as though in silent encouragement to himself to continue on. "I looked her up last weekend, just to see. She's remarried, to a doctor this time. Has two little kids who go to a private school out in the Berkshires."

I wonder if that's what he wanted to find or if he'd hoped that she was still shacking up with his father, considering that his and Dave's life have been a downward spiral. "What about your dad?"

"Dead." He says it with little emotion, as though discussing the weather. "Got stabbed in prison a few years ago."

My heart aches for him, bleeding for the little boy and the man he is now. "Marshall—"

He cuts me off with a shake of his head. "I'm not telling you this so you'll feel bad for me, honey. I'm trying to show you a trend. I struck my dad, and Dave landed in jail. He's spent his years out of it making sure I know how much I owe him for taking the fall, to the point that he went to the extremes and tried to get me kicked out of the NHL. I can understand why he's upset. The mother he always thought was his, wasn't. The man who was supposed to love him, beat him up on a regular basis."

Marshall's gray eyes gleam with frustration. "But the fact remains that I was caught in the crosshairs too. That day I grabbed a knife because my dad had hurt my mother to the point where I couldn't even make out her features. I didn't ask for my mom to place the blame at my brother's feet. Hell, I barely even understood what was going on I was so young. It was his choice to grab that knife and twist. It was his choice, and I've been dealing with the fallout of that for years now."

Even knowing that I should continue to stand my ground, I can't stop myself from pressing my hand to his heart. It thuds beneath my palm, heavy and fast.

Marshall places his hand over mine. "And then in college, Gwen, I agreed to a bet because I was the odd one out. It was wrong. It was fucked up, and I'm more disappointed in myself than you'll ever know. I guess . . . I guess what I'm trying to say is that I also don't have much reason to trust people, just like you."

My shoulders twitch. His words aren't a jab but I feel startled nonetheless. Because I hear what he's saying—he's standing here in my apartment making a move. A move that I was too cowardly to take two weeks ago.

I'm not too cowardly now, and when I make contact with the Fake Gwen in the wedding dress, I know what I need to do and what needs to be said.

Don't be the Old Gwen. Be brave, be you.

I open my mouth, fully prepared to apologize, to offer everything that I am to get him back. This is my opportunity to be the Gwen I want to be, the one who stands tall and strong and knows her own self-worth.

Marshall's throat works with a hard swallow. "Sometimes fate works in mysterious fucking ways that I'll never understand. But in the same breath that I should have told you everything a long time ago, I wish it wouldn't have taken me walking away to realize how much you wanted me."

35

GWEN

There's nothing for me to say but the truth.

"I know." Letting out a built-up sigh, I allow myself to sink down onto the couch. "I'm not proud of the way that I acted all these years, pretending that I didn't want you, shooting you down. I can give you all these fake reasons why, starting with your age and the fact that you're an athlete, but the honest-to-God's truth is that I allowed fear to rule me."

"Of what?" His voice is a seductive rasp as he takes the spot beside me on the couch.

"You called me out on it two weeks ago," I tell him evenly. "I'm scared of becoming my mother and of ruining everything that I touch. I'm terrified of placing my complete trust in a man, only for him to snatch it away and try out someone new."

My smile feels brittle as I continue, "I didn't want to become just like Adaline, but in not wanting to be her, I became someone else." I squeeze my eyes shut. "I hurt people, I hurt *you*. And still I maintained that shell around me, in the hope that no one could ever touch my heart."

I straighten my shoulders and lift my gaze to Marshall's face. "But you already had, whittling down my walls over the years. You cared for me and showed me what it was like to hold someone and know that they wanted only the best for me." I pause and look down at where I'm tracing little circles on my leg. "You showed me all of that and then I tossed you aside. I walked away when you called me out. You told me to get messy in love, and I fled like a coward."

"Sometimes, we have to walk away in order to see things clearly."

I think of Adaline and then the family playing in the snow, and then I think of my father and the last words he spoke to my mom right before their divorce. *Don't ever bail.* In a tight voice, I murmur, "And sometimes when we stop being so self-centered, we realize that if we didn't bail when things got tough, we'd be the happiest folks in the world." I meet Marshall's gaze head-on. "I bailed on you, and I have spent every moment in the last two weeks figuring out how I could make you realize how serious I am about our relationship." I point at the three cutout couples along the wall. "And, yes, I went to the extreme, but I've got no playbook and I figured the more extravagant the better."

Small as it is, I see a hint of a smile on Marshall's face. "It's the wealthy Bostonian in you."

I shrug, even though I'm tempted to laugh because he's probably right. "We started off as not-quite friends, Marshall. I let my head get in the way—"

"It's a beautiful head."

He surprises me by brushing my hair behind my ears, and I stop short of nuzzling his hands. "Thank you." *Remember to breathe.* Easier said than done. "Crazy as those cutouts are, and I'm seriously hoping you picked up the reference to your alleged bondage days, I want them to symbolize our path. I want the happily-ever-after. I want the children and the yap-yap dog and the debate on whether we should eat out or stay in bed all day." I swallow, hard, and then force myself to keep talking. "I want to live without fear, knowing that my best friend, the man I love more than life itself, is right by my side." My chest expands because *this is the moment*, and I refuse to mess it up. "You are that man for me, Marshall, only you. You've ruined me for anyone else."

His palms land on my thighs, and his voice is pure grit when he speaks next. "There's no one else for me, Gwen. No one. These last two weeks, I've only been able to think of you. I wondered how I could give you the space you needed when all I wanted was you by my side."

I choke back a sob, my hands going to his arms to pull him closer. "How can you forgive me so easily when I've screwed up so many times?"

"Because that's the definition of unconditional love, honey. How do I prove to you that I'm not complete without you?"

Heart beating erratically, I tilt my face up to his. "You have me. You have my heart and everything there is for me to—"

This time it's not his words but his lips that complete my sentence.

Oh.

My.

God.

He kisses me like it's our first time all over again. Another fantasy kiss—each one strips a part of my soul and sews me back together into a version of myself that I love all the more because I have Marshall with me.

His lips work mine, demanding and needy in a way that

I reciprocate fully. This kiss is urgent and hard and downright naughty.

Cradling the back of my head, he touches his tongue to my bottom lip, seeking entrance. I give it. I give him everything.

My fingers raking through his hair, my mouth moving under his, my breath held captive as he strips off my scarf (why do I even still have it on?), my coat, my boots. He never pulls away, as though worried I'll disappear, and then he slips his hands up my sides to cup my breasts through my sweater.

"*Marshall.*"

"Fuck," he groans, "you need to slow me down."

"No."

I yank him down onto the couch, pulling his body over mine. "You owe me at least another fantasy kiss."

He chuckles against my lips. "Pretty sure that you're getting greedy now."

"Pretty sure you're the only one I hear complaining."

Marshall's eyes darken with lust, and he takes advantage of our position, rolling his hips against my core.

"The jeans," I moan, "off, off, off."

"Desperate?" he taunts. "What if I tell you no?"

Here's to finding out.

I push him onto the floor, delighting in the way his eyes go wide with shock and then desire. Then my fingers are on the button of his jeans, slipping it free and tugging down his zipper until it hits the base. With a little help, I ease the fabric down his legs, taking his briefs along for the ride. "While I've enjoyed all the ways you like to make me warm, I've been thinking of all the ways that I could return the favor."

"Gwen, you don't have to—"

His words end in a masculine groan as I slick my hand over his erection and press my lips to the tip.

"Holy shit."

I glance up past his thick cock to see Marshall up on his elbows. His T-shirt has ridden up his hard stomach, and he looks like a fantasy come to life. Utterly. Delicious. "This is one fantasy kiss you didn't see coming."

I close my mouth over him, making sure to watch him for his reactions. He doesn't hold back. His fingers thread through my red hair, pushing the strands back so that he can see my face. With each downward thrust of my mouth, I give it to him exactly how he likes it.

Tight at the top, with a flick of my tongue under the head.

I do that, over and over and over again until he's both praising me and cursing me all at once.

"No more," he rasps, "I'm going to come, and I've been dreaming about that sweet pussy of yours."

I give his cock one more hard pull, which is apparently all he'll allow me. He strips off my clothes in record time, leaving me naked and waiting on my plush carpet.

"Hold on a sec," he murmurs, leaving my side to head for the kitchen.

I don't want to wait for him, and the memory of his lust-filled gaze as I made myself come over our video chat has my fingers dancing over my clit.

"You couldn't wait, could you." It's not a question, but I can hear his laughter as he drops to the carpet and crawls his body over mine. "I love that you're always so willing to show me what you like."

I feel his blunt fingers trace my slit, encouraging me to widen my legs for his big body. My breath catches at the first touch of his finger to my clit, and then I'm left panting when he thrusts into me with one finger.

No, two.

"That's always the magical number for you, huh, honey?" He drops a kiss to my mouth, feasting on me as his fingers pump in and out. "Two fingers to your clit, two fingers inside your pussy." Another deep kiss that leaves me moaning like a complete hussy.

Those magic lips of his descend down my body, kissing here and there. My limbs freeze at the first touch of his tongue. He groans deep in his throat, and I feel heat sweep up my chest. "Oh, my God."

The smooth glide of his fingers is replaced with his thrusting tongue, and I lose it. Right then and there, with no lead-up necessary. Fingers grasping my furry rug, I gasp and call out his name.

Another swipe of his tongue against my clit. A shiver works down my spine.

"You're sweet." He leans up to kiss me, devilishly and raw, and I taste myself on his tongue. "So damn sweet."

He pulls back to prop my legs over his thighs, so that he's nestled between my legs, his cock poised at my entrance. With his hands on my hips, it takes him only one thrust to enter me fully.

Wowza, wowza, wowza.

Shoulders bunching, he shifts his angle, hitting me just *there*.

"*Yes*." My fingers dig into his thighs, delighting in every thrust of his hips. "Please don't stop."

"Never," he growls, dropping his elbows to either side of my head so that he covers me fully. His chest meets mine, his breath whispering against my forehead. "I'm yours,

Gwen." He pulls out, nearly leaving me, before pumping back in sharply. "Always," he promises, "for as long as you'll have me."

My hands tangle around his shoulders, and I kiss wherever I can reach. His forehead, his nose, his lips. "Forever. I'll have you forever."

"Good."

He reaches down between our bodies, flicking his finger against my clit.

That one touch pushes me over the edge, sending me straight over. My thighs lock around his waist, unwilling to let him go. He never pauses, drawing out my orgasm as he keeps pace, working my clit until I come for a second (miraculous) time. Only then does he unlock my legs and push my knees up to my chest so that I'm his for the taking.

His mouth flattens, twisting in a way that turns his pretty-boy features into something darker, for me only, and then he comes with a low groan that I will never tire of hearing.

My head drops back against the rug as Marshall's body collapses on mine. "You've killed me," I mutter, tracing his spine with my fingers.

"You love me," he returns. "I love you, too."

Warmth spreads in my chest, and I hug him tight. "I love you, Marshall. I love you so much."

"You better." He presses a kiss to my mouth, then reaches for something on the coffee table. "Here, it's a tradition."

I glance up to see a blueberry pie in his hand. Laughter bubbles out of me. "You didn't."

He grins wickedly, though his gray eyes are so full of love. "Trust me, I did."

"There's no way I'm letting you near me with that thing." I scoot back, pushing him off so that I can scramble up to my feet. "The only way I'll let you come close to me with that pie is if it's on a plate."

"Aw, honey," he rumbles, stalking me down. "I just want my two favorite things. My girl and my pie."

I skip out of reach, knowing he loves the chase. Our laughter echoes in my apartment as I swipe his Christmas hat off the kitchen countertop and then take its place. My feet dangle against the side of the cupboards as I watch Marshall swagger past Fake Gwen and Fake Marshall and our fake little dog. His gaze is on me alone, and I love every second of it.

He dips one finger into the pie and licks it right off, giving a fake moan. "So good," he growls, "are you sure you don't want any?"

I take in his tattooed arms and his rock-hard body that's been put through the test during hours of practice and brutal hits. "I just want you," I tell him.

The final two feet between us disappear as he sets the pie down on the counter and lowers his face for a kiss. "I'll take it," he says, "and just so you're aware, I plan to score a hat trick tonight, honey. I hope you're ready for it."

I cup his jaw, taking in the man I love more than I ever thought possible, and touch my lips to his.

And then I dig my hand into the pie and spread it all across his chest.

Because what's love without a little mess?

The End.

X

Not ready to be done with the Boston Blades just yet?
Perfect, because the fourth Blades novel, featuring Holly & Jackson Carter, is now available on Amazon/Kindle Unlimited! Swipe right for a sneak peek!

PREVIEW OF BODY CHECK

Body Check is now available! Keep scrolling to read the opening scene from the latest in the Blades Hockey series, featuring Holly & Jackson Carter. It's a steamy second chance romance that will have you laughing out loud!

HOLLY

The groom is sporting hard wood.

And I'm not referring to the hockey stick he wields around TD Garden for the Boston Blades. No, I'm talking about the metaphorical type of wood—the one that sprang to life in his black tuxedo pants the minute his bride, Zoe, began the walk of all walks down the center aisle of Boston's historical Trinity Church.

My knees burn against the scratchy red rug as I angle my camera to snap a photo of the groom's awestruck expression. While Andre Beaumont—King Sin Bin to hockey fans across the country—may have hired me as his wedding photographer, I'm pretty sure he's not interested in having his erection memorialized in between pictures of Zoe's gorgeous, ivory lace gown and the flower girl prancing down the aisle like a cotton ball made of tulle.

Then again, it's the ball-busting kind of photo that his teammates and brothers-in-hockey-gear would kill to get their hands on, and Andre should have known better than to rope me into this gig.

Swallowing an ill-timed laugh, my fingers slide over the camera's familiar black, plastic frame.

Click.

One inappropriate photo down. Only one hundred-plus elegant ones to go.

Wedding photography isn't my thing. And, sure, maybe it's because I lived the Happily Ever After fairytale and came out on the other side with my gold band tucked away in my dresser and my newly signed divorce papers doused in wine, sweet-and-sour sauce, and dried tears.

It was a rough night.

Scratch that—it's been a rough three years.

Like a moth to a flame, I lower the camera and slide my gaze to the second groomsman standing to the right of Andre. My grandmother once called him "strapping." Accurate, I'll admit, albeit begrudgingly. He's built like a linebacker: tall and broad with muscular thighs that strain the fabric of his tuxedo pants. Dark brown hair that's casually tousled in the same style he's worn for years now. Even when he graced the glossy front page of *Sports Illustrated* last February, he looked exactly the same.

Some things change . . . he hasn't.

Hard, square jaw. Formidable body. Shrewd brown eyes that I imagine terrify his opponents on the ice when he comes barreling toward them.

Jackson Carter.

Captain of the Boston Blades.

Otherwise known as my ex-husband.

Those astute dark eyes meet mine now, and I wait for the rush of familiar emotions to hit me like a freight train. Only, before I have the chance to do my usual shushing of my heart, Jackson's full lips part and he mouths something that looks *suspiciously* like, "Did you just take a picture of his dick?"

And that right there, *that's* the reason why I've felt so lost for the last three years.

Our marriage didn't crumble because one of us cheated. Jackson isn't that sort of guy, and I've always been a one-man kind of woman.

It didn't combust in a ball of fiery flames because we fought like we were prepping our audition tapes for that trashy reality TV show *Marriage Boot Camp*.

No, we simply . . . grew apart.

He passed out on the couch.

I slept in the bed.

He ate meals with his teammates.

I chowed down on mine alone at my desk, late into the evening hours after my employees had already gone home to their families.

He reached out to Andre or the Blades goalie, Duke Harrison, when he needed to talk.

I acted like smothering my emotions was as easy as breathing.

Eleven years ago, I married the man who swept me off my feet during my first semester at Cornell University.

A year ago, we sat opposite each other at a wooden table, our feet locked on our respective sides instead of tangling together the way we'd always done, nothing but our signatures standing in the way of a divorce.

The cry fest with the Chinese food and wine came later

that night. No matter how alone I'd felt prior to finalizing our divorce, spending that first night in our house—empty but for the select furniture I'd kept—had been a hard pill to swallow. Accepting the fact that we'd failed at the *till death do us* part of our vows was even more difficult.

Camera feeling heavy in my hands, I lift my gaze from Jackson's mouth and return silently: "Blackmail."

His eyes crinkle at the corners, and my pathetic heart dives into an incessant *thud-thud-thud* that could rival the quick-paced tempo of an EDM song. *Dammit.* Those creasing laugh lines are more attractive than they have any right to be. Hell, the fact that I still find Jackson attractive at all feels like unjust punishment, doled out for some unknown bad misdeed I've committed in life. Considering my worst transgression of late is accidentally tossing half a burger into a recycling bin, the unyielding attraction seems a bit unfair.

He drags his thumb across his bottom lip, in that revealing way of his that tells me he's trying to wrestle back a grin, and I nearly hurl my camera at his head in retribution.

I can just imagine the newspaper headlines now: *Ex-wife of Famous NHL Player Interrupts Wedding of the Season by Flying Camera—Updates to Follow.*

Once upon a time, I'd made it my mission to make Jackson's infamous steel resolve disintegrate in inappropriate places. He always got me back—generally in bed with me fisting the sheets and his tight body powering into mine.

Now, I swallow hard at the memories and divert my attention to the bride.

Zoe radiates warmth and happiness. When her lips turn up behind the gossamer fabric of her veil, I readjust my grip on the camera and rise to my haunches. Knees cracking, I scoot back to avoid blocking someone's view. The five bridesmaids to my left all smile, as if on cue, and I catch a shot of them, too.

The light streaming in through the stained-glass windows paints them in a mural of jeweled tones, and I know—even if I make my living taking photos of professional athletes—that the picture will be one that's kept on their walls for years to come.

I get Zoe next, just as she steps up to meet Andre and her father gives her away.

Whether or not Andre is still sporting wood, I've got no idea. I keep my gaze above the belt, so to speak, as I step into the dance that's become as familiar to me as breathing over the last number of years: finding the best angles for the best photos.

Beaumont looks down at his bride like she's his greatest gift, and then he throws tradition out the window by lifting the veil and smoothing it back over her head with a mammoth-sized hand.

The Blades' toughest son of a bitch grins, looks at the priest, and announces, "Sorry, Father, I'll always be the worst kind of sinner."

"Andre—" Zoe's hands flutter upward.

He promptly cradles her face with one hand, binds an arm around her back, and, without giving anyone the chance to object, drops a heady kiss onto her mouth.

"Hell fucking yeah!" shouts one of the guys from the groom's side. "Get it, man. Get. It!"

Someone in the pews follows up with an equally boisterous, "Don't get her pregnant in the church, dude!"

The guests roar with laughter, palms kissing with thunderous applause.

I capture it all on camera:

Zoe's wide gaze as her fiancé steals a kiss before the ceremony officially begins.

The top of Andre's dark head as he glides his mouth over his bride's, his hand flexing at the small of her back, as though he's desperate to strip her out of the gown and touch her bare skin.

The bridesmaids whistling.

Father Christopher's red face and twitching lips.

My lens finds Jackson.

Click.

His hands dive into the pockets of his well-tailored pants.

Click.

He grazes his teeth over his lower lip.

Click.

Familiar brown eyes land on my face, startling in their intensity.

Click.

Long ago, he'd look at me just like he is now and whisper in that rough, endearing Texas drawl of his, "Always you."

The sentiment used to send my heart soaring.

Now he only averts his gaze, stubbled cheeks hollowing with a heavy breath, and turns back to the bride and groom.

Click.

The final shutter of the camera mimics the steady rhythm of my heart.

One inappropriate photo down.

Five too many pictures of my ex-husband already catalogued.

Father Christopher clears his throat. "Perhaps we can hold off on the impregnating until after we exchange vows?"

I snort.

And then the four-year-old ring bearer seals Andre Beaumont's sinner status for good. Thrusting one little arm up in the air as Andre releases Zoe and steps back, the kid shouts, "Mommy! Mommy, Mr. Beaumont has a sword in his pants! *I* want one that big!"

I find Andre's shocked expression with my lens.

Click.

I may not have the husband or the white picket fence or the two-point-five kids, but goddamn it, I love my job.

Some days, it feels like enough.

X

Want to keep reading? *Body Check* is now available!

Read or download now via Kindle Unlimited

JOIN THE FUN!

Did you love Gwen & Marshall? Do you want to stay updated on releases, sales, free books, and all that juicy goodness? If your answer is yes, consider signing up for my bi-monthly newsletter at www.marialuis.org/contact.

And, if you *really* want to delve into the world of my books, receive weekly short stories, and all the latest Maria Luis news before *anyone* else, then definitely join my Facebook reader group, Book Boyfriends Anonymous.

The only requirement?

You have a somewhat (un)healthy addiction to the men we read about in our romance novels ;)

Join **Book Boyfriends Anonymous** by searching: "Book Boyfriends Anonymous Maria Luis" in the search bar on Facebook.

DEAR FABULOUS READER

Hi there! I'm so excited that you decided to take a chance on Gwen & Marshall, and I so hope you enjoyed them! If you've never read any of my books before, my Dear Fabulous Reader section is where I give a few behind-the-scenes glances at the book. Are you ready? Let's begin...numerical-style!

1. Cheers, anyone? Although it might seem strange, there is actually some event space right above this iconic Boston restaurant. Inspiration struck, actually, from reality! A family friend held their wedding reception there—think fancy suits, servers dressed to the nines, and more finger sandwiches than you could possibly eat. Unfortunately, there were no super sexy hockey players that I recall being there!

2. Wintertime in Boston means (generally) frigid temperatures, hot chocolate, and...ice sculptures! Each year on First Night (New Year's Eve), a famous local ice sculptor tromps out to Boston's Copley Square to chisel gorgeously stunning sculptures for all to see. In *Hat Trick*, I took a little creative liberty and placed the event along the twinkling

harbor, but if you were to ever visit Boston on the search for ice sculptures, now you know where to find them!

3. In Massachusetts, athletes live *everywhere*. But there seems to be a very great hub of them in what locals fondly call the Three W's: Wellesley, Weston, and Wayland. A friend of ours (not the one who got married at Cheers!) is a very well-known gardener in the area, and he's tended to the lawns of everyone from Big Papi of the Boston Red Sox to celebrities on the big screen. One thing in common? Many of them tend to make the Three W's their home, so I opted to make Weston the town Marshall lives in. You'll remember that Gwen mentions it once, toward the end of the book.

4. Sometimes, characters pop into your head and they just won't let go. When Gwen showed up in *Power Play*, I hated her. Really, I did. I don't think I spotted one redeeming quality. (But I still wanted to know her story). Then, as I was writing *Sin Bin*, she kept popping up all over again. And that time, she was softer—just by a little—and I began to think . . . *I want to write your story*. My friends suggested that I don't do so. Readers of *Power Play* questioned my sanity—understandably so! No matter how hard I tried, though, Gwen would just not go away. And then in came Marshall Hunt, and I thought to myself . . . *this is the moment*. Gwen's journey isn't smooth. It isn't elegant. But it is *real* and full of mistakes and regrets, and sometimes—sometimes even when everyone is telling you to run for the hills and stop writing about a character who is hated—you just have to do what feels right. Writing Gwen & Marshall's journey felt right, and it was important for me to show that love isn't always easy and it isn't always smooth. Sometimes it's rocky as all hell, and you just have to jump in and buckle your seatbelt and prepare for a ride that will leave you breathless.

PREVIEW OF SAY YOU'LL BE MINE: A NOLA HEART NOVEL

The NOLA Heart series is now complete! Keep reading for a sneak peek of Say You'll Be Mine, the first book in the series—featuring a second chance romance that will heat up your kindles and keep you up at night reading.

SHAELYN HAD NEVER BEEN A RUNNER. Oh, she'd tried a few times after moving to New York City. Seeing all those fit women in their yoga pants and tiny sports bras jogging in Central Park had been the inspiration she'd needed to get her butt moving. After all, *her* thighs and derriere were the ones jiggling and making a mortal enemy out of every pair of jeans.

As it turned out, Shaelyn hadn't enjoyed running as much as she'd enjoyed seeing other people do so, and her outings to Central Park were thereafter limited to people watching.

But New Orleans . . . New Orleans was worse.

Halfway there, Shaelyn told herself as she spotted the stone tower of Holy Name of Jesus Church sprouting out over the treetops. *Just make it to that black trash bin and then you can die.*

She didn't make it to the trash bin. She barely made it another thirty feet before she hobbled over to one of the ancient live oaks lining the paved path. Pressing her palms to the ribbed bark, she rested her forehead against the back of her hands and swallowed fistfuls of humid air into her aching lungs.

Never again.

Shaelyn crumpled to the ground, with her back against the live oak and her hands settled on her bent knees.

This was all Brady Taylor's fault. She wished he hadn't looked so damn good the other day, dressed in a plain gray T-shirt and Levi jeans that were faded in all the right places. The problem with Brady was the *way* he filled out his clothes: his broad shoulders had stretched the thin material across his back, and good Lord, but the way the cotton had barely skimmed his stomach hinted at killer abs underneath.

Shaelyn's saving grace at the BBQ had been when Brady opened his mouth and revealed himself to be the same jerk she remembered all too well.

But still, here she was running in a futile attempt to shed the pounds she'd gained since high school. That Shaelyn cared at all about what Brady thought of her darkened her mood.

With a glance at her watch, she hauled herself up off the ground with a small moan of pain. Were her shins supposed to be stinging so badly?

She yanked on the hem of her shorts and waited for a mother pushing her baby in a stroller to pass before picking the wedgie from hell. Either her butt had grown in the last few months or the hot, humid air was making her swell.

With that spurring her on as motivation, Shaelyn ramped her fast walk up to a slow jog. She tried to think of anything else besides her burning calves and her tiny running shorts.

By the time Shaelyn made it back to her car, she was sweating from places she hadn't known existed. The clanging bells from Holy Name of Jesus Church marked 4 p.m across the street as a car parked behind hers beeped twice. She fumbled with her car keys, which she'd clipped to the belt loop of her shorts for safekeeping.

"Need help with those?"

Shaelyn jerked at the familiar masculine voice and nearly pantsed herself. Picking a wedgie in public, while sometimes necessary, was embarrassing, but losing her shorts in front of Brady Taylor, strangers, and the all-seeing eyes of her parish church might actually spell the end of her.

Then again, problem solved. Meme Elaine would have to find someone else to inherit their ancestral home, of course, but Shaelyn could work some serious magic from Upstairs.

"Nope, I've got it," she bit out. She didn't look at him. One glance and there was a decent chance of her good sense going MIA.

"You sure?" Black Nike tennis shoes entered her peripheral vision. "Looks like you might need a hand."

His toned calves were dusted with short, black hairs. It was a sign of weakness, she knew, but Shaelyn couldn't stop the upward progression of her gaze. Settled low on his hips were maroon basketball shorts with cracked-gold lettering running up the side. The first and second O's were missing, so that instead of Loyola, it read "L Y LA." She wondered why he wasn't wearing his alma mater, Tulane University, and then reminded herself that she didn't care. Her gaze traveled up to a faded-blue NOPD T-shirt that—

Shaelyn inhaled sharply as she realized just how awful *she* must look. Boob sweat was the least of her worries when her underwear had officially integrated itself between her butt cheeks. She reached up to smooth her short, curly hair, which she'd tamed with a headband straight out of the '90s. Her bedroom was proving to be a treasure trove of forgotten goodies.

"You've got something . . . " Brady reached out a hand toward her butt.

"Hey!" She swatted at his long-tapered fingers. He wasn't wearing his hat today, and she finally had her first glimpse of his blue-on-blue eyes. She'd once compared them to the crystal blue waters of Destin (where their families once vacationed together in Florida every summer), and she was annoyed to find that time had not dampened their appeal. Straightening her spine, she snapped, "Hands off."

Holding both hands up, he dipped his chin. "You might wanna check out your behind then." Those blue eyes crinkled as he grinned, with small laugh lines fanning out from the corners.

Shaelyn twisted at the waist. Three leaves were stuck to her butt, suctioned to the fabric of her shorts as though hanging on for dear life. Sweat, apparently, was the proper glue foliage needed for attachment.

She was never working out again.

"You got it?" Brady asked, humor lacing his husky drawl. "I'm good with my hands, if you need help."

An image of Brady's large hands cupping her butt snapped her into action. She swiped at the offending leaves, sending them fluttering to the ground. "I'm good. Thanks."

His sweeping glance, one that traveled from her tennis

shoes all the way up to her face, left her wondering if he liked what he saw or if he was glad he'd dumped her years ago. Finally, he murmured, "I can see that."

The key ring came loose from her belt loop with an extra hard tug of desperation, and she started for her car. "Right. Well, nice to see you."

Brady effectively ruined her escape by leaning against her car door with his arms crossed over his hard chest. Hadn't she suffered enough today without having to deal with him, too? Boob sweat, wedgies, and leaves suctioned to her ass were all a woman could take, thank you very much.

She gestured at him. "Do you mind?"

His answering smile was slow and easy. "Not at all."

Her fingers curled tightly around the car keys. "I've got somewhere to be."

"Yeah?" His tone suggested that he didn't believe her. "Where are you going?"

She toyed with the idea of blowing off his question, but if there was one thing she knew about Brady Taylor, it was that he was annoyingly persistent. "I've got a bachelorette party tonight."

"Oh, yeah?" He said it differently this time, as if intrigued, perhaps even despite himself. "Didn't realize you had many friends left in N'Orleans?"

She scowled, placed a hand on her hip, and then realized that she must look about five seconds away from throwing a good ol' Southern princess tantrum. Hastily she folded her arms over her chest to mimic his stance. With determination she ignored the way her sweat-coated skin fused together.

"For the record, I do have friends." She didn't, not really, but he didn't know that. "And secondly, my job is hosting a bachelorette party."

He seemed to digest that, his full mouth momentarily flattening before quirking up in a nonchalant smile. "Where do you work nowadays, Shae?"

The bells of Holy Name chimed again. She really had to be going, but something stopped her from walking around the hood of her car, climbing in, and speeding away. She didn't want to think about what that *something* might be.

"I work at La Parisienne in the French Quarter. On Chartres."

One of his black brows arched up in surprise. "The lingerie joint?"

Only a man would call a business that sold women's underwear a "joint." Rolling her eyes, Shaelyn let her weight rest on her right leg. She bit back another moan of pain. "It has a name, but yes, I work at the 'lingerie joint.'"

"And they host bachelorette parties?"

She shrugged. "Sometimes. Tonight we're cohosting it with The Dirty Crescent."

"The sex toy shop?"

"Yes."

His blue eyes glittered, and when he asked, "Can I come?" his voice slid through her like that first shot of whiskey she'd downed in his grandfather's office years earlier. Shocking at first, and then hot and tingly as it heated her core.

Then he ruined everything by laughing.

Nothing ever changed with him.

"You're such a jerk," she snapped. She stepped forward and pushed at his chest to urge him away from her car. He didn't budge, which only infuriated her. How dare he tease her like he hadn't broken her heart? So what if she'd been young, naïve, and fifty shades of stupid? Being a gentleman was not overrated.

He was still laughing when he caught her by the shoulders. "I could arrest you for harassment." His hands were warm on her exposed skin, hotter, maybe, than the late afternoon sun toasting the back of her neck.

Shaelyn glared up at him, not the least bit pacified by the mischievous glint in his blue eyes. His thumbs stroked her collarbone. Once, twice. If she'd been a weaker woman, she would have curled into his embrace. "You should arrest yourself."

"For what?"

"For being an ass."

His head dipped, his breath a whisper against her ear. Goosebumps teased her flesh. "You gonna do it yourself? Maybe buy a pair of new 'cuffs from that party tonight and put them to good use on me?"

Want to keep reading? *Say You'll Be Mine* on Amazon!

ACKNOWLEDGMENTS

No book would be complete without saying a million thank-you's to everyone who helped make *Hat Trick* what it is today—

Najla—thank you so much for this gorgeous cover! I can't get over how beautiful it is . . . and I still can't get over how I changed my mind about couples at least four times. This couple, though? They are the one.

Kathy—with every book, you push me to go harder and to give more. I wouldn't be where I am today as a story-teller without you.

Tandy—thank you for shining up this manuscript and making it sparkle!

Dawn—girl, there are not enough ways to thank you. To keep it short: thank you for your friendship, thank you for having my back, thank you for reading my books and always catching my "hardwood flowers" and "popcorn bowels." And, truly, thank you for being you.

Viper and Brenda—thank you a million times over for being the amazing beta readers that you are! Your feedback brought Marshall & Gwen to a higher level, and I appreciate the time you give to reading my work more than you will ever know.

To the bloggers who have shared all things *Hat Trick*—I could not have done this without you! Words cannot express how much appreciative I am for everything that you do.

Terra & Sam—my Boozers Who Write, my ride-or-die's, my . . . you get what I'm putting down here. Y'all are amazing, and thank you always for talking me off the ledge.

Jami—Sometimes you meet people and just know you're supposed to be friends and be each other's rock—you're my rock, girl. Or should I say...rock star? Too much? Maybe too much, LOL.

Joslyn—what else do I say but that you're amazing and I'm so happy to have you in my life? Truthfully, thank you for always being there and for always listening. I'm so happy to have you in my life!

To my family and friends, you know who you are. Thank you for putting up with me on my showering days and my non-showering days; when I'm on deadline and I forget to eat; when I'm sitting on my couch and texting you random photos of cover models and asking if you'd "do him." Thank you for it all.

To my BBA pack—this author life would be so much more lonely without you. I'm honored to know all of you, and I hope to one day meet all of you in person!

And, lastly, to my readers—thank you for taking a chance on my work, and for reading my words. Without you, my dream of being an author would not be my reality.

ALSO BY MARIA LUIS

NOLA HEART

Say You'll Be Mine

Take A Chance On Me

Dare You To Love Me

Tempt Me With Forever

BLADES HOCKEY

Power Play

Sin Bin

Hat Trick

Body Check

BLOOD DUET

Sworn

Defied

PUT A RING ON IT

Hold Me Today

Kiss Me Tonight

Love Me Tomorrow

FREEBIES (AVAILABLE AT WWW.MARIALUIS.ORG)

Breathless (a Love Serial, #1)

Undeniable (a Love Serial, #2)

The First Fix

ABOUT THE AUTHOR

Maria Luis is the author of sexy contemporary romances.

Historian by day and romance novelist by night, Maria lives in New Orleans, and loves bringing the city's cultural flair into her books. When Maria isn't frantically typing with coffee in hand, she can be found binging on reality TV, going on adventures with her other half and two pups, or plotting her next flirty romance.

X

Stalk Maria in the Wild at the following!
Join Maria's Newsletter
Join Maria's Facebook Reader Group

Printed in Great Britain
by Amazon